Easy Bake Coven:

Book One of the Vivienne Finch Magical Mysteries

J.D. Shaw

For Mom,

Who always read to her children each night and imparted her love for books.

For George,

My soul mate, best friend, and editor extraordinaire without whom this book would not exist.

Special thanks to my mentor, Jeanne Cavelos, for believing in my work and her dedication to the craft for making writers the best they can be everywhere.

Prologue

Mona had always been a woman who liked to be in control, even though the results rarely worked in her favor. As a little girl, she refused help from her older sisters as she worked the little plastic oven that cooked with a single light bulb. They would say she put in too much water, or that the frosting was too thin, but she insisted they let her do it by herself. Sure enough, the little baked treat ended up about as appetizing as frosted cardboard. She had done it without help and that was all that really mattered she told herself.

As a teen, she defied the caste system of the local high school by becoming a cheerleader even though her family lived on the wrong side of town. Although she executed the routines with flawless determination, she never could unseat Missy Collins and her perfect blond hair from the lead position. While no one could argue she was indeed a cheerleader, her invitations to the after-game parties always seemed to get lost in the mail.

When she graduated from community college with a degree in business administration, she envisioned herself leading a small company to global success. But the reality turned out to be five years in a corner office in New York City with no window and endless paperwork. While her ideas to take the company in a new direction sailed on golden wings, her own were clipped as the company refocused its brand appeal and started fresh, minus her position.

Like some fairy tale princess suffering from a

dire curse, she was ultimately rescued by a handsome young man named Richard Clarke. Through his job at city hall, the doors began to open that had for so long been locked to her. She attended the best parties, met the best people, and eventually had the best wedding that even Missy Collins would have envied. Tired of the metropolitan life, Richard convinced Mona to leave for a quiet town upstate where they could put down roots. Within two months, they had departed the concrete jungle for the quiet shores of the Finger Lakes.

Settling in Cayuga Cove, Richard landed a decent job in local government and quickly rose up the ranks to eventually be elected Mayor. Mona, charged with serving as the first lady, went about setting up committees to address problems in the town and implemented ideas on how to fix them. Her first few forays into civic activities proved fruitful and at long last she had a taste of the success that always seemed to elude her.

Today was going to be one of the grand moments that she enjoyed so much. She was leading the ribbon cutting ceremony for the new *Sweet Dreams Bakery* opening on Main Street not only as the Mayor's wife, but as the chairwoman of the newly resurrected town historic commission. Through her efforts, the town was going to be transformed into a destination like no other along the lucrative *Cayuga Wine Trail*.

She had taken the largely ceremonial role handed to her and crafted it into something others would look upon with awe and wonder.

Perhaps one day, they would present her with a plaque or plant a tree in the park to honor all her hard work? She would accept, naturally, but vowed to remain humble and gracious.

When the large scissors used for ribbon cuttings were plunged into her chest that early morning, she wasn't all that surprised she was going out in a blaze of glory. As so often happened in her life, the other shoe had finally dropped.

Knocked off balance, she was pushed into the dumpster filled with white trash bags and left alone as her murderer fled into the early morning drizzle.

Thank God she had written her obituary years before, she thought before she died. Richard would never have been able to compose such a moving tribute without her help.

Chapter 1

"Mother, you can't measure dry ingredients with a liquid measuring cup." Vivienne Finch cringed as the confectioner sugar spilled over the top of the glass and scattered all over her freshly mopped black and white checker tiled floor of the soon-to-open *Sweet Dreams Bakery*. Thank heaven the health inspector had already cleared her to operate the day before.

Nora Finch peered over her bifocals, having never followed the optometrist's advice how to use them properly. Dressed in a stylish gray fisherman's sweater and a simple plaid skirt, she looked hopelessly out of place in the confines of the kitchen workspace. "That's nonsense." She gingerly set the full measuring cup on the stainless steel counter. "I've measured everything this way for years and never had a problem.

Vivienne suddenly knew why Nora's holiday fruitcakes were hearty enough to anchor a sailboat. "I really could use some help assembling the Linzer cookies. Just stick the tops on and dust them with the sugar. After all, they're for your rummy club tonight." She grabbed the broom and dustpan from the corner to sweep up the mess her mother had left on the floor.

Nora happily moved over to the marble island where the mostly finished cookies awaited. "Would that be more helpful?" She smiled sweetly. "I wouldn't want you to have to rush getting ready for your date with Joshua tonight." She began to hum a tune to herself, her usual habit whenever she knew the jig was up on whatever plan she had set in motion.

'So that's why you're here.' Vivienne thought to herself and exercised control to not roll her eyes. All mothers seemed to have a sixth sense whenever their children did so and she didn't have time to get into another heated discussion. "I haven't exactly committed to that just yet." She knelt down to sweep up the confectioner's sugar off the floor.

"Vivienne, you're my daughter and I'll love you no matter what."Nora said as she plucked a cookie up from the tray. "Don't you want a man to sweep you off your feet?"

"I'd rather have a man sweep the kitchen and maybe once in a blue moon lift the toaster oven up to clean the crumbs underneath."Vivienne answered as she emptied the dustpan of sugar into the trash.

Nora stared at the cookie in her grip, still warm from the oven. It was soft, sweet, and so terribly easy to crumble. Just like her daughter's will. "Honey, I don't want to alarm you, but you do work in a bakery surrounded by sweets. If you don't get a man to sweep you off your feet soon, he's going to need a bigger broom."

"Gee, thanks." Vivienne sighed.

Nora clucked her tongue in response. "Well, my darling daughter, I have good news. Mother has accepted the date on your behalf because you're so terribly busy with the opening."

Vivienne's face warmed as she considered her response. "Mother, how could you do that when you know the grand opening is three days away? I'm barely keeping up as is."She walked the dustpan over to the trash can and dumped it with a little more vigor than was actually needed. A small cloud of white lifted into the air.

"I did it because you'll continue to find excuses to not go out with him." Nora worked slowly on the cookies, refusing to make eye contact with her daughter. "You do have a knack for always finding activities to get you out of things."

Vivienne was about to get into one of their usual heated discussions when the phone rang just in the nick of time. She took a deep breath, leaned the broom against the counter, and then answered. "*Sweet Dreams Bakery*, how can I help you?"

The voice of her best friend, Kathy Saunders, greeted her in response. "I was driving by just a few seconds ago and I couldn't help but notice Mommie Dearest in the kitchen."

"Yes, that's right." Vivienne kept her voice in her business professional tone. "Would you like to place an order for that?"

Nora looked up from the cookies she was working on and pointed to her watch.

"Meet me for some coffee in fifteen minutes at Clara's?" Kathy offered.

"Absolutely, I can do that. I'll see you soon." She hung up the phone and turned to face her mother.

"I hope you're not wasting precious time that could be better spent at the salon." She adjusted her glasses once more as she looked over her daughter's appearance. "You should take the rest of the day off and treat yourself to a day of beauty."

"If he can't be attracted to me, crow's feet and all, maybe it just isn't meant to be." Vivienne countered.

Nora shook her head as she finished assembling

the last cookie on the tray. "At least take time to clean up the flour streaks in your hair."

"What flour streaks?" Vivienne puzzled.

Nora put her hand to her mouth. "Oh dear, I didn't realize how bad the lighting was in this place."

Vivienne bit down on her lower lip in response to her mother's barb about her auburn hair and the occasional white strands that appeared more frequently these days. "I don't have time to get it colored if that's what you're driving at."

"Just try to be gracious and act like everything he says is just fascinating." Nora walked over to her daughter and began to inspect just how many white strands had invaded her hair. "He's a fine catch."

"Mother, please." Vivienne brushed her hands away from her hair. "I need to run down to the grocery and pick up some more cake flour."

Nora backed away. "I have some errands to run myself." She squinted in an effort to read the face of the wall clock.

"It's one forty-five." Vivienne smiled.

"That means that Eunice Kilpatrick is still on lunch down at the bank. She always short changes me when I make my withdrawals." Nora grabbed her purse from the nearby counter and gave her daughter a hug. "I better hurry before she gets back."

"I thought Eunice was one of your best friends? Isn't she usually your team mate?"

"She is." Nora smiled sweetly as she picked up her tray of cookies. "But she gets to gabbing so much she never pays mind to what she's counting out and don't even get me started on keeping track of cards played." She paused for a quick inspection of her appearance in front of the oven glass. "Last week I ended up with ten deposit slips and some coins in my purse when I made a withdrawal from my casino fund." She waved goodbye and disappeared out the front door onto Main Street.

Vivienne relished the moment of peaceful quiet in the bakery. The ribbon cutting was still three days away, but she wasn't all that worried. It was just going to be a simple ceremony with the mayor and members of the small business community on hand to give their support. What could possibly go wrong with that?

Twenty minutes later, she walked into *Clara's Diner* and was greeted by the gentle tinkle of the little brass bell above the door. The owner, Miss Clara Bunton, handed change to one of the regulars. Like most of the males in the town, his outfit consisted of a pair of jeans with ragged bottoms, a flannel shirt, and some sort of hat with the logo of a favorite sports team.

Clara, however, was consistently the same no matter the day. She was a thin woman in her sixties with cheeks that always had a little too much blush on them and permed brown hair with curls a bit too tight. As usual, she was dressed in a perfectly pressed pink uniform with a decorative white lace collar. She worked the cash register by the front door, as she had for the past thirty years, keeping an eye on the bottom line and the actions of the staff. "Vivienne, I was just thinking about you today."

"Hello Miss Clara." Vivienne scanned the empty diner booths for Kathy. As was the normal for any of their planned activities, she kept up her perfect streak of running five minutes late. "I'm going to need a strong cup of coffee."

Clara grabbed a menu from under the counter and set it on the table of a nearby booth. "Flying solo today?"

"I'm meeting Kathy here."

Clara was joined by Stephanie Bridgeman, the newest waitress who was still learning the fine art of how to properly wait tables. "The special today is Yankee Pot Roast." Stephanie awkwardly searched her small apron pockets for her order pad and pen but only found sugar packets and a crumpled napkin.

"Sounds delicious, but I'll just have coffee." Vivienne smiled at the young girl. Stephanie was one of the locals who had recently graduated high school but who couldn't afford to go to college. Like so many of the farm families in upstate New York, they were just making ends meet.

"Would you like cream and sugar?" Stephanie asked, setting several sugar packets on the table as she continued her search for a pad and pen.

"Please." Vivienne winked at Clara. "I have to admit I'm tempted with Miss Clara's pecan pie over in the baker's case."

Stephanie's eyes brightened. "Can I get you a slice?"

"I deserve a little treat after all my hard work these past few weeks." Vivienne reasoned. "Pecan pie is one thing that I'm not going to touch at the bakery. I could never compete with Miss Clara's famous recipe."

"You get the coffee, Stephanie." Clara ordered. "I'm going to make sure Vivienne gets one of the bigger slices."

"I really shouldn't indulge like that." Vivienne replied. "But mother did say I should treat myself to something nice today."

Clara chuckled in response. "You're such a sweet girl. It's hard to believe that Nora is your mother."

"Believe it." 'You two are like a pair of magnets.' Vivienne thought to herself. 'Flip them one way they are thick as thieves. Turn them over and they can't push away fast enough.' They were friendly enough in person to each other, but deep down there was some sort of intense rivalry of who could have the more perfect version of everything. Clothes, cars, home décor, friends, even garden flower beds.

The bell over the door jingled as Kathy entered. As usual, her attention was drawn to the screen of her smart phone.

"I'll go get your pie." Clara reached down and gave Vivienne's hands a gentle squeeze before leaving to supervise Stephanie who seemed to be having trouble working the double brewer system.

"The bakery isn't in flames, so I take it Nora must have left." Kathy joked as she slid into the booth. As the owner of the *Trade Winds Clothier*, she was always stylishly dressed no matter what the occasion. Her shoulder length blond hair was swept up into an elegant style that was both business-like and sexy. Her makeup was flawless. Thanks, in no small part, to the hundred dollar consultations with the experts at the *Nouveau You* salon in town.

Stephanie slid an enormous slice of pecan pie, in front of Vivienne. "The coffee is brewing again. It should only be a few minutes."

"Thanks." Vivienne glanced around the table but found no napkin or flatware.

"Can I get you anything?" Stephanie asked Kathy.

Kathy, never one to mince words, nodded. "Some napkins and flatware would be a good start."

Stephanie slapped her forehead in response. "Oh my God, I'm so sorry."

"It's okay, sweetie." Vivienne narrowed her eyes at Kathy. "I'm in no hurry to take on these empty calories."

Kathy glared back at her friend and rolled her blue eyes in response. "I'll just have a coffee, black."

Stephanie pulled out her order pad from her apron pocket and scribbled.

"Carbohydrates be damned." Kathy added. "Give me a piece of the pecan pie too."

Vivienne shook her head and smirked. "Bad moods burn calories."

"Then I should be able to have the entire pie and not worry about my figure." Kathy drummed her fingernails on the vintage red Formica tabletop.

Stephanie let out a nervous laugh and rushed back to the kitchen area where Clara was dealing with a coffee grinder that Stephanie had overfilled. The pre-measured cup to capture the freshly ground beans spilled a cascade of aromatic powder onto the floor behind the counter. "I'm sorry about that Miss Clara."

Clara shook her head at the mess. "I'll get the broom and dustpan."

"Geez, what put you in such a good mood today?" Vivienne asked as the smell of the pecan pie made her stomach grumble in anticipation.

"Mona Clarke." Kathy confided. "She and her sycophants were poking around my store and pointing out all the flaws in my choice of décor. She practically called it tacky."

"The mayor's wife said that?"

"The queen bee said that." Kathy folded her hands together on the table. "A fitting title since she's always buzzing around other people's business these days."

"I've never had many encounters with her." Vivienne offered. "She's always in such a hurry whenever we meet."

"Count your blessings!" Kathy interrupted. "She and that women's small business group can shove their plans where the sun doesn't shine."

"Whoa!" Vivienne leaned forward toward her friend. "I have no idea what you're talking about."

"That's because you're not operating as a business yet." Kathy explained as Clara walked two mugs of coffee over to the table and set them down along with some napkins and some flatware. Stephanie followed suit and slid a much smaller slice of pecan pie in front of Kathy before returning to finish cleaning up the coffee mess.

"I will be in three days." She glanced around for some wood to knock on but found nothing except polished chrome and vinyl. "Barring any unpleasant surprises, that is."

"You want an unpleasant surprise?" Kathy asked. "Try the *Cayuga Cove Women of Small Business Association* on for size." She took a big sip of coffee. "They have come up with a proposal to refresh main street stores and shops with a classic look of yesteryear. New sidewalks and awnings, fancy street lamps and scalloped facades. Each business will be limited to a simple wooden sign hanging over each entrance with two simple spot lights for nighttime illumination."

"I read something about that in one of their flyers that came in the mail the other day." Vivienne recalled. "Didn't the newspaper have an article explaining how the state funding fell through recently?"

"It did." Kathy continued. "I was all for making Main Street look more appealing to shoppers, but I can't afford to front the cost of all those cosmetic changes to my store. Those simple wooden signs start at seven hundred dollars and go up from there depending on the color and style of the fonts."

"I don't understand where the problem is." Vivienne speared the pecan pie with her fork and took a small bite. "Without state funding, it will be tabled until who knows when. Problem solved."

Kathy wielded her fork like a knight with a sword. "Here's the real kicker." She stabbed a tiny piece of her pecan pie. "This was Mona's pet project and as the director of the association she refused to let it go. So right after that little roadblock, she and a few of her devoted followers started digging through the town records and now they're planning on reviving the Historic Commission to force the changes she wants through antiquated town codes."

Vivienne swallowed another sweet bite of pie and washed it down with her coffee. "Can they really do that? Strong-arm the merchants?"

"I don't know for sure, but her group is planning a meeting soon." Kathy shook her head. "It sounds like Mona Clarke is getting ready to force our hands to make the town look the way she envisions it."

"Having each of the business owners on Main Street write the checks." Vivienne finished the thought. "I certainly won't be in any sort of financial position to do that for the first year."

"You might not have a choice." Kathy added as Clara appeared with a coffee carafe. "Not if you want to continue to do business on Main Street."

"Are you two talking about Mona Clarke?" Clara asked.

"Yes." Kathy nodded. "Be glad you're not on Main Street."

"But I am only one street away." Clara added as she refilled Kathy's mug. "Something tells me Queen Mona isn't going to stop with just one street."

"We're assuming that all this is legal." Vivienne handed her mug to Clara to refill. "It could take years for anything to get implemented."

Clara pointed out the window to the twenty foot tall metal sign that was shaped like a coffee mug. Framed by a red outline of neon tubing, it had been a beacon for the late night bar crowd for years. "Jake, God rest his soul, was so proud of that design. It would break my heart to get rid of it." Her eyes clouded up for a few seconds as she thought about her late husband who had passed more than a decade ago, leaving her as sole owner of the business he had loved so much.

"Jake's sign is a part of our history here." Vivienne agreed. "I'd even go so far to say that it should be protected with historical status."

"It's not like I'm one of those blasted chains out on the interstate." Clara topped off Vivienne's coffee. "I'm making just enough to keep afloat and pay my bills. Heaven knows how much a lawyer would cost."

"Which I'm sure is what Mona and the others on the commission are probably counting on. Hoping we all tuck tails between our legs and skulk off." Kathy savored another bite of pie, enjoying every second of the decadent treat she rarely allowed herself.

"That woman has got some nerve." Clara added with a scowl. "Do you know that she actually bought one of my pecan pies here a few weeks ago and was going to enter it in a baking contest at the State Fair?"

"How did you find out?" Kathy was intrigued.

"I was there myself to enter the very same pie." Clara smiled. "So when I ran into her at the check in line, she was mortified. Next thing I knew she was saying how she had a terrible migraine and she slipped away with that pie stashed under her arm before she could enter it."

"Are you sure it was one of yours?" Vivienne asked.

"She didn't even have enough sense to take the little heart made out of pecans from the middle of the pie." Clara shook her head. It was her own little trademark that everyone in town knew identified her famous pecan from others. "I never did like her much. After that incident, she's never set foot in here again."

Vivienne stomach turned a few knots. She wasn't sure if it was the sugar rush or the topic of conversation. "All these local politics just makes my head spin."

"Just don't sell her any of your baked goods during fair season." Clara smiled.

The tinkle of the door bell startled the three women as a tall man in a deputy's uniform ducked inside the doorway. "Good afternoon, ladies." His voice was low and smooth, with an accent you couldn't quite place. "I hear this diner has the best coffee around."

Clara winked at them both and straightened the lace collar on her uniform. "You've heard right, Mister..."

"I'm Joshua Arkins, the sheriff's new deputy."

Vivienne swallowed hard and began to choke on a piece of pecan pie. Her face turned bright red as she tried to contain the loud hacking.

Kathy handed her the coffee mug. "Drink some of this."

Vivienne took it from her and downed the hot liquid. It did the trick and sent the stubborn pecans down her throat where they belonged. "Thank you." She squeaked out.

Joshua and Clara stared at Vivienne making sure she could breathe.

"Everything's fine." Kathy defused their concern. "Thank you."

Joshua removed his brown deputy hat and allowed his thick black hair to gleam in the afternoon sunlight that was streaming through the window blinds of the diner. "Glad to hear it."

Clara waved Stephanie over to the front. "Here at Clara's we always have a complimentary cup of coffee for the sheriff and his deputies."

Stephanie quickly filled a ceramic mug with some coffee.

Clara grimace in response. "Use one of the paper cups and be sure to put a cardboard sleeve on it."

"Oh right." Stephanie blushed and rushed to complete the order per Clara's instructions.

"I could have it here I suppose." Joshua smiled at Clara. "Sheriff Rigsbee wants me to get to know the town better."

"Why, of course!" Clara smiled warmly and directed him to one of the little stools that lined the counter. "Would you like to see a menu?"

"No thanks, I don't want to spoil my appetite for dinner. I've been setup on a blind date tonight." Joshua sat down on the stool, where his long legs barely folded under the counter.

"Just kill me now." Vivienne whispered to Kathy.

"What are you talking about?" Kathy whispered back. "He's adorable."

"I'm the blind date tonight." She tried to lower herself in the booth.

"Get out." Kathy tapped her hands with excitement.

"Nora." She explained.

"Damn." Kathy admired Joshua's body a few more times and then pouted. "This may be the only time I wished your mother was my own."

"Stephanie, can we have our check please?" Kathy snapped her fingers.

"What are you doing?" Vivienne's eyes widened.

Kathy winked at her. "I have a business to run and you need time to get ready for your date with mister tall, dark, and handsome."

"You sound just like her." Vivienne muttered under her breath.

"Hey, if you don't want to go out with him I'm more than happy to act as the proxy." She grabbed the check as Stephanie dropped it off. "This is on me."

"Okay, okay. I'll do it." Vivienne snuck a glance at him and for once wasn't disappointed by her mother's choice. He was a very handsome man and, based on how he was charming Miss Clara, had a good personality to match.

"Color me so surprised." Kathy raised her finely shaped eyebrows and handed a ten dollar bill to Stephanie. "Keep the change, sweetie."

"Thanks!" Stephanie gushed at the generous tip.

"Excuse me." Kathy removed herself from the booth and walked slowly, her hips swaying side to side with great effect to show off her trim figure. As she passed Joshua, she pretended to drop her purse. "I'm such a butterfingers." She tossed her hands up to her mouth and feigned embarrassment.

Joshua bent down to retrieve her purse which afforded all the women a great view of his rear. He filled his fitted brown pants out quite nicely, a testimony to the many hours of hard work spent at the gym.

Clara mouthed a silent 'Oh my God!' to Kathy in response.

"Here you go, Ma'am." Joshua handed her purse back with a smile.

"Ma'am?" Kathy extended her hand with perfectly French-manicured nails to him in response. "I'm Kathy Saunders, owner of the *Trade Winds Clothier* on Main Street."

"Joshua Arkins." He took her hand in his where it disappeared into his enormous grip.

"Feel free to stop by when you're out and about on patrol." She cooed. "I like to know those brave souls who serve and protect the public."

"I'll do that." He smiled at her, flashing white teeth that were straight and well cared for.

"Always nice to see you, Miss Clara." Kathy waved goodbye and exited the diner with a little extra swish in her step.

"You too, Kathy." She waved back as the door to the diner slammed closed, ringing the bell.

Vivienne chose that moment to try to make a quick exit from the diner. She smiled at Joshua and waved to Clara. "See you soon, Miss Clara."

"Don't be a stranger, Vivienne." Clara smiled back.

"Vivienne?" Joshua looked at her in surprise. "You wouldn't happen to be Vivienne Finch would you?"

Her cheeks flushed warm. "Uh, yes I am. I'm opening the new bakery on Main Street."

"Your mother is a very nice lady."

"Yes she is." She was surprised how weak and hollow her voice sounded.

"Honestly, I was a little worried about this blind date tonight." He took a little sip of coffee. "I've never had good luck with them before."

"Oh?" She tried to force a smile but feared it came across as a pained grimace across blushed cheeks.

"Your mother suggested seven thirty to pick you up, is that still okay?" His steel blue eyes seemed to look right into her soul.

"Actually, eight would work better. I have something to take care of when I finish at the bakery tonight." She made a mental note to stop at the Monarch grocery and pick up a hair coloring kit on her way home.

"See you then." Joshua nodded and turned his attention back to Clara. "You're right. This coffee is the best I've had Miss Clara. Is it a dark roast?"

Vivienne stepped out the door and enjoyed the cool autumn breeze that blew across her face. She could actually feel her heart flutter a bit, which was a welcome change from the butterflies in her stomach.

Chapter 2

"Damn!" Vivienne mumbled as the bottle of auburn number three slipped from the grip of her gloved hand and splashed into her pedestal sink with a thud. A splatter of red, not unlike the color of blood, sprayed the shiny white bowl and proceeded to drizzle down in crooked rivulets toward the drain. Keeping one hand on her lathered hair, she reached for the bottle and set it back on the shelf above the spigot.

Why had she decided to color her hair tonight? She was usually better at warding off her mother's barbs about her declining appearance. No, it wasn't because of her mother. It must be the stress from opening a new business. No, she changed her mind again. Deep down it wasn't all that bad. She had worked out a five year business plan, crunched the numbers, and conducted local research. All signs pointed to a recipe for success. The actual answer, she feared, was much worse. It was Joshua and those stunning steel-blue eyes. For the first time in many moons, she actually had a crush.

She set the egg timer for thirty minutes and proceeded to clean up the mess of red that had invaded her normally pristine white-tiled bathroom. Every so often, she would catch a glance into the mirror at her reflection and she wasn't thrilled with what she saw.

There were times she could still see that awkward teenager girl who didn't fit in with the popular crowd at the high school. She had to work at the local pizzeria carrying pitchers of beer and slices of supreme pizza while all the popular girls drove to the mall in Ithaca on Friday nights and bought the latest designer fashions and expensive makeup that the magazines raved as 'must haves'.

Not that she regretted her formative years for a minute. Truth be told, they gave her a sense of how a small business should run. She would often stay late with the owners, watching as they balanced their books and took inventory of what to re-order for the next big weekend. There was no doubt that she was able to start her own business thanks to the long hours spent near those searing hot ovens.

As for the popular girls, a few of them probably found a husband with a good job and settled down to start a family. A handful most likely came to their senses and worked on degrees in college to create the life they dreamed of. But most probably had their youth slip away and had no choice but to work menial jobs at whatever corporate retail chain was hiring. She wondered if they ever had any regrets as the new generation of popular girls walked by the store windows with their noses in the air, mortified to be seen shopping in a discount chain. Father time was indeed cruel when he began to take back the fleeting gift of youth.

The timer buzzed her back to reality and Vivienne completed the coloring ritual by dunking her head under the faucet of warm water and letting the excess dye drain away. After she finished, she admired the new red color that reflected back from the mirror. Gone were the wisps of white that betrayed her illusion of youth. She was once more a confident woman in her mid thirties who wasn't afraid to give her appearance a little spit and polish to look her best when needed.

A half hour later, she reverted back to that shy teenager when she used her fingers to part the blinds in the living room window. It was ten minutes after eight and there was still no sign of Joshua. She had called her mother earlier to confirm that she had given him her address and to fish for any more surprises that she should be aware of. Nora was famous for laying little traps for the men she set her daughter up with. There would be the little photo album filled with blank pages that she would produce from her purse, explaining how much she wished to fill with pictures of grandchildren.

Or the time the owner of *Cameo Bridal* had asked Vivienne to model a dress at a wedding show in Syracuse and her mother made sure the picture was front and center in the style section of the *Cayuga Tribune*. Nora was an old pro at making sure the men she sent out into the field of battle were properly trained to capture her daughter's heart.

At twenty-five minutes past the hour, she could take no more and dialed Kathy's number from her cell phone. It rang three times before she answered.

"I'm sincerely hoping this is just a random purse dial while on your hot date." Kathy's voice was stern.

"Guess again." Vivienne peeked once more out the window at Sunset Terrace, which remained quiet and free of traffic. Normally, this was something she loved about renting the simple two-bedroom Cape Cod that she called home. Tonight, however, it really irked her.

"Oh, honey. What happened? You didn't chicken out did you?"

"Trust me, I did not put myself through two hours of hair, makeup, and wardrobe changes to sit on the sofa and catch up on the television shows stored on the DVR." She paced back and forth on the cream wall-to-wall carpet, somewhat unsteady in the heels she wore only to funerals, weddings, and the occasional holiday party.

There was an awkward silence between them before Kathy cleared her throat. "I'm sure you look fabulous."

"Don't sugar-coat it for me." Vivienne demanded. "Am I being stood up?"

Another awkward silence passed. "He is a man of the law. Perhaps there was an accident out on the highway?"

"Or maybe he took one look at me at the diner and thought better of tonight's date."

"Vivienne, you know that's not the case." Kathy's voice was emphatic enough to almost be believed.

She parted the blinds once more to peek out. "Well, he did bring up the date at the diner in front of Miss Clara and Stephanie…"

"And why would he do that if he was going to stand you up?" Kathy asked.

"I suppose you're right. I can't believe I'm this nervous about going out on one of my mother's blind dates. Usually, I'm cool as a cucumber." Vivienne was surprised to hear a little laugh emerge from her mouth.

"That's because the men she sends rarely make it up the front steps before you shoot them down." Kathy laughed back. "Remember the guy who bought those organic gluten-free, sugar-free, fair-traded chocolates?"

"The ones that tasted like tree bark?" Vivienne laughed out loud.

"I believe you said that tree bark, dipped in swamp water, probably tasted better." Kathy continued with a snort.

"I didn't send him away because of those foul chocolates. I sent him away because he didn't believe in deodorant." Vivienne cackled.

"The alluring scent of natural musk," Kathy continued, "How on earth could you resist that?"

A knock at the door startled Vivienne. "Oh my God, I think he's here." She dropped her voice down to a whisper.

"So hang up and answer the door." Kathy whispered back. "And call me later with all the details."

Vivienne ended the call and slipped the phone into her purse that was perched on the end table. She took a deep cleansing breath and then opened the door with a radiant smile.

Joshua Arkins stood at the top of her front stairs and he looked even better with the porch lamp reflecting off his chiseled features. He was much taller than she had remembered, easily a few inches over six feet. Now out of uniform, he was dressed in a pair of khaki pants and a dark green polo shirt that defined the best parts of his chest in all the right ways. "I am so very sorry about being late but we had a late booking down at the office."

"Are you late?" She lied like a pro and then, to seal the deal, craned her neck back to the small wall clock in her entryway. "I lost track of time myself."

Joshua flashed his mega-watt smile and gave his

brow a quick wipe. "That's good to hear. I wouldn't have blamed you for slamming the door in my face."

"I would never do that." She gestured to the living room behind her. "Would you like to come in for a minute?"

"Thank you." He followed her into the living room where she sat down on her white sofa that was draped with one of her grandmother's hand-knitted afghans. "Can I get you something to drink?"

"No, thank you." He glanced around her living room and took a seat next to her. "This is a beautiful home."

"It's rented." She blurted out and then laughed. "Sorry, I don't know why I just spit that out."

"Wish I had found a place like this when I moved to town."

She could feel his body heat emanating like her steam radiator during a cold snap in January. He was no doubt just as nervous as she had been and that was the magic trick that allowed her to relax just a bit. "So where did you move to?"

"I found a duplex over on Meier Lane." He answered quickly. "But it doesn't have a quarter of the charm of this place. Look at that cove molding."

She was impressed. He wasn't one of those men who only seemed able to memorize sports scores and the names of Hooters waitresses. "The landlord told me most of these homes were built right before the depression. They were actually owned by the railroad and rented to workers and their families. After the railroads went bust, the homes were bought up by newlyweds who soon outgrew them as they created the baby boomers."

"You like history too?" He relaxed a bit with his posture, allowing his hands to move from his lap to the sofa cushions.

"Always have." She glanced at the wall clock and cleared her throat. "Well, if we're going to grab dinner we better get a move on."

He looked at the clock in surprise and lightly slapped his head. "I apologize again."

She put her hand on his and there was a moment of silence between them. He was unusually warm to the touch and she felt some sort of extra protective aura being so close to him. No doubt it was just her subconscious not letting her forget that he was an officer of the law. "No need." She rose from the sofa and he followed suit.

"So where's a good place to eat other than *Clara's Diner*?"

"Are you fond of Chinese?" She asked as she walked over to the end table and clutched her purse.

"Love it."

"Shall we take my car or yours?" She opened the front door, letting in a breeze that smelled faintly of wood smoke from the neighbors who had wood burning stoves to heat their homes. Mixed with the earthy smell of fallen leaves, it was a smell she felt defined the country-style of upstate New York.

"After showing up late, the least I can do is save you some gas money." He winced as the words came out. "I didn't mean it like that."

She laughed it off. "It's fine. I'm nervous too."

He led her to his blue Jeep Grand Cherokee, which was spotlessly polished. "I'm so glad to hear you say that." He opened the passenger door for her.

"Thank you." She slid into the passenger seat and was pleasantly surprised that the new car smell was still quite strong. The floor mats were clean and the door pockets weren't shoved full of wadded up drive-thru napkins. Joshua was light years ahead of her other blind dates.

A short drive later they were seated in a cozy corner booth inside the *Shanghai Sunset* restaurant. The lighting was soft and subdued, to allow the small votive candle on the table to be the star. The décor of wooden booths and chairs upholstered in red fabric, against the dark cherry wall panels carved with scenes of temples and pagodas from the Far East, was both exotic and romantic. The gentle sound of a single lute, played softly from the ceiling speakers as they enjoyed their dinners.

As the waiter placed her order of house special fried rice on the table, she ignored the chopsticks and went straight for the standard utensils. "I never could master chop sticks." She stabbed a shrimp with her fork and popped it into her mouth. "Mother always said my fingers were too stubby."

Much like Vivienne, Joshua avoided the chopsticks as they always seemed to end up either in his lap, on the floor, or sometimes both. "This is so much better than those greasy little take out places in the city."

"What city would that be?" She asked as her fork speared another shrimp off the blue and white patterned plate.

"Take your pick." He winked at her.

"I've never lived anywhere but Cayuga Cove." She revealed.

"There's something to be said for having that kind of stability." Joshua added as he finished the last of the noodles with a little slurp.

"I suppose you could look it that way." She set her fork down across the plate and pulled the napkin from her lap. She dabbed her lips gently and quickly ran her tongue across her teeth to hopefully snag any wayward vegetables that might have become lodged in-between the spaces.

"The cities these days are getting more like war zones." He added as he performed the same napkin ritual.

"I guess I should be thankful that Cayuga Cove is such a peaceful place. Why, you hardly ever hear a siren going down the street except during the Fourth of July parade."

"That's definitely something to be thankful for." Their waiter cleared their plates and set a check billfold down on the table along with two fortune cookies. Joshua snagged it quickly and reached into his back pocket for his wallet.

"Let me leave the tip." She offered.

He shook his head and smiled at her. "That just wouldn't be right."

Her heart fluttered again as she found herself not wanting the evening to come to an end so soon. "You are too generous."

He tucked a credit card into the slot at the top of the billfold and the waiter appeared seconds later to whisk it away. Joshua picked up a fortune cookie and handed it to her. "But I insist you read your fortune cookie aloud."

"That's fair." She opened the cellophane

wrapper and cracked the cookie into two clean pieces. She unfolded the little slip of paper and squinted to read the tiny writing in the dim lighting. "You have hidden talents that will pay off in bed." Her hands flew up to her mouth the moment she finished.

His eyes widened in surprise. "Say what?"

She suddenly felt like slapping her forehead in response. "It's just a thing my best friend Kathy and I do. We always finish fortunes with the words 'in bed'." She felt her cheeks flush red. "Not that I was suggesting anything like that tonight." She gingerly sipped her tepid Oolong tea while mentally chiding herself for blurting out such a suggestive thing.

"I think that's cute." He opened his with a single squeeze and ended up with several crumbled cookie bits. He fished out the fortune and held it close to the candle on the table. "Never say never", he paused for dramatic effect, "in bed."

As if in slow motion a nervous laugh escaped, along with some of the tea in her mouth, which created a small spit take much like the kind that had been the staple of so many comedy movies.

Joshua broke out into a hearty laugh and reached across the table to pull her hands away from her mouth. "Well that's a first."

She caught his hands in hers and their fingers intertwined. "This is why I don't go out on many dates."

The waiter returned with the billfold and credit card. "Is everything okay?"

Joshua nodded to her in response. "Would you care for more tea?"

She repressed a laugh. "I'm fine, thank you."

"Do come back." The waiter smiled and left them alone with the votive candle, the cellophane wrappers, and the tea-soaked table cloth.

Chapter 3

One the best things about being an early riser was experiencing the gentle quiet of the town as she drove her little red car to work each morning. The sky transitioned from the soft tangerine of sunrise to a vibrant periwinkle blue as she pulled into her private parking location at the rear entrance to her bakery. It promised another fine September afternoon, the kind that just begged to be spent sipping cider at one of the local orchards.

As she walked up the three concrete steps that led to her back door, she skidded on a pile of greasy waxed papers and nearly toppled forward. "Not again." She moaned.

The sanitation company, although prompt with their service, was getting terribly lax with cleaning up the trash that spilled out of their trucks as they lifted the nearby dumpsters to empty them. Just the other day, they had dropped an entire bag from the pizzeria that was two doors down, which spilled a mess of half-eaten crusts and half-finished sugary sodas all over the two parking spots that were designated for her business. She had cleaned up the disgusting mess on her own, not wanting to step on or over the revolting mix of trash.

Making a mental note to call the company and politely ask that they exercise more caution when removing waste, she fished the brass key out of her purse, tripped the lock, and stepped into the back supply room.

There were two days left before her grand opening and today started the first of the big stocking days to fill the store with the non-perishable items that would supplement her delicious baked goods.

But before any of that could be started, the first order of business was to have a steaming mug of English breakfast tea. She walked over to the large desk that was a mess of invoice papers, receipts, print-outs of recipes, and several paint color samples that she had passed on for the walls but liked enough to perhaps try in one of the bedrooms in her home. Hidden amongst the chaos, there was her trusty little electric kettle. As was the ritual each night, she filled it with water so it would be ready to go the next morning.

A few minutes later, with a mug firmly in her grip, she turned on the spotlights above the sales floor and looked over the progress she had made since securing the space a month ago.

Thanks to the beauty of the exposed brick wall on one entire side, she had saved money by only having to paint the opposite wall a pleasant shade of light yellow. It reminded her of a bright spring day and she instantly felt her mood elevated whenever she looked at it. She hoped her future customers would also feel inspired like that when they stepped in through the door and searched for the perfect item to satisfy their sweet tooth.

Along the exposed brick wall, she had installed simple chrome wire shelves to display the selection of various coffees and teas, some cute aprons and oven mitts, and a smattering of cookbooks that were still packed into large boxes in the back stockroom.

But the majority of the floor space was filled with her three glass display cases that would soon house decadent chocolate, vanilla, and peanut butter flavored whoopie pies. There were simple white trays that would display dozens of homemade cookies and brownies and vintage glass domes that would showcase the pies and cakes that would vary according to the season. But most importantly, her famous lemon-raspberry layer cake with white coconut frosting would take the prime location in the front display window. She had taken the blue ribbon two years in a row at the county fair with it.

Whenever a potluck dinner invite came in the mail, she knew her hosts would be disappointed if she arrived with anything but that. "You should sell this." They would insist between chewing mouthfuls of her cake. It had taken plenty of time and effort, but at last she had followed their advice and now they would see it every time they passed by her store window.

As fall was gearing up to full swing, she had decided to go with apple and pumpkin themed baked goods for the start. If those were a hit, she could easily carry them over into October and early November before switching to the winter wonderland of Christmas baking.

Taking a seat at one of the three bistro-style tables that took up the remaining floor space, she opened a spiral-bound notebook that contained her 'to do' lists and went over the agenda for the day.

As she sipped her tea and let the liquid warm her throat, the peaceful morning was interrupted with the sound of a man and woman having some sort of argument.

She couldn't help but wander over to her empty display window to see what all the fuss was about. She had a clear view of the couple arguing across the street and was shocked to see Joshua in his deputy uniform writing a ticket in front of Mona Clarke's gray luxury sedan.

"This is outrageous!" She shrieked, her voice transmitting easily through the thin glass of Vivienne's store. "I was only parking here for a minute. And on official city business, I might add."

"Which is directly in front of a fire hydrant," Joshua interrupted, "And clearly marked as a 'no parking zone' with several signs."

Mona put her hands on her hips. "That's because there is never any parking on this street for anyone thanks to all the tenants who live above the businesses."

"I'm not the parking commission, ma'am." Joshua finished the ticket and handed it to her with a black-gloved hand.

"Do you even know who I am?" She took a step toward him, defiantly.

"Mona Clarke. Fourteen hundred Presidential Circle." He recited from memory.

"I'm the mayor's wife and as I tried to tell you I was conducting vital city business when you so rudely interrupted me." Her voice was stern and cold, as if she were addressing some petulant teenager.

"This vehicle isn't one of the city fleet." He reasoned.

"I'm doing my civic duty to save the taxpayers money by using my own vehicle and gasoline." She sniffed.

'That's a hot one.' Vivienne thought to herself as she took another sip of her tea and watched the argument continue to unfold outside. It was proving to be better than anything on daytime television these days.

"You can take it up with the city manager or the Mayor if you desire, Mrs. Clarke." Joshua kept his voice flat and at a professional yet controlled volume.

"Why don't you give tickets to all these cars that hog up the streets so people can't shop?" She asked him. "Aren't they supposed to use odd/even parking?"

"A blocked fire hydrant is a clear danger," he insisted, "One that could cost lives if a fire broke out." He gestured to the other cars around her. "Everyone else is legally parked."

She snatched the ticket from his hand. "This isn't over, you know. My husband is going to hear about this. He will personally visit Sheriff Rigsbee to let him know how displeased he is with this sort of nonsense."

He tipped his hat to her. "You have a good morning Mrs. Clarke."

She stomped away from him and yanked open her car door. "I wouldn't get too cozy settling in here. This is a small town and people who make waves don't usually end up staying terribly long."

"I'm going to pretend I didn't just hear you make a threat against an officer of the law." He warned her. "Now please move along."

She disappeared into her car and slammed the door with enough force to make sure he knew she meant business. Vivienne couldn't help but feel bad for Joshua who had the misfortune of seeing the real Mona Clarke. She kept her public persona up so well that it was rare to see her true colors. Kathy and Clara certainly weren't exaggerating the other day at the diner.

As Joshua started to get into his patrol car he paused for a moment and then looked right at Vivienne.

She gave him a little wave and went to open her door to see if he wanted to come in and see her new store.

He nodded politely and then sped off in a hurry leaving her alone on Main Street once again.

She removed her hand from the door knob and sighed. "Must not be a good time." She spoke to herself and went back to her lists.

* * *

The next time she glanced at her watch it was quarter to three in the afternoon. She took a step back to admire the wire shelves that were now filled with all the items from her stockroom. She had rearranged everything several times until deciding on the perfect placement for easy viewing and purchasing.

The echo that she had become so used to hearing inside the store was less noticeable as she walked over to the counter where her new register was installed. Next on her list was the tedious task of programming all the individual department buttons to help her keep track of inventory and sales. The clerk at the warehouse store had tried to steer her toward one of the new fancy 'point-of-sale' terminals, but she never was much of a fan of computers. True, she had grown up with them as a child of the 80's, but they never seemed to like her and the feeling was mutual.

She did have a computer at home, but it was only used for email and for browsing the internet while shopping at Christmas. How it worked was a mystery. One she was very happy to leave as such. As long as it turned on and did what she asked, she was happy.

She pulled out the rather skimpy manual that was barely four pages, two of them in Spanish. As she pressed the power button, the machine hummed and emitted a shrill beep to announce that it required a roll of receipt paper.

Nora stepped through the front entrance with her usual greeting yodel of "Yoo hoo." As she closed the door, she stopped in her tracks. "You colored your hair!" She gushed.

"Thanks for noticing and hello to you too, Mother." She tore open the plastic wrap around the receipt spool and dropped the paper into the proper slot.

Nora joined her at the counter. "It's such a rich color, really goes well with your pale complexion." She turned her attention to the new cash register. "I didn't think they still made these things."

"Yes, they do." Vivienne answered as she closed the receipt bin and turned her attention back to the manual and the tiny section of how to assign different departments to specific keys.

"Most of the stores I shop at have these wonderful computer terminals." Nora continued. "Just amazing what they can do with those."

"That's all well and nice." Vivienne's brow furrowed as the instructions did not yield the information she hoped for. "But I'm not coordinating a

NASA launch, just selling cakes and cookies."

"There's no need to get snippy." Nora chided as she set down a large shopping bag from *Trade Winds Clothier*.

Vivienne looked up from the manual. "Kathy said she was having a good sale. Looks like you found some things."

"It's never too early to start Christmas shopping." Nora sat down in one of the bistro chairs and sighed. "I hope to have all of it done before Thanksgiving."

"What about Black Friday?" Vivienne thought of the many cold nights spent with her mother outside waiting for stores to open with door buster sales. Each year the openings seemed to come earlier and earlier and the behavior of the eager crowds grew worse and worse.

"It's getting a little too crazy, even for me." Nora answered as she looked around at the stocked shelves. "Is that really the best place to display the aprons?"

"It makes sense." Vivienne answered.

"About no longer shopping on Black Friday or the aprons?" Nora asked.

"Both."

Nora chuckled. "You sound so much like your father used to."

Vivienne missed her father, even after five years of not having him around anymore. She thought of him often, usually whenever something good happened. "I wish he could be here to see this."

"He sees it." Nora was quick to answer. "He sees more now than he ever did."

"I know." Vivienne's voice grew soft. "I just miss him."

"I do like where you have the cookbooks." Nora changed the subject. "Do you have any Rachael Ray ones?"

"She's not a baker." Vivienne reminded her.

"She had some actress on her show the other day, that one from that show we watch on Sunday nights." Nora snapped her fingers. "You know who I'm talking about."

"Are you talking about the blond that plays Sandy Briar on 'Retribution'?"

"Yes!" Nora smiled. "She was a real class act, I must say. They made some kind of vegetarian club sandwich together."

"I've been so busy here I haven't paid much attention to daytime television." Vivienne set the manual down and pushed 'program cash register' to the bottom of the list.

"Speaking of our nights, how was yours?" Nora coyly asked.

"It was fine."

"You didn't chicken out, did you?"

"Why does everyone jump to that conclusion first?" Vivienne asked.

"Who else thought that?" Nora asked.

"Kathy."

Nora's eyes narrowed. "She was nicer than usual to me at the store. Must be she was fishing for information too."

Vivienne threw her hands up in frustration. "You all don't have to tip toe around to find out what I'm doing in my private life. Why don't you just ask me what you want to hear?"

"This isn't the Spanish Inquisition." Nora interrupted. "I was just wondering how you two sparked."

Vivienne took a moment to compose her emotions. She knew that the stress of opening the store was growing as the grand opening crept closer to reality. She didn't wish to take it out on everyone around her like so many others seemed to do these days. "He was a gentleman in every sense of the word." She revealed and pulled up a chair to sit down across from her mother.

"I'm so glad." Nora gushed with pride. "Hard to believe he's still single."

"We had dinner at Shanghai Sunset."

"So what did you learn about him?"

Vivienne paused for a moment and then realized how little he had talked about himself. She actually couldn't think of anything new or personal that he had shared during their date. "Not much."

"Where's he from?"

"He mentioned a city, I think." She thought back to their conversation over dinner. "But I don't recall if he gave a specific name."

Nora shifted in her chair. "That's a bit odd."

"Is it really?"

"That's the topic of conversation when you're new in a small town." Nora replied. "I'm surprised that he never brought it up."

"Well we had a great time, despite the lack of personal information." Vivienne took her mother's hand in hers and gave it a little squeeze. "Thank you for setting us up."

Nora smiled at her daughter. "So you're going to go out with him again?"

"Yes." Vivienne thought carefully of her answer and amended it to curtail any gossip. "If he asks me again, that is."

"He'd be a fool to let a successful small business woman opening her own shop in this terrible economy slip away." Nora gestured to the bakery with pride. "Not to mention such a beautiful daughter."

"Thanks, Mother."

Chapter 4

It was right at the peak of dinner hour that Vivienne stepped into the Monarch Grocery store and snagged one of the smaller grocery carts, stashing her green fabric grocery bags on the lower rack near the wheels. As she pushed her cart along through the produce aisle, she stopped to admire the display of apples from some of the local orchards. There were so many varieties to choose from, but she had her favorites when it came to baking.

The Northern Spy apple, with its partly green and red coloring was the one her grandmother always picked on their fall orchard visits. It was a hearty apple, with a tough exterior that allowed it to keep much longer than the other varieties. It was the perfect choice for her grandmother, who had grown up during the depression and always looked for the best value for her money.

She found a half-bushel and placed it into her cart with the intention of turning out some rustic apple blossoms for the grand opening. As she wound through the displays of vegetables, she picked up a small bag of salad mix that would serve as a quick dinner at the bakery when she finished programming the register.

She had just turned the corner toward the deli counter when she nearly bumped carts with Kathy who appeared to also be on a dinner scouting mission. "They just let anyone shop here now, I tell you." She joked.

Kathy blinked for a moment before recognizing her best friend. "You colored your hair. It looks wonderful."

"Did you finally go see Marie at *Nouveau You*?"

"I did it on my own." Vivienne smiled and moved her cart to the side so a harried mother with four hyper children could get past her. "But thanks for the compliment regardless."

"I was just thinking about you, actually." Kathy smiled.

"We must have some weird psychic connection, like identical twins?" Vivienne admired the Caprese salad on the Mediterranean olive bar. The succulent red tomatoes and creamy pieces of fresh buffalo mozzarella tossed together in olive oil with fresh basil certainly looked tempting, but the ten dollar a pound sign next to it curbed her appetite quickly.

"How did the date with Deputy Dashing go?" Kathy guided her cart over to the international cheese case and added a small wheel of brie to her collection of groceries.

"His name is Joshua Arkins." Vivienne corrected. "It was actually better than I could have hoped."

"That's so good to hear." Kathy motioned for them to move down to the bakery section where one of the workers was putting out some freshly baked bread.

Vivienne followed her, careful to not run over one of the hyper children who was now sprawled on his back and spinning in a circle on the polished floor as his clueless mother picked out luncheon meat to be sliced for sandwiches. "He was thoughtful and had none of that macho male attitude that you'd think would come with a cop."

"Nora actually snagged someone good this time?" Kathy picked up a small loaf of multi-grain bread and examined it for flaws. Satisfied with her choice, she tossed it into her cart and moved on to the meat department with efficient speed.

"I'm as surprised as you." Vivienne hurried to keep up behind her. She paused to pick up a package of boneless chicken breasts.

"You're better off getting the club pack of a dozen breasts rather than a four pack." Kathy pointed to the price per pound information.

"But I don't need that much. It's just me for dinner most nights." Vivienne reasoned.

"Divide them into bags and store them in your deep freeze for later." Kathy picked up a rib eye steak and placed it in her cart. "I'm sure you'll find all sorts of recipes to use with your slow cooker when you're at work. That's what I do."

"You're amazing." Vivienne shook her head. "You squeeze a nickel until the buffalo poops at the grocery, but don't bat an eyelash at dropping a hundred dollars on a makeup consultation."

"You can't put a price on beauty." Kathy grinned. "Well, actually, I guess you can."

"One hundred dollars, to be exact." Vivienne mentally did the math and decided to go with the club pack. She could very well be cooking dinner for two if more dates with Joshua followed and she sincerely hoped they would. "I need to visit the toothpaste aisle."

Kathy led them to the health and beauty section where a plethora of personal care products beckoned with flashy packaging promising more quantity or better performance for the same low, low price. She stopped at the shower gels and flipped the tops to sniff some of the scents. "So when is the next date?"

Tossing her usual brand of whitening toothpaste into the cart, she pulled out a crumpled sheet of notebook paper from her pants pocket and went over her grocery list. "Probably not until after the store opens."

Kathy pulled out her smart phone and pulled up her grocery list from one of the many apps installed. She shook her head at her friend's lack of interest in technology as she updated her items and glanced at the latest status messages on her social network site. "Maybe we should check his *Social Butterfly* page?"

Vivienne scooted over to Kathy and tried to peek at what was on the screen. "Can you do that?"

"Sure." She tapped her slender fingers across the digital keyboard on her phone. "Hardly anyone uses smart phones as phones anymore."

Vivienne marveled at how adept her friend was with electronics. "I don't get how people are so into reading other people's everyday thoughts. What's so exciting about what they're cooking for dinner tonight?"

"I think I found his profile." Kathy smiled and then frowned. "Damn."

"What is it?" Vivienne suddenly became very interested in whatever everyday thoughts Joshua was having. Had he blabbed she was a bad date who spit green tea all over the table?

"He's cocooned."

Vivienne just stared at her friend. "What on Earth does that mean?"

"He doesn't post anything public. You have to friend him to see anything other than his profile picture." She held the phone closer and nodded. "But he takes a great picture."

"Let me see." Vivienne reached for the phone.

Kathy handed it to her. "If you were more connected with the technological world, you'd have been on his friends list by now."

Vivienne had to admit that her friend was indeed right about the photo on Joshua's profile. He was handsome and masculine, showing off his smile that she so enjoyed on their date the previous evening. "Do you think you could setup *Social Butterfly* on my computer at home?"

"I've only been offering to do that for like two years now." Kathy took her phone back. "When's good for you?"

She thought of the remaining tasks to get accomplished and felt guilty pushing it all aside for her fascination with the new deputy. "I probably should wait until after the store opens."

"Oh my God, live a little." Kathy scolded her. "Let's do a quick dinner at your place and I'll set it up while you toss together a chef salad."

"What do you think he has on there?" Vivienne wondered aloud. "Do you think he said anything about our date?"

"If he did, I'd dump him." Kathy's voice dropped a bit. "You don't want a boyfriend blabbing every intimate detail."

"A lesson learned from past experience?"

"I need some cooking spray." Kathy changed the subject and pushed her cart toward the end of the aisle.

"I also forgot my shopper's club card and I need to borrow yours, so don't sneak off to the checkout without me."

Vivienne shook her head and followed. "I'm right behind you."

Back at her home, Vivienne couldn't help but feel like a school girl playing hooky as she tossed together a simple chef salad to share with Kathy. There were so many little things to finish. She really should have been eating dinner at her bakery.

Kathy was hard at work on the desktop computer that was tucked into a corner in the living room and almost forgotten under piles of junk mail that threatened to bury it. "This thing is a dinosaur." Kathy complained in front of the boxy monitor that flickered every now and then from age.

"I've got better things to spend money on." Vivienne brought the salad bowl over to the dining room table and placed it in the center. She had chopped up some left over deli meat from the fridge, thrown in some cherry tomatoes and cucumber slices, and even mixed up one of those Italian dressing packets in one of those cheap glass cruets from the grocery store.

"If you had a modern computer this would have been done an hour ago." She leaned back in the chair. "I didn't know dial up was still around anymore."

Vivienne rolled her eyes and placed the salad tongs in the bowl. "Dinner's ready."

"I'm starved." Kathy rushed over from the computer and took a seat. "Hey, this looks pretty good for one of those pre-packaged salad kits." She eagerly placed some salad in her bowl.

"I always jazz them up a bit." Vivienne said as

she sat down to enjoy her dinner. "So how's it going over there?"

"It's going." Kathy drizzled her greens with some dressing and passed the cruet to Vivienne. "Give it another five or ten minutes."

As she speared some salad with her fork, she thought about what she had seen this morning in front of her store. "Did I tell you I saw Joshua giving Mona a ticket this morning?"

"No." Kathy was intrigued. "Do tell."

"I couldn't hear everything from inside the store, but she had parked in front of a fire hydrant and kept insisting she was on some sort of official city business." Vivienne explained as she drizzled a little more dressing on her salad.

"That woman has no shame." Kathy agreed. "So did she put up a fight?"

"She was loud and even made kind of a threat about him living in a small town and rubbing people the wrong way." Vivienne thought back to the ugly incident and hoped Joshua wouldn't judge everyone on the bad temper of a spoiled woman like Mona Clarke.

"Get out." Kathy nearly spit out her salad in shock. "She threatened him?"

Suddenly aware that this dinner conversation could spiral into town gossip emanating directly from the *Trade Winds Clothier* store, she worked quickly to downplay it. The last thing she needed when opening a new business was to get on Mona Clarke's bad side. "It wasn't really a threat. It was something stupid she said in the heat of anger."

Kathy shook her head in amazement. "Still, that's quite an aggressive move on her part. I swear, starting this Historic Commission has gone right to her head."

"It certainly has lit a fire under her." Vivienne agreed.

"I'll bet there are plenty of people who'd love to see her get burned." Kathy laughed.

After finishing their salads, they moved back to the computer where Kathy sat Vivienne down in the basic office chair she had found at a yard sale and forced her to learn the fine art of social networking.

Kathy used her smart phone to capture a good picture of Vivienne in just the right pose with the most flattering lighting they could provide. Using some basic photo editing software, she softened the image and it was soon uploaded to the new *Social Butterfly* account. "We've got a great picture and all your basic information on there."

"What's the next step?" Vivienne glanced at the computer screen.

"You need to start sending friend requests. After they approve it, you'll be able to follow their status messages and look at any photos they have added.

"Wow." Vivienne couldn't help but be impressed.

"You can even make ad for your business and use it for all sorts of free marketing." Kathy explained. "I often put little one day specials on the *Trade Winds* page and it can drum up business on a slow day."

"Now that's something useful."

"But let's get that friend request to Joshua." Kathy reached over her and typed his name in the search box. A few clicks of the mouse later his picture was smiling on Vivienne's monitor. "It's sent. Now you'll have to wait until he logs on and approves it."

Vivienne scanned the main page and pointed to the icon that looked like a patch of little flowers. A red number one was highlighting it. "What's that?"

"Click and see." Kathy instructed.

She did just that and Kathy's picture appeared. "Kathy Saunders wants to join my friend garden?"

"Congratulations. I hear she's fabulous."

Vivienne accepted the request and Kathy explained the basics of reading the profile and how to post status messages and share links to interesting web pages. Nearly an hour and half later, she was shocked to see how it consumed her free time at an alarming rate. "I have to go back to the store and get that register programmed."

"Is it really after eight?" Kathy checked the designer watch on her wrist. "Let me help you load the dishwasher."

"No need to do that. I'll just deal with them when I get home." Vivienne shut the computer down. "Thanks for all your help."

"Welcome to the twenty-first century, darling." Kathy smiled. "We've been expecting you."

Chapter 5

It had taken four snooze button presses before she was able to part herself from the warm covers of her bed the next morning. She had returned to her store after dinner and managed to not only program the cash register, but she had finished the kitchen setup for the morning baking. It was nearly three in the morning when she briefly considered pulling an all night session like a twenty year old college student. But her thirty-six year old body refused to allow that and she went home to get a few hours of shut eye.

As she swung her legs over the edge of her queen bed, she shoved her feet into a pair of comfortable white bunny slippers that Nora had given her as a Christmas present last year. The sunlight was streaming in through the lavender curtains of her bedroom. As usual, she walked over to greet the morning from her second floor window. It made her happy to see that the big sugar maple next to the sidewalk was starting to display its peak foliage. The green leaves were now a fiery red and yellow mix that just begged to be collected and waxed for her window display at the store. Mother Nature always provided the best decorations for this time of year.

After retrieving the newspaper from her front steps, she inhaled the air that was crisp and a bit colder than the day before. There hadn't been a heavy frost yet, but she was certain one was on the way. Cayuga Lake provided a micro-climate that allowed for temperature fluctuations that were especially productive for grapes. As such, wineries had sprung up all along the shoreline, with more opening each year. The tour buses made regular visits along the wine route, but lacking a winery in the town area they never stopped in town. She began to wonder if perhaps Mona Clarke had the right idea but was just going about it the wrong way.

With a mug of hot coffee in hand, she slid into the chair in front of the computer and turned it on. This felt strangely different from her usual routine of sitting on the sofa and casually browsing the newspaper for interesting articles about local happenings.

Following the instructions Kathy had given her, she was excited to see the little flower garden icon highlighted with a red number one above it. She moved the cursor, clicked the mouse, and a picture of her mother appeared on the screen. `Nora Finch wants to join your friend garden`, the text underneath it had explained.

She sighed and took a sip of her coffee. How long had her mother been social networking? She hadn't even known she could use a computer. She must have taken one of the free classes at the senior center. Why couldn't she have taken something like needlepoint or photography? As her finger hovered over the mouse to accept the request she paused. Did she really want to give her mother this much insight into her social life? Then again, denying one's own mother as a friend seemed rather harsh and she was sure it would lead to more arguments than she really cared for in the future. With a click of the mouse she and her mother were now officially friends, at least according to *Social Butterfly*.

As she scrolled the status page, she found a link

that Kathy had posted sometime last night. It led to the page of the *Cayuga Cove Historic Commission* and an artist rendering of Main Street after all the proposed improvements. Vivienne navigated to the 'What's New' button and clicked on it. She found that the first meeting to discuss the Main Street Renovation Project was going to be held in the library at seven tonight. In tiny text at the bottom, there was mention that it was open to the public.

She wasn't sure she'd have to time to attend given all the baking that needed to get done to fill her cases, but she was going to try her best to be there. The future of her business could be at stake and she probably should be as proactive as possible to make sure it remained her livelihood.

As she parked her red Toyota Matrix near the dumpsters behind the bakery, she was happy to see that no wayward trash had been deposited from careless trash pickup. The sun was shining strong and bright on another fine morning. It warmed her face as she walked to the back door. She felt energized to start the non-stop baking fest and fill her store with tempting goodies.

An hour later, she had her four commercial grade convection ovens filled with batches of peanut butter, sugar, ginger, and oatmeal raisin cookies. Thanks to the dual industrial mixers, she was able to churn out batches in record time but still, she was running a little behind schedule and it made her just a little nervous. Did she need to hire an assistant? It was the one question she couldn't really answer at the moment. Only time would reveal that.

There had been no argument outside her store

this morning, and the space where the bright yellow fire hydrant reflected the sunlight had remained open. As the smell of cookies filled the air, she walked over to the display window and looked out at Main Street.

Despite nothing being open, the road was filled with cars from all the tenants who rented the apartments above the businesses. Mona Clarke had been right about the lack of parking for customers and once more she felt she had a good point. True, some of the spaces opened up as the tenants left for their jobs, but most remained full for the day and it could be a challenge to find parking for some of the businesses.

Just how far was one of her customers willing to walk a cake back to their car? What about rain or snow? She doubted people would trudge very far through puddles or dirty snow banks to buy some cookies.

Another hour of baking passed. Now that the first batches were cooled, she began to fill the glass display cases with some of the goods. She placed paper doilies down on the trays, arranging the cookies in neat rows that would look attractive from the customer side of the case. Thanks to hours as a child spent learning cursive in grade school, she was able to hand script little price and product identification cards that perched on spiral place card holders above each product. It gave the store a special homemade touch that felt nothing like the impersonal corporate coffee shops and bookstores that spread like weeds across America's retail landscape.

The air was now perfumed with the scent of decadent chocolate mocha brownies. Some plain, others swirled with cheesecake and peanut butter. As she continued to write up little signs perched on one of her bistro tables, she was startled by a knock on the front door. She looked up and saw the smiling face of Mona Clarke standing outside.

"I'm afraid I'm not officially open until tomorrow morning at ten." Vivienne said as she opened the door.

Mona Clarke smiled at her, dressed in a royal purple jacket that probably cost as much as one of the commercial ovens in the bakery. "I saw the closed sign, but I thought a little sneak peek might be okay for the Mayor's wife."

Vivienne was at a loss for words. She had so much to do, but the chance to get some inside information from Mona was too much to resist. She gestured for her to enter. "What a delightful surprise. Come in."

Mona breezed into her store, trailing some sort of floral perfume that completely overpowered the baking smell. "What a beautiful little shop you have." She gushed, taking in the view.

Vivienne closed the door and gave her apron a quick pat down to shake off some of the flour that had spilled during her morning baking. "Thank you. I did most of it myself, except for the electric and the plumbing."

"It's just so charming and warm." Mona walked over the display case and admired the fresh cookies inside. "These look absolutely scrumptious."

"Would you like a free sample?" Vivienne asked. "I've got plenty on hand."

Mona removed her coat and set it on the back of one of the bistro chairs. "That would be wonderful, dear." She knelt down to check her reflection in the glass of the case, making sure her light blond hair, swept up into a fancy style with a bejeweled clip, was still picture perfect.

"I was just about to have some tea." Vivienne sailed into the kitchen area and turned on the electric kettle. "How about some honey lemon?"

"Don't go to any trouble." Mona answered as she sat down.

"It's no trouble at all." Vivienne put the tea bags into two ceramic mugs and returned to the table with two peanut butter cookies on a small saucer.

"I don't know if you're aware of the *Cayuga Cove Women of Small Business Association.*"

"I just received one of your newsletters the other day, actually." Vivienne answered.

"Wonderful." Mona folded her hands together on the table, catching the late morning sunlight with her diamond encrusted wedding band. "I'm the Director and we'd love to have you join our little group."

"That would be nice." Vivienne answered politely. "Aren't you also involved with the Historic Commission?"

"I am indeed." Mona reached for a cookie and took a tiny bite as a knock on the front window startled them both.

Vivienne saw the smiling face of Victoria Clemens peering in. She was dressed in workout sweats that somehow looked better than any of the everyday clothes she wore.

Victoria gave a little wave and then continued on what must have been her morning power walk to work off breakfast. 'How many calories could Irish coffee actually have?' Vivienne wondered to herself. Given Victoria's trim figure, she doubted a sugared doughnut or deep-fried fritter ever crossed her Botox-enhanced lips.

Mona waved back and then let out a little sigh. "Unfortunately, we already have the voting member chairs filled."

"Oh, I wasn't interested in joining that." Vivienne corrected.

"But the meetings will be open to the public, of course." Mona added with a little smile. "We're not expecting much of a turnout for the first one." She took another bite of the cookie. "These are just divine."

"Thank you." Vivienne retuned a smile. "So why are you expecting a small turnout?"

Mona paused for a moment, as if she were composing her thoughts in advance before speaking. "Well, I hate to say it but our agendas will probably be quite dull for the general public's attention. First meetings usually lack a cohesive flow."

"I would think quite the opposite to be the case." Vivienne leaned forward in her chair. "If you're going to be taking on the challenge of updating Main Street to attract more tourism, I think that'd generate quite a bit of buzz."

There was an uncomfortable silence as Mona listened to her words and processed them. "I guess we'll find out tonight for sure."

The tea kettle whistled and Vivienne jumped up to grab the hot water. "I'm hoping to be there if I can catch up on all the baking left to be done."

"Great." Mona's tone was flat.

Vivienne poured the hot water into the mugs

and returned to the table. "I think that once the right plan is presented, you'll find everyone happy to jump onboard for bringing in those tour busses that zoom by along the wine trail."

Mona sipped her tea and nodded thoughtfully. "It will have to be sooner rather than later."

Vivienne took a sip of her tea. "Why is that?"

"Well, for one thing those tour companies plan their bus tours about a year in advance. In order to entice them to add us to their routes, we need to be able to present them with our plan by late October." Mona explained as she took another sip of tea.

"I didn't know that." Vivienne took care to keep mental notes for Kathy who would no doubt want all the details.

"Not many people do." Mona sighed. "They think these bus tours just meander about the roads and stop wherever it looks interesting. But the truth of the matter is you really have to pitch your town to their corporate planning board. Even after that, there's a terrible amount of competition along the wine trail and it's just getting more crowded with each season."

"Is this what you're going to explain at the meeting tonight?"

"Yes, along with some other minor details." Mona pushed her chair back and stood up to retrieve her coat. "I hate to rush off, but I have a rather important issue to take care of this afternoon."

"Thank you so much for stopping by."

Mona slipped her coat on and walked over the display of teas. "I may have to start a standing order for some of these blends for the meetings. All that speaking can be murder on the vocal chords."

"Just say the word and I'll write it up." Vivienne stood up from the table and extended her hand.

Mona gave her a firm handshake. "Let's add a dozen cookies or so to that order." She turned to leave and then pivoted back around on her expensive-looking designer heels. "What time is your grand opening tomorrow?"

"Ten." Vivienne's voice cracked as she thought about all the last minute details that were going to have to get completed.

"I'll see you tomorrow morning with the giant scissors." Mona winked and sailed out the door, trailing her perfume once again.

Chapter 6

"You must be crazy." Kathy raised her voice from behind the counter of her store.

"I'm telling you, she's not as bad as she seems." Vivienne had four cakes baking in her ovens. Thanks to her mother offering to watch the store, she had been able to slip away for a little break to catch her friend up with her morning encounter.

"Are you sure she didn't slip something into your mug of tea when you weren't looking?" Kathy folded her arms across her chest.

"Nice as could be." Vivienne insisted. "She was nothing at all like the woman arguing with Joshua the other morning."

Kathy rapped her French-tipped nails on the countertop nervously. "Now I'm positive she's up to something."

Vivienne had made steady progress with her baking schedule and she was quite certain she would be able to make the meeting tonight after all. "Want me to save you a seat at the meeting?"

"I thought your new friend didn't think there was going to be a big turnout?" Kathy raised an eyebrow.

"She's just an acquaintance." Vivienne corrected. "Despite what she thinks, I imagine it will be quite full.

"Oh, it will be." Kathy started typing on the keyboard of her computer.

"What are you doing?"

"I'm sending out a group message to all the local merchants I'm friends with on *Social Butterfly*." Her fingers flew across the keyboard. "I will need you to save me a seat because this meeting is going to be packed."

Vivienne wasn't sure if her friend was doing it for the good of the Main Street merchants or just out of spite for her dislike of Mona. Either way, a healthy crowd turnout was a good thing. More ideas could be brought up and perhaps everyone would walk away with a better understanding of the whole situation. At least, she hoped it would turn out that way. "That's a great idea."

Kathy finished the message and sent it along. "I'm glad you agree."

"I better get back to the bakery before Nora decides to try her own recipes." Vivienne glanced at her watch and was surprised it was still only ten minutes to two. The day was cooperating for once.

"See you at seven." Kathy waved as Vivienne left her store.

* * *

As Vivienne pulled open the glass door to the Cayuga Cove library, she inhaled the scent of old books that always conjured images of trips with her mother for story hours. Nora had instilled a love of books and reading from an early age in her daughter. As an only child, much of her social interaction outside of the school yard had happened in a seated circle on a large braided rug in the common room of the library.

The librarian would read a book to the children, usually acting out the parts with funny voices and asking the children to provide the sound effects. After a snack of cookies and fruit punch, she and the other boys and girls were allowed to browse the rows of colorful books and choose one to check out. It would transport her to different worlds where dogs could be red or rain clouds could drop scoops of strawberry ice cream.

Her moment of sweet nostalgia was interrupted when Clara Bunton's voice startled her from behind. "This had better be worth closing down early tonight."

"Stephanie isn't quite ready to be left alone yet?" Vivienne followed in step with Clara as they breezed past the circulation desk and headed for the set of double doors that led to the conference room. She was still dressed in her pink uniform, but had put a simple white sweater over it to keep the evening chill away.

"Don't get me wrong, Harold is a capable cook and I trust him like a member of my own family." Clara explained as she waved to Harriet Nettles, the town librarian. "But his field of vision rarely leaves the grill."

"So how did you find out about the meeting?" Vivienne could smell the faint scent of fried food as she followed Clara. "Was it through *Social Butterfly*?"

"What's that?" Clara asked as they approached the doors which were thrown open revealing the oak-paneled walls that had oversized lithographs of famous novel covers framed like art prints hanging haphazardly. Harriet Nettles was a great librarian, but her interior decorating skills left much to be desired.

"It's this social networking program on the computer." Vivienne could hear the murmur of many voices from the conference room and it sounded rather crowded.

"Me use one of those infernal devices?" Clara

laughed. "Kathy came in for lunch and told me all about it."

As they stepped into the room, Vivienne surveyed the scene with disbelief. There were ten rows of folding chairs, split by the aisle, with five on each side. The first eight rows were full and several more patrons slipped in behind them and claimed more space. "We better find a place quick and save a chair for Kathy."

Clara guided her to the second to last row on the left and removed the white sweater from her shoulders. She placed it over the aisle chair and then sat down next to it. "Done and done."

Vivienne sat next to Clara and began to scan the crowd of faces for people she knew. She recognized Tony DiSanto who owned *The Leaning Tower of Pizza* shop two doors down from her bakery. He was talking to Evelyn Hart, who ran the *Lakeside Gift Emporium*, his hands a flurry of gestures that seemed quite emphatic.

Two uniformed police officers stood watch at each end near the front of the room where several folding tables had been placed. Vivienne had hoped one of them would be Joshua so she could say hello again in person, but it wasn't meant to be.

A swath of burgundy cloth had been draped over the tables, giving the entire scene a look of official business. At the center, a tabletop podium of light oak was adorned with a golden placard that had the image of the town flag ringed with the words '*Cayuga Cove Historic Commission*' around the edge. Atop the podium, a small wooden gavel rested waiting for a hand to bang it to call the meeting to order.

There were small name cards arranged in front

of the four chairs that flanked the podium, along with small microphones. Vivienne squinted to read the names, but was too far away to make them out. She knew that Mona Clarke would be seated at the center podium, ready to lay out her plans to the town. Would she use her charm like this morning at the bakery? Or would she take a more aggressive approach like she had with Joshua when he wrote her the ticket?

"So does this count as a second date?" Joshua tapped Vivienne on the shoulder from the row behind her.

She craned her neck around in surprise. He was dressed in civilian clothing again, this time a blue flannel button down shirt and a pair of dark denim jeans and tan cowboy boots. "I was just thinking about you." She gushed and felt her cheeks burn slightly.

Clara turned slightly to face him with a smile. "What brings you here, Deputy Arkins?"

"Social Butterfly had a notice about a big meeting tonight concerning the future of the town." He answered in his matter-of-fact voice that refused to give up the location of his accent. "It sounded like something important."

"Isn't that the computer thing-a-ma-jig you were talking about earlier?" Clara asked Vivienne.

"Yes." Vivienne answered. "I haven't had a chance to use it much."

"That's a relief." Joshua added with a smile. "I thought maybe you were avoiding me."

Vivienne felt her jaw drop slightly in shock. "Whatever gave you that idea?"

"I sent you a note about going to this meeting together but I never heard back." Joshua feigned a sad face. "I thought maybe getting ignored online would hurt less?"

"I was waiting for your friend request to be accepted." Vivienne was quick to the defense.

"I did this morning." Joshua waggled his eyebrows at her.

The heat from her cheeks seemed to radiate to the rest of her body. She had been so busy with baking and getting the store ready she hadn't checked her computer at home at all. Heck, she hadn't even been home since she left early in the morning. "I've been busy down at the shop." She stammered.

He reached over and placed his hand back on her shoulder. "It's okay. I know how busy you've been and I was just teasing."

She loved the feel of his hand on her body. It was warm and she wished he would leave it there for the entire meeting. "Tomorrow is the big day. I hope you can make it for the ribbon cutting at ten."

He pulled his hand away and scratched the goatee on his chin. "I'm pretty sure that I'm free, unless someone in town decides to act up and break a law."

"Like Mona Clarke?" Vivienne regretted the comment the moment it passed her lips.

Joshua's eyes narrowed a bit and he took a deep breath. "Don't remind me."

She hated bringing the subject up, especially when Mona was going to be speaking to the room in a few short minutes. "I thought you handled the whole deal like a real professional." She tried to smooth the awkward moment over. "Frankly, I don't know what the big fuss was about."

He nodded politely and leaned back against his

chair. "Thank you."

"And this doesn't count as a second date, by the way." She gave a nervous laugh.

His demeanor softened for a moment. "I'm glad to hear that."

She turned back around as the Historic Commission officers filed into the room and marched up the middle aisle with purpose. As Kathy had explained at the diner a few days ago, the board was composed of five women. First to appear was Victoria Clemens, a tall brunette who had never actually worked a day in her life. She had married well to Stephen Clemens, whose family operated the *Harvest Glen Winery* on the West side of the lake. She wore a high-end designer outfit that made her look like a model strutting down the fashion runway.

Suzette Powell followed next in line, a petite woman with a dark brown pageboy haircut who looked nervous at the amount of people in the room. Having the misfortune to follow behind Victoria, her modest outfit looked rather frumpy and she kept biting her nails only to catch herself and drop her arms rigidly at her sides. She ran a small catering company out of her home named *The Formal Affair*. More than a few people had gossiped about the unfortunate coincidence with the name, as her husband Brad Powell was a notorious ladies man who had his share of affairs over the years.

Third in the line that proceeded down the aisle, Mary Ellen Bryce was composed and confident. As the assistant principal at Cayuga Cove Elementary, she frequently clashed with parents when their children violated any of the school's policies. She was a strong supporter of conformity and many parents in the town still seethed over the pricey school uniforms they were required to buy each school year thanks to her expertise at intimidating the school board and its weak superintendant.

Cassandra Pembroke held tightly to a large yellow notepad as she marched up the aisle. She was a rather plain looking mother of four grown children who seemed content to keep company in her large home with several pampered cats. She seemed out of place amongst the other officers on the board, but Vivienne knew that back in her glory days she had been quite a social climber with stunning looks to match.

She had married and later divorced a chief financial officer for one of the big banks in Manhattan during the boom of the eighties. Although she had secured a generous amount of alimony, the tempestuous separation had taken its toll on her looks and eventually she just stopped trying to re-capture her youth. Yet, she was the one to call whenever you needed an important contact for anything, and most certainly Mona Clarke wanted to keep in her good graces for needed favors down the road. After all, she had provided several big names for Mayor Clarke's election campaign that opened their checkbooks for generous donations that practically all but assured his election the previous year.

Last, but certainly not least, Mona Clarke kept several paces behind the others and frequently stopped to nod hello and shake hands with some of the members of the audience who wished to do so. Like her husband, she had learned the fine art of the firm handshake and sincere look. Even when someone had shouted 'Queen Mona' in the crowd, she ignored it and continued to the podium with her usual grace. Taking her place behind the podium, she tapped the gavel five times and brought order to the room. "Order please."

The general murmur of conversation died off as people hushed each other. Kathy glided into the room just as Harriet Nettles closed the doors. She slipped into her chair and shoved her purse down by Vivienne's feet. "Sorry I'm late. Something came up that I couldn't put off."

Vivienne moved her legs awkwardly to the side as Kathy's oversized handbag took nearly all the floor space below her. "You're just in time." She whispered back as the members sat down at the table to face the audience.

"I call this meeting of the *Cayuga Cove Historical Commission* to order." Mona spoke firmly as the microphone amplified her voice over the speakers in the ceiling.

The other board members looked a bit flustered at what to do next. Some fidgeted with pens and paper. Others poured glasses of ice water and looked out at the crowd nervously.

Mona took charge immediately. "I'd like to start this first meeting by thanking all the members of the community who have taken time out of their busy schedules to attend tonight. We look forward to hearing your valuable input this evening."

"We need to defend our businesses." Someone shouted from the crowd to which Mona banged the gavel three times in response.

"Please, I must ask that all comments and

concerns be raised at the appropriate time." Mona scanned the room with her eyes, defying another outburst. Satisfied with the quiet, she set the gavel down and continued. "As I said, I appreciate everyone's time and I'm sure that you're all going to agree that our plan will benefit the entire town."

Clara gave Vivienne a slight poke with her elbow. "Do you think Julius Caesar started his last speech that way?" She whispered.

Vivienne smiled and gave her a wink. "Et tu Brute?"

Over the next half hour, Mona proceeded to explain her plan for the refurbishing of Main Street. She utilized a computer and projected several artist renderings of what the building style would look like onto a large screen behind the board members. "As you can see, our design will give all the businesses on Main Street a cohesive look that will entice shoppers to explore and discover. Our inspiration for the design started with Market Street in Corning, New York." She displayed a series of images as she spoke. "Which when combined with elements from downtown Salem, Massachusetts and the coastal charm of Ogunquit, Maine, will add up to a unique locale irresistible to tourists."

Vivienne had to admit, the drawings certainly did make Cayuga Cove look like one of the picturesque seaside towns that dotted the New England coastline. The colors and styles were uniform and pleasing to the eye, as were the decorative wooden signs for each of the businesses. The artist had even produced four images of the street decorated for each of the seasons and several oh's and ah's came from the assembled audience.

Just as she had done in the bakery with Vivienne, Mona went on to explain how the cosmetic changes would entice tour bus companies to make the town a stop on their lucrative wine trail runs and how the increase in business would bring much needed tax money into the local economy. "By investing in the future, you are helping not only to create a beautiful town to call home," she paused for dramatic effect, "You are going to create a stable tax base that will help keep costs to taxpayers at a manageable level."

Her remarks were met with a smattering of applause. "It's a win-win deal for everyone."

There were quite a few disgruntled moans afterwards and a low murmur began to stir.

"I move we open the floor for discussion." Mary Ellen Bryce spoke up sensing the energy of the assembled crowd. As assistant principal it was second nature to use her voice to command attention. Vivienne half expected her to flip the lights on and off as was the norm at so many school assemblies.

"I second the motion." Suzette Powell spoke into the microphone a little too closely which caused some feedback. She cupped her hands around it which only made more noise.

Victoria pulled Suzette's hands away and the feedback disappeared, much to the relief of the room.

"Discussion is approved." Mona tapped the gavel. "There is a microphone set up on the far right of the room, please line up and speak clearly."

Several patrons jumped to their feet and created a line along the right wall. "Excuse me ladies." Kathy grabbed her purse and hustled over to the end of the line.

First to speak was Raymond Meeker. He cleared his throat and tapped the microphone with his right hand. "Testing?"

"The microphone is working." Mary Ellen replied, her voice taking a more harsh tone than before. She squinted at the long line of questioners. "Given the length of the line, I suggest we limit each person to one question."

"I agree." Mona gave her approval. "Please proceed."

"My name is Raymond Meeker of *Meeker Jewelers*." He spoke just a little too slow, as if placing an order at a fast food drive-thru speaker. "My concern is the funding for this project."

"What is your exact concern?" Mona asked.

"The state is flat broke right now." Raymond wrapped his thumbs around the red suspenders he wore over his starched white dress shirt. "Are we supposed to foot the entire bill for this on our own?"

Mona put on her best smile. "Think of it as a short term personal loan to the town." She took a sip of her ice water and swallowed hard. "You see, once we get all these improvements made, your investment is going to pay off double, maybe triple when all those tour busses pull into town and mob the local stores. If the state-funding is approved down the road, each business will be reimbursed equally."

"Do you want to put that in writing?" Raymond asked her.

"I'm not a psychic, Mister Meeker." Mona shook her head. "I can't guarantee an exact return any more than I could predict the next lotto numbers."

"Then why not wait on this until the state can provide funding?" He asked.

"He might have a good point." Cassandra Pembroke spoke up much to the surprise of everyone. "If not full funding, perhaps we can work out a deal for matching funding?"

"That could take years." Victoria Clemens interrupted with a wave of her bejeweled right hand. "As someone who knows the wine trail inside and out, I can tell you the longer we wait, the less chance we will ever get put on the map."

"As someone who knows banking from the inside out, I think we need to put more effort into funding this project through grants and government loans." Cassandra snapped back.

"Your ex-husband knows banking inside and out." Victoria cast an icy glare at Cassandra. "I hardly think that qualifies you as a financial manager of this project."

"Any more than being married to a winery owner qualifies you as a vintner." Cassandra rebuffed the challenge.

"I told you putting her on the board would create problems." Victoria tried to whisper to Mona, but the microphone picked it up and amplified regardless.

Mona put her hands up in protest. "Ladies, please. This is a hot bed issue to say the least, but we are not here to make personal attacks on who is qualified to do what." She gave a stern look to each end of the table. "Next question please?"

"I'm Tony DiSanto, from *The Leaning Tower of Pizza*." He was dressed in a pair of flour-stained black workpants and a simple white button up shirt that had faded red tomato sauce stains on the sleeves. "So just how much is this going to cost each business owner? Is everyone going to be charged the same amount for the refurbishment?"

Mary Ellen pulled out an electronic tablet device and tapped the screen with her slender fingers. "If we go with the plan presented as of tonight, divided by the number of shops on Main Street, each business would spend approximately three-thousand and fifty dollars and some change."

An elegantly dressed woman with a bun of salt and pepper hair atop her head approached the microphone next. "I'm Evelyn Hart from *Lakeside Gift Emporium*." She spoke softly. "That's quite an investment from each business. I can't speak for everyone here, but I'm not afraid to tell this board it hasn't exactly been a banner year for my store." She raised a piece of paper up and adjusted the gold wire frame glasses on her nose. "My profits are actually down forty percent from last year."

"We're not asking you to refurbish the inside of your shops." Victoria Clemens fielded the question. "We are only talking about a small cosmetic change to the exterior of each business and a uniform sign to tie it all together."

"That's easy for you to say." An anonymous male voice shouted back from the audience. "You don't have a business on Main Street."

Victoria peered into the crowd to try to find the source of the challenge but failed. She brushed her long brown hair back with her hands. "As a matter of fact, *Harvest Glen Winery* is going to open a small tasting room and gift shop on Main Street next spring. So I do have a stake in this, thank you."

Several more members continued to barrage the board with questions about footing the bill and how much everything was going to cost. Mona and her officers did their best to provide answers but the crowd wasn't too convinced by their efforts.

At one point, the discussion turned to the issue of tenant parking on the street and the board was raked over the coals by several apartment dwellers who resented the proposed plan to make them park in lots two streets over to provide ease of customer access.

"One last question and we must close discussion and move on." Mona's voice was strained from her impassioned pleas and saleswoman techniques.

Kathy stood before the microphone. "Kathy Hemmings, owner of *Trade Winds Clothier*."

"Hello Miss Hemmings." Mona's voice was cold. "It's so nice to have such an active participant in the audience." She gestured to the audience. "I hear we have you to thank for such a vigorous turnout tonight."

"Hello," Kathy replied back in an equally cold manner, "and you're most welcome."

"What is your concern?" Mona locked eyes with her.

"Is it true that you're using this issue as a springboard to launch your campaign to run for mayor after your husband's term ends?"

There was a collective gasp in the room. Mona cocked her head to the side. "Whatever gave you that idea?"

Kathy reached into her purse and pulled out some papers. "I have copies of an interview you did with an online magazine, *A Byte of Upstate*, about running for office in a small town."

"I was referring to my husband running for office." Mona was quick on her defense. "The magazine misquoted me and I tried to get them to print a follow up to clarify that."

Kathy quoted from the paper in her hand. "I feel that as a woman running for office, you need to do something beyond mere campaign promises to convince voters you are serious about the job. The truth is that the voting public often gets things wrong and it's the job of elected officials to make them think they're right."

Mona rolled her eyes. "I never said that."

"It's right here in print." Kathy shook the paper.

"It's nothing more than slander by a zealous media outlet to get attention." She gripped the edge of the podium so tight the color drained from her hands. "I've hired a lawyer to pursue legal action if needed."

"Convenient." Kathy nodded and turned to face the crowd. "I've posted a link to the magazine article on Social Butterfly for those of you who want to read it for yourselves."

A general murmur broke out as Kathy stood at the microphone. She began passing out her printed copies of the article to eager hands nearby.

"As there are no more relevant concerns about this project, I move for a vote to go forward with phase one of the proposal." Mona raised her voice.

"What's phase one again?" Suzette asked the board.

"The historic commission has the power to re-zone parking to prevent obstructed views of historic buildings." Mary Ellen reminded everyone. "Main Street will be re-zoned with one hour parking in front of all businesses."

There were several angry shouts from the apartment tenants in the audience.

"All in favor of phase one?" Mona asked.

"Aye." Victoria was first to answer.

"Aye." Mary Ellen added her approval.

Suzette looked nervously around the room. She wrung her hands together for a moment. "Aye," she stammered meekly.

"Opposed." Cassandra spoke with extra emphasis, which brought a cheer and a few whistles from the apartment tenants.

"I vote yes." Mona slammed her gavel down. "Motion passes and will be given to town officials tomorrow morning." She motioned to the police officers at the back of the room who moved forward and stood at each side of the long table. "Our next session will convene two weeks from tonight. This meeting is adjourned." She tapped her gavel again and sat down as the crowd reacted to the event.

The officers kept watch on the crowd as they began to argue with each other about who was right and who was wrong. "This isn't good at all." Joshua spoke up from behind Vivienne. He extended his arm to escort her from the meeting.

"I've never seen anything like it." Vivienne gave him her arm and said a polite goodbye to Clara.

They left the library and stepped out into the air which had grown quite a bit colder since the sun set. "I wish Kathy hadn't done that."

"I'm actually kind of glad she did." Joshua smiled.

"I guess I was raised to believe there is a time and place to bring things up." Vivienne watched as her breath condensed and floated upwards toward the stars above.

"If Mona Clarke wants to get into politics, she better get used to it." Joshua walked beside her on the sidewalk along Main Street. "It's a dirty game."

"That's why I never want to be a part of it." Vivienne replied. "Give me cakes and cookies and recipes any day."

"Speaking of the bakery," Joshua thought aloud, "I should have some officers on standby at the grand opening."

"Who'd want to hurt me?" Vivienne asked.

"Mona Clarke." Joshua replied. "Given the mood tonight I think it might be a wise idea."

Vivienne balled her hands into fists and shook them in the air. "This is just what I needed for publicity and I have my good friend to thank for that."

They arrived in front of the *Sweet Dreams Bakery*. Joshua gestured at the display window that was filled with decorated cakes and cookies. "Once everyone sees this they'll forget all about tonight."

She reached around his waist with her arms. "You think so?"

"I never lie." He looked into her eyes.

"That's good to know." She replied as he pulled her closer and then kissed her fully on the lips.

"I hope that wasn't too forward." He whispered in her ear.

"Not in the slightest." She reached up and ran her fingers through his thick head of hair.

They kissed once more, only this time it was longer. He nibbled slightly on her right ear. "I better let you get back to setting up your store."

She let out a sigh. "I suppose you're right." She fished around in her pants pocket and pulled out her keys. "I made something special for you earlier tonight."

"Oh?" He raised his eyebrows.

"But it tastes better warmed in the oven, so you'll have to come back tomorrow to try it." She stuck the key into the lock and turned the brass tumbler.

"I can't wait. Goodnight Vivienne."

She pulled the door open which caused the little bell to ring. "Goodnight Joshua."

He waved goodbye and disappeared into the night. She shut the door and let her heart slow down from its frenzied beats.

Chapter 7

Despite burning the midnight oil once again, Vivienne had started her day a full hour before her alarm had gone off. Her mind had been working overtime creating lists and checking items off as she got dressed in one of her better outfits she had purchased from Kathy's store. It was a navy blue A-lined sleeveless dress, paired with a tailored jacket and a faux croc belt. It would be fancy enough for the media at the ribbon cutting ceremony, yet she could lose the jacket and slip her logoed apron on to work comfortably through the rest of the day. Heels, of course, would be impractical so she packed a pair of basic black flats to change into after the grand opening.

As she was about to leave, the telephone rang and a quick glance at the display showed Nora's cell number. She shook her head and grabbed her car keys off the hanging wooden rack. "Not this morning, mother."

The gorgeous sunny mornings she had grown used to, failed to repeat today. Thick gray clouds shrouded the light and threatened rain. As long as it held off for the ceremony she wasn't going to complain. She backed down the small driveway of her little home and hummed along with one of those catchy pop songs that played on the radio as she started the ten minute drive to work.

As she drove along Spruce Street, she passed *Clara's Diner* and the usual morning regulars that assembled inside. She wondered who would become a regular at her bakery. Who would claim one of the bistro tables and regale her with town gossip each morning?

Making a right at the red light, she turned onto Main Street and accelerated past the post office and county courthouse. Both buildings had bundled corn stalks and some pumpkins placed as decorations and it made her smile that her favorite time of year was coming once again.

Since it was just after seven-thirty in the morning, most of the businesses on the street were still dark. However, there were a few exceptions. The lights at *Weiss Chocolatier* were on as two employees busied themselves with stringing leaf-shaped garland inside the display window of homemade boxed chocolates and fudge. *Hummingbird Floral* was open for business as the owner, Brian Amberry, watered the rows of hardy mums that lined the sidewalk area in front of his store. He waved to her as she drove by, giving her horn a little toot. Vivienne made a mental note to stop by and pick up a few pots to put in her store for some dazzling fall color.

Passing the darkened storefront of *The Leaning Tower of Pizza*, she put on her turn signal to pull into the alley when she noticed Joshua's deputy cruiser in front of her store along with several other police cars and an ambulance. 'He certainly is true to his word about keeping things secure.' She thought before braking suddenly as her eyes spied the bright yellow ribbon around her store and one of those wooden barriers which blocked all entrance to the alley. Her heart dropped in her chest when she realized it was crime scene tape.

With nowhere to park, she had to swing an awkward 'u' turn and park where Mona had received a ticket, directly in front of the fire hydrant. She hurriedly jumped out of car and dashed across the street as fast as her high heels could carry her. She no sooner reached the edge of the yellow tape, where a few curious onlookers were observing the commotion, when Joshua appeared from the alley. "What happened?" She asked breathlessly as the onlookers murmured to each other.

"Vivienne, you'll have to stay outside the crime scene for now." Joshua's voice was low and professional.

"Is it my mother?" She felt tears welling up in her eyes as she recalled ignoring the phone call. "Did something happen to her?"

"It's not Nora." Joshua assured her.

Without thinking she fell into his embrace. "Oh thank God. I'd have never forgiven myself if something had happened."

He kept her in his embrace for a moment as she caught her breath. "I didn't mean to scare you like that."

She pulled her face away from the black leather jacket that he wore over his brown uniform. "It wasn't you. I scared myself."

"I'm sorry this had to happen on your special day." Joshua tried to comfort her.

She could hear the_ voices of emergency responders talking to each other, radios crackling from the response vehicles. A sudden flash erupted from the back alley and she blinked in surprise. "What happened?"

He looked around for a moment and pulled her out of earshot of the growing crowd that was gathering in front of her store. "It's Mona Clarke. She was found dead in a dumpster out back."

Vivienne felt her knees go weak and she grabbed onto the edges of his jacket for support. "Someone killed her?"

"Yes." He kept his voice low. "But right now we've got some of the state troopers on the scene and we're keeping a lid on the details. Promise me you won't say anything."

"I promise." She replied.

"Vivienne, she was found in your dumpster."

Her mind flashed to a horror scene of splattered blood and gore. "Has someone told her husband yet?"

"We've already sent someone to pick him up." Joshua's face was grim. "They need him to verify her identity before they can transport the body up to Rochester for an autopsy."

Vivienne shook her head in disbelief. "I never thought something like this could happen here. Who would do such a thing?"

"Given the mood at the meeting last night, I'd say there is a long line of suspects." Joshua added.

Vivienne, once again steady on her feet after the shock, stepped back from Joshua and stared at the crime tape. She couldn't help but think of Mona talking about those giant novelty scissors used to cut the ceremonial ribbon. "It's so unreal. She was just in my shop the other day to get a sneak peek."

"When was this?"

"Yesterday morning." Vivienne stepped to the side of Joshua as two burly men in medical garb began to wheel a gurney up the alley. A simple black body bag rested on top as the metal frame rattled and echoed between the buildings.

"Don't be surprised if you get called in for some questions." Joshua explained as he turned to face the men.

"Am I a suspect?" She asked.

"As someone who was with the victim less than twenty-four hours before her death, you're going to get questioned." Joshua replied and went to assist them with loading Mona's body into the ambulance.

"But it wasn't anything important."

Joshua slammed the back doors. He rapped on the window a few times indicating they were good to go and turned to face her as the ambulance pulled slowly away. "Every ounce of information can help to solve a crime. No matter how insignificant it may seem. I'll be in touch." He tipped his hat and walked back down the alley where several state troopers were gathered in a tight circle.

With nothing left to do, Vivienne crossed the street only to find the parking enforcement officer sliding a ticket under her wiper blade. "I'm leaving." She tried to explain.

"There is no parking allowed in a fire zone." The officer who couldn't have been more than twenty explained. He had a pencil thin blond mustache that she imagined he had grown in an attempt to look older.

"I'm the owner of *Sweet Dreams Bakery*." She pointed across the street. "My parking space wasn't available this morning due to the emergency."

"I'm sorry ma'am." He tapped the little device that created the violations. "But I can't cancel the ticket once it's printed."

Suddenly, Vivienne could understand why Mona had become so upset. She hadn't been parked more than a few minutes and there certainly wasn't a fire that required access to the hydrant. "There are never any spaces on the street this early. I was concerned something had happened to my mother inside my business."

"I'm going to have to ask you to move your vehicle or it will get towed." The young officer explained. "The towing and impound fee alone would be a few hundred dollars."

Vivienne shook her head and removed the ticket. She wanted to scream and yell and stamp her feet, but she couldn't. Joshua would surely hear of it and worse, she would probably get thrown in jail for obstructing justice or something. "I'm moving it now."

"Thank you for your cooperation in this matter." His voice was downright cheerful, as if he wasn't used to winning so easily without a fuss.

She slid into her car and stuck the ticket inside the armrest where several receipts and other papers had accumulated. She was all dressed up with no place to go. As she put the key in the ignition and turned the engine over, she gave one last look at the crime scene in front of her bakery and sighed. A couple of rain drops splattered onto the windshield. Mother Nature sure could have a rotten sense of timing, she thought as she pulled out onto Main Street and sped away.

By the time she had turned back onto Spruce Street, the rain had become a steady deluge and she found it necessary to turn the wipers up to high. The bright red neon of *Clara's Diner* sign called to her like a beacon. With a sharp turn, she pulled into the parking lot and dashed inside.

Clara waved from her post at the front register. "Vivienne, have you been down on Main Street this morning?"

Vivienne ran her hands in an attempt to fix her hair which had become damp and slightly messy from her morning ordeal. "I just came from there."

"Did you find out what happened? Everyone's dying to know what's going on." Clara inquired as the sound of Harold pounding on the little order bell interrupted her.

"I couldn't get past the crime tape." Vivienne took a seat at the first counter stool.

"Did it involve your bakery?" Clara's eyes widened. "What happened?"

Vivienne wanted to tell her what she knew, but Joshua has asked her to keep quiet until they could make a formal announcement. "I don't know yet." She lied. "I saw the ambulance guys loading a body bag."

"Good heavens." Clara walked over to the counter and set a coffee mug up in front of her. "No one we know I hope."

"All I know is that the body was found in my dumpster." She took a deep breath. "And that it wasn't Mother."

"Thank heavens." Clara grabbed a carafe of fresh coffee and poured it into the mug.

Vivienne poured some cream into her coffee and swirled the liquid with a spoon watching the color change from black to tan. She thought about the standing order for tea that Mona had placed. She wouldn't require that anymore. Nor would she require cookies or anything else for the committee meetings. Would the committee even stay together after this? Had this been the work of someone to stop the process all together?

"Penny for your thoughts?" Clara asked.

"I could use a penny right now." Vivienne took a sip of coffee, thankful it chased away the chill from the morning cloudburst. "To offset the loss of all those baked goods that will go unsold."

Clara reached over and placed her hand on Vivienne's. "You and your business will survive this."

"I hope you're right." Vivienne gave a little smile but she knew the effort was half-hearted at best. "Who'd have thought *Sweet Dreams Bakery* could turn into a nightmare?"

Chapter 8

After enjoying a cup of coffee and a sympathetic ear to listen at the diner, Vivienne returned to her home and changed from her damp dress clothes into her comfy gray sweats that were usually reserved for lazy Sunday mornings of clipping coupons from the newspaper. She planted herself in front of the computer and navigated to the *Social Butterfly* site.

She found the little flower patch icon was highlighted red with the number one above it. She moved the pointer over and clicked. Josh's picture appeared along with a message that he had accepted her invitation to join his friend garden.

Another click brought up the profile that had been hidden from her and Kathy the other day. Much to her dismay, it didn't reveal as much as she hoped. There was a column with some basic vital statistics that revealed he was six foot five inches tall and was born on January tenth. He was thirty-three years old and had graduated from the State University in Albany, New York with a degree in criminal justice.

As she further explored the profile, it revealed that his hobbies were kayaking on the Finger Lakes and nature walks. There were only two photos posted in his online album, the close-up cover picture and one of him in uniform that looked like a standard class photo from police school.

The ringing of her telephone made her jump. She picked up the receiver without even glancing at the caller ID display. "Hello?"

"Oh thank God, I thought you were dead." Nora's voice was emphatic. "Why didn't you call me?"

"I'm sorry, Mother."

"I just saw it on the early local news and my heart nearly exploded." Nora continued.

"I just got home a short time ago myself." Vivienne kept staring at the picture of Joshua and it bothered her how secretive he was.

"What did the news say?" Vivienne asked.

"Only that a body was discovered in the alley behind your shop. Were you the one who found it?"

"No, thank goodness." Vivienne's stomach turned at the thought of finding Mona's body.

"Any idea as to who it is?" Nora pressed.

Remembering her promise to Joshua, she held the vital information back. Nora loved good gossip. More than loved, she thrived on it, as the women in her weekly rummy games could more than attest to. "They wouldn't say. I was stopped outside on the sidewalk."

"What about your grand opening?" Nora asked.

"I think cutting the yellow crime scene tape with those giant scissors might put a few people off." Vivienne snipped without thinking.

"Hold your fire." Nora interrupted. "I just wanted to know if you were okay."

"I'm fine." She felt guilty about taking the tone she did and chalked it up to her frustration. "I'm sorry, Mother. I didn't mean to snap at you."

"I just wanted you to know that I'm willing to help with whatever you need to get opened."

"Thanks." Her voice had softened. "I don't know when they'll let me into the shop again."

"I'll bet by later tonight." Nora reasoned. "Maybe you could ask Joshua about that?"

"I'm sure he has his hands full right now." Vivienne rolled her eyes. "And yes, we had a wonderful date the other night."

"You did?" Nora sounded genuinely surprised. "I'm so glad to hear that."

"I wanted to say thank you for setting it up."

"You're welcome dear." Nora replied. "So when do you think you'll go out again?"

Vivienne stared at the handsome picture of Joshua on her monitor. "You'll be the second to know."

"I love you, darling daughter." Nora closed the conversation with her usual nickname. "Call me later."

Vivienne no sooner hung up the phone before it rang again. The number for *Trade Winds Clothier* appeared on the display. "Hello Kathy."

"Oh my God, are you okay?" Kathy asked breathlessly

"I'm fine and so is Nora." She revealed.

"What happened?"

Vivienne left the computer chair and paced around her home as she filled Kathy in with the basics, withholding the true identity just as she had done with everyone else. She was starting to realize how much she despised keeping secrets. They were so much work.

She was just about to finish her conversation when the phone line clicked to indicate another call was coming through. It was from the *Cayuga Cove Sheriff's* office. "Kathy, I have to go. I'll call you later."

"You better." Kathy demanded and hung up.

"Hello?" Vivienne's voice cracked as she took the other call.

"May I speak to Miss Vivienne Finch?" It was a woman's voice.

"This is she."

"Sheriff Rigsbee would like you to come in for an interview today. Would two o'clock work?" The woman on the other end asked.

"Sure." Vivienne glanced at her wall clock and it was still only a quarter to eleven. "Do I need to bring a lawyer or something?"

"No ma'am." The woman replied in a completely neutral tone. "Do you know the location of the Sheriff's office?"

"You're located in the annex building off the county courthouse?" Vivienne asked.

"Yes ma'am."

"See you at two." Vivienne hung up the phone and suddenly felt a little nervous. She had watched so many shows on television where characters went into questioning and how eventually someone cracked under the pressure. At least Joshua would be there to make her feel better.

"Please have a seat, Miss Finch." Sheriff Zeke Rigsbee gestured to a simple metal chair that was in front of his desk. "Thank you for coming down today." The desktop was cluttered with folders and files, mesh baskets labeled 'in' and 'out' and an assortment of pens and pencils. Vivienne noticed small photos of his wife, Sally, and their two children Nicholas and Sarah, who were both college students out-of-state.

"It's no trouble at all." Vivienne took a seat facing him. The office was smaller than she had imagined it would be. A drab tan color had been painted over the cement block walls in a futile attempt to warm the room but it did just the opposite. It felt cold and sterile. Even the green philodendron plant, dangling its long vines and leaves from a dish garden atop a filing cabinet, seemed washed out and lifeless.

Zeke Rigsbee was in his early fifties, but in surprisingly good shape for a man of his age. He didn't have the paunchy belly like the small town sheriff's on television and in movies. His thinning dark hair was parted neatly on the side, and his sideburns were cropped and neat. He sat down after her and folded his hands across the desk. "I know that this has been a terrible day for you."

"You can say that again." Vivienne craned her neck to look behind for any sign of Joshua.

"Are you expecting someone else Miss Finch?"

"I thought Deputy Arkins was going to be here too." She turned back to face him.

"Normally he would, but I was informed of your existing relationship and it wouldn't be kosher to proceed given the circumstances." His bushy eyebrows raised slightly in response.

"I wasn't aware we were actually in a relationship." Vivienne perked up.

"Relationship, a date, even just close friends, it's too personal when it comes to an investigation." He straightened his back against the chair. "I have a few questions concerning your encounter with the victim, Mrs. Mona Clarke."

"I'll help however I can." Vivienne answered. So Joshua had defined them as a relationship to the Sheriff? She didn't know why that surprised her so. It was a good sign, but was she comfortable using the term relationship so early? What did that mean exactly?

"Miss Finch? Are you listening to me?" Sheriff Rigsbee's voice raised a notch in volume.

"I'm sorry." She blinked in response. Her cheeks flushed warm and she felt silly for letting her mind wander during the question session. "This is all such a shock."

Sheriff Rigsbee studied her and his expression seemed to indicate he didn't buy her cover story. "Yes it is. Would you like me to repeat the question?"

"Yes please." She leaned forward and pushed all thoughts of Joshua from her mind.

"At what time yesterday did Mrs. Clarke enter your establishment?"

Vivienne tried to recall that exact time but she was stumped. She remembered having something baking in the oven. "It was sometime in the late morning. If I had to guess I'd say ten thirty or so?"

"You don't recall looking at a clock?"

"No." Vivienne shook her head. "I had timers set on all the ovens because I was baking for the opening. Looking at the clock would just make me more nervous about running out of time."

Sheriff Rigsbee scribbled down her statement as she spoke. "Did you expect to see her that morning?"

"No, my day was really too busy to spend time socializing."

His pen sailed across the yellow notebook paper in a fluid motion, having taken many statements over his years as sheriff. "How did your meeting with Mrs. Clarke come about?"

"She must have been walking by and saw me working in the bakery." Vivienne explained. "She knocked on the door and asked if she could get a sneak peek at the business."

"Then what happened?" He waited for her answer.

"I invited her in for a cup of tea and a peanut butter cookie. We talked about the *Cayuga Cove Women of Small Business Association* and the historic commission meeting taking place that night."

"How long did you talk?"

"Not long, perhaps fifteen minutes? Before I knew it she said she had something to take care of and placed an order for some tea and baked goods for the upcoming meetings." Vivienne raised her eyes to the ceiling, noticing that one of the tiles from the drop ceiling wasn't completely settled into place. How did they end up like that? It never ceased to bother her that no one ever took the thirty seconds to fix it.

"Have you any idea where she was headed?" He flipped the notepad paper over to continue writing.

"She never said. I thanked her for stopping by and then she left." Vivienne finished.

"Did anyone else come into the bakery while you were together?"

"No." Vivienne scrunched her lips together. "Well, not exactly."

"What do you mean?"

"While we were in the store, Victoria Clemens knocked on the window and waved." Vivienne recalled. "She was all smiles and sunshine."

"But she never came inside?" He scribbled the name on his notepaper and circled it.

"No. She looked like she was power walking or something."

Sheriff Rigsbee put his pen down and scratched his chin with his right hand. "Thank you for coming down today Miss Finch."

"Is that all?" She had hoped to find out some more details about what happened, but he had made sure she did all the talking. Vivienne figured it was some sort of investigator tactic to weed out fact from fiction.

"Yes." He stood up from his chair and smiled. "If we need anything else we'll give you a call."

She pushed the chair back and rose to her feet. "You know where to find me."

"Just to be on the safe side, we're asking you let us know if you'll be leaving town during the next few days."

"Am I still a suspect?" Her voice unexpectedly raised an octave.

"It's simply standard procedure during any investigation, Miss Finch." He ushered her out of his office with a smile. "No need to worry yourself over anything."

"Oh, that's a relief." She smiled back as they passed the registration desk where a matronly looking officer was working the desk and answering a phone that never seemed to stop ringing.

"If you think of anything else, please don't hesitate to call or stop in." He opened the front door, allowing a blast of chilled autumn air to swirl in along with a few stray leaves.

"Thank you, Sheriff Rigsbee." Vivienne stepped out and took in a deep breath. The reality of the police questioning hadn't been anywhere near as lively as she had imagined.

As usual, the real deal failed to live up to the hype of the crime shows on television.

Chapter 9

As she watched the local news on the television in the living room, she hated seeing her display window surrounded by that awful yellow tape. Gossip had spread fast and the entire town had become aware of Mona's death. The burden of keeping that secret had now passed and she felt a little better not having to hold back with her friends and family.

The reporter on the scene didn't have any specifics, only reporting Mona had been killed in the alley behind her bakery and the body was transported to Rochester for an autopsy by the medical examiner.

She was surprised to see the image of Victoria Clemens appear on the screen with a microphone near her face. Vivienne reached for her remote and turned the volume up.

"The Cayuga Cove Women of Small Business Association has suffered an immeasurable loss today. Mona Clarke was a champion for so many business owners here locally. My thoughts and prayers are with her husband, Mayor Clarke, and their family during this time of great sorrow." Victoria looked calm and composed, but perhaps that was simply shock. She didn't know if they were close friends or merely worked together on committees, but she was clearly taking charge by granting a small interview.

As the news changed over to the weather report, Vivienne turned it off and walked over to the computer. She was about to turn it on and browse *Social Butterfly* for status messages about Mona's death when there was a knock at her door.

She rushed over to the window and pried the closed blinds apart with her fingers. Nora was standing outside with a small cardboard box in her hands.

"Hello Mother." Vivienne opened the door. "What brings you over on a book club night?"

Nora stepped inside the living room and set the box down on the small accent table next to the sofa. "I thought about our conversation today and I figured you could use these."

Vivienne peeked into the box and saw a smattering of old books, some rather faded and tattered. "What are they?"

"It's a bunch of old cookbooks and recipes from Nana Mary." Nora pulled out an avocado green cloth-covered book. The outer edges of the pages were yellowed with a combination of age and cigarette smoke as Nana Mary always had a cigarette in one hand and a spatula in the other whenever she cooked.

Vivienne pulled out a little tin box that had 'My Recipes' written in light blue pen. "This is wonderful. Are you sure Nana Mary won't mind you giving these to me?" She opened the top and found at least fifty index cards stuffed inside.

"She wanted me to give them to you the last time I visited her." Nora shook her head. "But her memory has been failing so much lately she'll probably forget all about them."

"I didn't think her memory was failing the last time I saw her." Nana Mary Darden had been living at the *Whispering Oaks* assisted living facility for almost five years. Despite being ninety years of age, she had remained quite independent and sharp witted. Light housekeeping and general household maintenance helped to ease her daily tasks, but that had been all the assisting she had required or wanted. Vivienne tried to visit her at least twice a month, usually on quiet Sunday afternoons.

Nora put her hands on her hips. "Yesterday I went to drop off a little box of that rocky road fudge from *Weiss Chocolatiers* that she likes so much. Well, I no sooner stepped into her apartment when she shushed me because she was busy catching up on gossip."

Vivienne smiled. "Well, you know how social she is."

"She was talking to a crow that was perched outside the window." Nora tossed her hands up for emphasis. "Does that sound normal to you?"

"Are you sure she just wasn't pulling your leg?" Vivienne pulled out a faded book with pictures of cakes and pies on the cover.

"I didn't stay long enough to find out. She insisted I give you these books and that was that." Nora eyed the collection. "I've never been much of a cook so they'd do me no good."

"I'll treasure them." Vivienne smiled. "This is just what I need to get inspired to do the opening again."

"When is that going to be?"

Vivienne shrugged. "Well, I think it'd be tacky to do it before Mona's service. I'd guess a week or so?"

Nora pulled at the sleeve of her gray pea coat and focused on her wristwatch. "Good heavens, I'm running late."

"What's the book this time?" Vivienne wondered.

"It's something about a red balloon and a little boy's ghost I think." Nora wondered aloud. "Ever hear of it?"

"Didn't you read it?"

"I kept falling asleep after the first chapter." She gave Vivienne a little kiss on the cheek. "I'll just nod my head and say how moving it was."

"What if it's a horror story?" Vivienne asked.

"I can still be moved by a little boy's ghost, darling daughter." Nora laughed. "Besides, I'll just blame the wine if it comes to that."

"Have fun." Vivienne waved as her mother rushed off to her car and drove away.

She shut the door and grabbed the box. As she sat on the sofa she pulled out the rest of the contents. What looked like a journal tumbled onto the floor and caught her attention. "What's this?" She asked herself.

It felt warm to the touch as she picked it up. The cover was lined with creases and cracks and appeared to be made of black leather. It was secured by one of those little metal locks that were often found on diaries. She tried to pry it open but it held fast against her efforts. Over the next few minutes she had tried to open it with a butter knife, a thumb tack, a straightened paper clip, and a bobby pin. Yet, it stubbornly refused to give up its secrets.

She gave up and reached for one of the other cloth-bound cookbooks inside the box when she slid her index finger across a sharp edge of paper and was rewarded with a fine cut. She pulled her hand back to examine the wound and a drop of fresh blood splashed onto the lock. She stuck her finger in her mouth and tried to wipe the blood off the lock with her free hand.

There was a tiny gurgling sound as the blood disappeared into the key hole. With a sudden 'pop', the cover flew open with a start. Vivienne jumped back in surprise.

The journal's pages were not the usual lined paper. Instead, it was filled with those uneven pulpy pages that were quite thick and sturdy. She couldn't believe it. The blood must have lubricated the old lock like oil. She reasoned that her previous efforts to open it no doubt helped with the process. She had learned over the years that things that seemed mysterious and creepy often just turned out to be a series of random luck and coincidence merging together.

Using the soft light from the table lamp behind the sofa, she could barely make out the date of the first entry but it appeared to be March 28th, 1692. She squinted and held it closer to the light to make sure she had read it right. Yes, there was no doubt it was indeed the correct date. Why on earth would Nana Mary have an old book like this tucked in with her cookbooks?

She continued reading the first page. *'Little Dorothy Good has been accused and we must flee into the wilds for our very lives. That a four year old child could be accused of witchcraft is beyond comprehension, but fear blinds those who should know better. Even though the threat of being attacked by hostile natives is quite real, the larger threat of our coven being exposed leaves us no choice but to flee Salem and start a safe haven far away from this madness. We are leaving tonight under cover of darkness, may the Goddess protect us.'*

"This can't be real." Vivienne gasped out loud. A lost journal from the Salem witch trials? This had to be some sort of novel that was made to look like such a thing. She flipped to the back of the book to find some sort of barcode or publishing information but there was none. There were pages of handwritten journal notes, strange drawings of symbols and letters she didn't recognize, and the unmistakable smell that very old books had.

With the opening of her store delayed, she had unexpected free time to investigate this little mystery. Her first stop tomorrow morning would be at the *Carriage House Antiques* on Main Street. The proprietors, Tristan and Nathaniel, were experts at decoding the past.

Chapter 10

Vivienne had never really shopped at *Carriage House Antiques* before. She had browsed the charming nooks and crannies of the large Victorian home that was filled with antiques from bygone years many times. But whenever she turned over one of those little price tags, her purse cried uncle and her knees went weak.

As she sat in a newly upholstered wingback chair holding the journal, Nathaniel finished ringing out a customer who had purchased a most unusual looking desk lamp shaped like an owl. "This will go perfect in your study." He smiled and handed the receipt and change. "I'll let you know if I get that Tiffany lamp at the auction next week."

"Oh, please do." The customer, one of the blue-rinse ladies that most likely frequented *Pearl's Beauty Shop* over on Cayuga Circle, nodded eagerly. "You know my number."

As she left, Nathaniel closed the door and sighed. "I wish there were more Mrs. Rathbun's in town."

"She must really have a keen sense of style." Vivienne reasoned.

At that moment, the heavy crimson drapes that hid the backroom area from customer view parted and Tristan emerged. He was dressed in a dark blue two-piece suit that was tailored to fit every inch of his trim body. "Actually, she has a loaded bank account and the good sense to avoid those glittery widow traps otherwise known as casinos."

Nathaniel laughed and joined them both in the small consultation room where clients could peruse auction catalogs. He was dressed more casually than his husband. Wearing a hunter green polo shirt, khaki dress pants, and well-worn loafers, his easy-going style fit his friendly personality perfectly. "She's single-handedly paid our mortgage for the past six months with her purchases.

"I sure hope she likes baked goods." Vivienne chimed in. "I could use a customer like that."

Tristan adjusted his necktie and collar. "If you bake things in the shape of owls, I'm sure she'll buy them."

"So what brings you here today?" Nathaniel asked.

Vivienne lifted the journal from her lap and set it atop the cherry wood table that had one of those checker boards built into the top. "I was wondering if you could help me with this."

"What is it?" Tristan asked.

"It looks like a personal journal, but I'm thinking it may be an old novel that was supposed to read like one." Vivienne explained. "It was found in a box of old cookbooks that my Nana Mary wanted me to have."

"May I?" Nathaniel asked as his hand hovered over the worn leather cover.

"Yes, but take care not to lock it. I had a devil of a time getting it to open last night."

He turned the cover and began sifting through the pages. "So what makes you think this might be a rare book?"

"Well, the first entry is dated in 1692." Vivienne explained. "I know it looks old, but I'm having a hard time believing it's really that old if you know what I mean."

Nathaniel leaned over to Tristan and showed him the contents. His red hair glimmered from the *Tiffany*-styled lamps suspended above. "It's a journal for sure."

Tristan's brow furrowed. He turned a few more pages. "What entry are you referring to?"

"The first page has an entry mentioning the Salem colony." Vivienne leaned forward in her chair. "I didn't find any publishing information though."

Tristan set the book down in front of her. "Show me."

She flipped the pages back to the beginning and pointed to the entry she had read last night. "This is what I'm talking about."

Nathaniel shrugged at Tristan. "I don't see anything but blank pages."

Tristan nodded. "Me either."

Vivienne shook her head. "Are you two pulling my leg? Is this some sort of early Halloween prank?"

Nathaniel's face betrayed no sign of humor. "I was going to ask you the same thing."

Vivienne tapped her finger on the entry that was crystal clear even in the soft lighting of the store. "Neither of you can see the words on this page?"

Tristan shrugged. "I'm sorry, Vivienne. All I see is one blank page after the next."

Nathaniel glanced at his watch, having lost interest in the prank he was certain she was pulling. "Based on the condition of the cover and the yellowing of the pages, it's probably over a hundred years old. As for any value, well..."

Not wanting to be seen as a lunatic, she decided to play along with the Halloween prank idea. "Okay, I give up. You got me. Kathy pulled this one on me the other day and I thought I'd give it a try."

Tristan scratched at his dark brown goatee and smiled. "Good one, Vivienne."

Nathaniel let out a little chuckle. "You almost had me there for a minute too." He folded his arms across his chest and let out a sigh. "It's nice to know another Halloween fanatic will be moving onto Main Street."

"If you go all out with decorating this year we won't stand out so much." Tristan added. "Maybe we can even work on some cross promotions?"

"That's a great idea." Vivienne retrieved the journal and closed it with a snap. "I did actually have another reason for coming in today." She tried to think quickly of what it was. "I was thinking of adding a few vintage baking supplies to my store for some decoration." The lie rolled off her tongue with surprising ease.

"I just saw some copper gelatin molds at an auction in New York about two weeks ago." Tristan recalled. "They'd look stunning mounted on a wall display."

"I was thinking about those different sized whisks and measuring cups from last week?" Nathaniel added. "I think it was a set of six. You could put some in your front window and really draw some attention."

Vivienne could only imagine what this little jaunt to their store was going to cost her. She put on her best smile and tried to act interested. "I'm afraid my budget is quite small for that kind of thing now. Maybe a few months down the road I'd like to add some of those?"

"Sure." Tristan was quick to reply. "Next time I'm at auction I'll try to pick up a few things."

"Oh, you don't need to go to any trouble just yet." Vivienne could almost feel the dollar bills disappearing from her purse. She shifted uncomfortably in her chair.

"Don't feel pressured to buy them." Nathaniel sensed her discomfort. "How about you place them in your store and if someone wants to buy them you direct them to us?"

"That's so kind of you." She rose from the chair. "It's a deal." She glanced at a gorgeous grandfather clock that nearly touched the ceiling with its impressive height. "Well, I've taken up enough of your time as it is."

"I'm sure we'll see you at the service for Mona Clarke." Tristan added.

Nathaniel poked his partner in the ribs in annoyance. "If you're going, that is."

"Have they set the date?" Vivienne asked the pair.

"Not yet." Nathaniel answered. "I'm sure the investigation is holding things up."

"It's such a tragedy." Vivien offered. "Not to mention the fact I don't know when I'm going to have my grand opening."

"I'm sure that the turnout will be impressive, regardless." Tristan spoke up. "Despite how people felt after that meeting the other night, I'm sure they will still attend out of respect."

"Were you at the meeting too?" Vivienne wondered.

"I was." Nathaniel nodded. "But I hate speaking in front of crowds so I just watched the fireworks."

Tristan sighed. "I was out of town picking up that owl lamp for Mrs. Rathbun. But I really wish I had been there to see it all in person."

"I told you all about it." Nathaniel protested.

Tristan wrapped his arm around him. "Honey, I love you dearly but you are not a good gossip."

Nathaniel shrugged. "I report the facts."

"Yes, you do. But it's like reading an article in a newspaper about Elizabeth Taylor versus watching a trashy television movie about her." Tristan smiled. "It's just more exciting when you have Lindsay Lohan's poor acting powering the train wreck."

"See what I have to put up with?" Nathaniel smiled at Vivienne.

"How do you two feel about the proposed changes to Main Street?" She asked.

"I'm all for it." Tristan eagerly chimed in. "The buildings are looking rather tired and worn down lately."

"But we don't think forcing the issue with the business owners is the right approach." Nathaniel countered.

"We can't rely on Mrs. Rathbun to keep us afloat every month, honey." Tristan's voice was firm. "Mona was right about making the changes sooner rather than later. Besides, she said our business needed only minimal changes. A few hundred dollars tops. We already have a wooden sign and she told us that she was using that as the base model for all the other stores."

"Well, that's convenient." Vivienne added.

Nathaniel nodded in agreement. "It's a divisive issue to say the least. But we're flattered that Mona chose to use our store as a springboard for change."

"Well, I really have taken too much of your time today." Vivienne pulled herself up from the comfortable chair.

"So how's that handsome deputy of yours doing?" Tristan took her by the arm and escorted her toward the door. "He certainly is easy on the eyes."

Nathaniel took her other arm. "We heard it was a blind date your mother set up. You sure are lucky."

Vivienne swallowed hard. "Boy, news sure travels fast in this town. Did you hear about our first date too?"

"We heard it was a cozy dinner for two at *Shanghai Sunset*." Tristan added with a laugh. "Nora stopped in here yesterday to see if we had any good finds at the auction."

"News travels fast, but my mother moves at the speed of light." Vivienne joked. "Well, it was a wonderful date and I'll leave it at that."

"Tell him he's welcome to stop by our store and visit anytime." Nathaniel interrupted. "Business is sure to pick up with a handsome guy like that standing in the showroom."

Vivienne broke out into a hearty laugh. "You two are crazy but I love you anyway." She gave them each a little kiss on the cheeks. "Thank you so much for your help and keep me posted if you hear about when the service is going to be."

"We'll save you a seat next to us." Tristan waved as she left the store. "We'll save one for the handsome deputy too."

As she walked down Main Street, she flipped open the journal and made sure the entries were still there. As she suspected, they were quite clear under the gauzy sunlight of the overcast day. Why couldn't they see it? Was she going mad from all the stress of opening her business and Mona's murder?

No, she decided as she climbed into her car and turned the engine over. She wasn't crazy. She was going to go to the source of the book and get answers. She pulled out into the light traffic and set course for the *Whispering Oaks* assisted living facility. She'd have the answer.

Chapter 11

Despite the overcast day that almost made the scenery around the lake resemble an old black and white film, the drive along Cayuga Circle was quite pleasant. Here, most of the grand Victorian homes from the old days stood proudly on their manicured lawns that overlooked the lake. The homeowners were a mix of established old family money and new wealth that had sought refuge from the concrete jungles of New York and New Jersey. The driveways were paved and smooth, with luxury cars tucked inside gingerbread decorated garages that matched the colors of the homes. Front porches were decorated with corn stalks and pumpkins and ribbons of orange and black. There were no tacky crashed witches against the old oaks, nor were there white sheets twisted to make little ghosts holding hands. The mood was refined and elegant and also a reminder that this area was monitored by a strict homeowners association.

She pulled into the parking lot of the two-story building that housed the *Whispering Oaks* assisted living facility and found a spot near the picnic tables were staff members often enjoyed meal breaks on nice days.

With the journal tucked safely under her right arm, she entered the facility and was greeted by the cheerful face of Sandy Cumberland at the reception desk. "Hello Vivienne. Mary didn't tell me you were coming to visit today."

"It's a surprise." Vivienne replied. "Is she upstairs?"

Sandy checked the schedule on her computer. "She's probably at the bingo game in the recreation hall."

"When did it start?" Vivienne hated to interrupt the game, especially if Nana Mary was on a hot streak. She's never hear the end of it.

"It's almost over." Sandy looked at the clock near her desk. "I'd guess another ten or fifteen minutes."

"I better wait here." She smiled back.

"You should go down to the ice cream shop and try the new pumpkin pie ice cream. It's heaven." Sandy offered.

Vivienne was always impressed with the facility. In fact, it looked very much like a nice hotel in a larger city. The walls were wood-paneled in rich honey oak, the plush carpeting a pleasing green shade that brought to mind a summer lawn. There were no clinical white walls, nor the trace of urine smell that one associated with nursing homes. No corkboards with paper decorations stapled up amongst activities flyers. The residents who called this building home needed only minimal care. Once that situation changed, they were required to leave. It was the perfect fit for Cayuga Circle, Vivienne thought to herself. Rules and regulations were followed, protocols observed.

She had taken Sandy's advice and wandered down to the small ice cream parlor that the residents often enjoyed when their families came to visit. The young man working behind the counter was well groomed and wore an old-fashioned red and white striped shirt that was tucked into a pair of black pants. "I hear you have pumpkin pie ice cream?" She asked.

He nodded. "Sure do. Would you like a cone or dish?" He asked politely.

"A dish please." Vivienne found cones too messy.

The young man, whose metal nametag read Jonathan, pulled out a little cardboard dish with pink polka dots on it and plopped a fairly large scoop of orange-tinted ice cream inside. "Would you like whipped cream and a cherry?"

"No, thank you." Vivienne wanted nothing to disrupt the taste of the ice cream.

Jonathan placed the dish on the counter along with a plastic spoon and some napkins. "Would you like anything else today? We have rock candy on special, buy one get one free?"

"I'll just take the ice cream today." Vivienne repeated. "How much do I owe you?"

"Two dollars even." He replied.

She opened her purse and gave him a five. "Keep the change." She smiled warmly.

"Thank you so much." His eyes sparkled.

As she left with her treat, she had a feeling the residents rarely tipped. It was a different generation, she reminded herself. These were people who lived through the depression and believed one had to work hard for their money. She put a spoonful of ice cream into her mouth, and her tongue was treated to a mixture of pumpkin, graham cracker, and caramel. It tasted amazingly just like a slice of pie.

"Bingo." Nana Mary's voice startled Vivienne from behind. She whirled around to find her holding a little stuffed bear dressed in a witch's outfit. "I was on a hell of a hot streak today, let me tell you." She was dressed in a cream-colored sweater and a pair of lavender linen pants. Vivienne guessed it was an outfit Nora had purchased for her from one of her excursions to the retail outlets near Waterloo. Her short white hair was cut and styled in a pleasing look with a slight body wave, as the facility employed a rather talented beauty and barbering staff.

"Nana Mary", Vivienne held out her arms for a hug, "I didn't want to disturb you."

Nana Mary hugged her warmly. "You never disturb me." She pulled away with an impish grin on her face. "Your mother on the other hand…"

"She means well." Vivienne held out the ice cream. "Have you tried this pumpkin ice cream yet?"

"So much I'm sick of pumpkin already and it's not even Halloween yet." She gestured toward the elevators. "It's so nice you took time out of your busy schedule to visit me."

They walked into the elevator and rode it to the third floor where Nana Mary's apartment was located. "So what's up with the witch bear?" Vivienne asked.

"It was a door prize during intermission." Nana Mary smiled. "I won fifty dollars on a full card game today."

"You always have good luck." Vivienne knew that *Whispering Oaks* had a special agreement with *Our Lady of the Lake* church over on Lakeshore Drive. The nuns set up a bi-monthly bingo game to raise money for their Christmas toy fund and the residents appreciated getting to play a bingo game for real money without having to leave their comfortable home. Although it lacked the big jackpots of the regular games in the church hall, it was still well attended and something the residents always looked forward to.

Once they were settled in apartment 3-F, Nana Mary took her usual seat in the Amish-crafted rocking chair near the picture window. "Nora told me she set you up on a date with a handsome deputy."

"She did indeed." Vivienne revealed. "His name is Joshua Arkins and he's a very nice man."

"I can't believe Nora picked a good one. She's usually so lousy at it." Nana Mary chuckled. "Except for your father, that is. She got that one right, thank goodness." As she rocked back and forth in the chair she rested her fingers under her chin. "So I heard there was some foul play downtown."

"Yes." Vivienne began to grow tired of discussing the subject. "I wasn't able to open my bakery because of it."

"But that's not why you're here." Nana Mary's green eyes sparkled. "You're here because of the book."

Vivienne had almost forgotten the journal tucked under her arm. "Yes. How did you know?"

"I had a feeling you'd be coming sooner or later once Nora remembered to give you the cookbooks." Nana Mary chuckled. "And she thinks I'm the one with the failing memory."

"Well, she did have some concerns after her last visit. She had mentioned you talking to a bird outside the window?"

Nana Mary let out a hearty laugh and then snorted.

"What's so funny?" Vivienne wondered.

"It's just a game I was playing on your mother. She's always watching me, waiting for some random ailment to strike. So I decided to give her something to scratch that itch."

"Nana Mary, you are terrible." Vivienne found herself chuckling at her grandmother's wit. "She was really worried, I think."

Nana Mary waved her hands. "Oh, pish tosh. She'll get over it."

"So you know about this book." Vivienne held it out to her. "What is it?"

"Why, your heritage of course."

Vivienne felt her jaw go slack. "Come again?"

Nana Mary took a deep breath and composed herself. "It's a collection of spells and wisdom more properly known as a grimoire."

"Come again?"

"It's a book of magic," Nana Mary explained, "Spells and such that have been in our family for generations."

"You're pulling my leg." Vivienne smiled. "I'm not as easy to fool as mother."

"I'm serious." Nana Mary's voice was firm. "This is something I've been waiting to tell you for a long time."

"I can't believe what I'm hearing." Vivienne shook the journal in her hands. "This is a book of magic? Not the kind about pulling rabbits out of hats or sawing ladies in half, right?"

Nana Mary leaned forward in her rocker and pointed her left index finger at Vivienne. "You're here because you tried to show it to someone and they didn't see anything but blank pages, right?"

Vivienne blinked in response. "How did you know that?"

Nana Mary rocked slowly back and forth in her chair. "The same thing happened to me when I found the book." She shrugged in response. "I thought maybe I was losing my marbles early on too. It happens to everyone."

"Nana Mary, you're telling me that you're a…"

"A witch?" She finished the sentence. "Yes, I'm telling you exactly that my darling granddaughter."

"This isn't real." Vivienne reasoned. "Magic is just sleight of hand card tricks and coins pulled from ears."

"For most people it is anyway." Nana Mary agreed. "But for those of us skilled in the craft we know different. We don't have to accept the status quo of life, hoping to make lemons into lemonade. We get to bend the rules a little in order to get the most benefit from certain situations."

"Mother is a witch too?"

"She's I-N-O class."

Vivienne bit down on her lower lip. "What's that?"

"In-name-only." Nana Mary clarified. "For two hours on Halloween night she wears a silly black hat while handing out fun-sized candy bars to kids like most of the regular folks."

"So she's not like you?"

"Or you either." Nana Mary smiled. "You see, real magic is powerful. It comes from nature and nature knows how to portion it out so that things remain in balance." She glanced out the window as a gentle breeze rattled the bright red leaves of a sugar maple tree outside. "To keep things in order the power skips a generation. Sort of a failsafe mechanism, if you want to get technical."

Vivienne rubbed her hand across the worn cover of the grimoire. "Why tell me now?"

Nana Mary returned her gaze to Vivienne. "Because there's trouble brewing in town and you're going to need magic to get through it in one piece."

"What are you talking about?"

"You're in danger, my dear. There's a dark force moving through the town, something that isn't playing by the rules of magic."

"Nana Mary, you're frightening me."

"Good. Use your fear to your advantage. You'll need all your energy to focus on learning the craft and protecting yourself from harm." Nana Mary pointed to the book. "The lock opened after it tasted your blood. The grimoire has sensed the capability within you and now it offers its secrets."

Vivienne glanced down at her finger where the paper cut had been. It was almost completely healed. "You'll have to forgive me for acting strange, but this is an awful lot to take in. I don't know where to begin or even if I fully believe in magic."

"That doesn't matter, my dear. The magic believes in the power of you." She reached down into her sweater and pulled out a long chain with a round pendant attached. It had a five-pointed star engraved into a thick piece of silver. "My final spell was cast the other week. The magic is draining away little by little with each passing day."

"You're not a witch anymore?"

"I'll always be a witch." Nana Mary smiled warmly as she fingered the pendant. "But the spell book and all its power has now passed on to you. It's the way things have always been and how they are supposed to be."

"But I have a business to open, a new relationship to pursue." Vivienne counted them off on her right hand. "Now I have to add apprentice witch to the list? I don't have time for all this."

"Make the time, darling granddaughter." Nana Mary insisted. "Start at the beginning of the book and don't skip ahead. It will all start to make sense, I promise." She reached out for a hug. "Now hurry along home and start learning. Oh, and you better keep this conversation from Nora. If she hears a word of this she'll really think I lost my marbles."

Chapter 12

After leaving Nana Mary's apartment, she ended up at her mother's home after all. It was like living in a day dream, having a magic book that no one else could read. She couldn't resist testing the theory one more time. Just to be sure.

"So I found this journal tucked into the box of books you gave me the other day and I thought it was interesting." Vivienne sat at the kitchen table of her childhood home across from her mother. Nora was fond of picking a new motif for her kitchen about every two years and the most recent choice for a decorating theme turned out to be apples. Café curtains to dish towels to little apple salt and pepper shakers. If it had an apple on it, it was in her collection.

"What's so interesting about it?" Nora took a sip of her tea from a mug with a picture of a basket of apples on it.

Vivienne slid the grimoire across the table. "Take a look."

Nora reached over and opened the cover. Her eyes narrowed. "My word, that's something."

"What is?" Vivienne practically shouted with excitement.

"This book is so musty, phew." She turned her face away from it and grimaced. "It's old all right. I'd probably toss it in the garbage."

"What about the pages?" Vivienne pressed.

"They've probably got mold spores on them." She closed the book and pushed it back to Vivienne. "I better spray the table down with some Lysol after we're done."

"Were they blank?" She asked.

"Shouldn't they be?" Nora adjusted her glasses in annoyance. "My eyes aren't that bad, dear." She sighed and sipped some more tea.

"I was just curious." Vivienne shrugged. "I didn't want to toss it if it had some sort of sentimental value."

"You're starting to sound like Nana Mary now." Nora clucked her tongue. "You should be getting more sleep. It's very important according to this article I read in one of my magazines. There's a quiz that even helps you to find the estimated number of hours of sleep that you need."

"I was going to go back to the bakery today and start the destroyed product list. Sleep isn't high on the priority list at the moment." Vivienne ran her fingers along the worn cover of the journal. It felt warm to her, almost alive. A few times, out of the corner of her eye, she could have sworn the cover looked as if it were breathing.

"Is that for your insurance?" Nora asked.

"It's for tax purposes." Vivienne clarified. "I need to keep a record of everything."

Nora raised an eyebrow. "I never wanted to run a business because of all those infernal tax laws. It's hard enough trying to run a household on a fixed income."

Vivienne knew different. If given the chance, Nora would run a business just to keep up with Clara Bunton. Even though Clara didn't start a business, as a widow she inherited one and managed to keep it going. It was one of the few boasting points that Nora had no chance of topping. "I let the professionals at *Dowling Tax and Payroll* deal with all the fine details. Everything is done on computer now so you're in and out in less than an hour."

But she had spent more than an hour and half with her mother. She seemed to be getting into a habit of giving away time too freely and it simply had to stop. Vivienne pulled her red Toyota into the alley which led to her parking space. Even though it was afternoon, the shadows seemed darker and more ominous than she remembered. After parking her car in the usual spot, she looked at the dumpster where Mona's body had been left. Well, not this particular dumpster as the other one was probably locked up as evidence. But they all looked the same. Dark blue, rusted edges and lids, with faded property identifiers the disposal company had spray painted haphazardly on the sides. With keys in hand, she locked her car up and scurried up the stairs to the back door.

A loud meow startled her and she nearly dropped the grimoire in response. Appearing from behind the dumpster, a large tom cat blinked at her with his golden eyes. His ears were ragged from old battle wounds, and a patch of gray and white fur was missing from above his right eye thanks to a recent fight. "Hello there, Mister Tom Cat." She smiled and knelt down on the stairs. "Looks like you've had a rough couple of days too."

He raised his tail and gave it a few good shakes as he observed her behavior. He meowed once more as if telling her the introduction was strictly on his terms.

"I'm not going to hurt you, fellow. I just wanted to say hello." Vivienne snapped her fingers at him.

He watched her carefully for another few seconds and then charged up the stairs and rubbed against her knees. She carefully stroked the coarse fur along his back and he purred in response.

"I haven't seen you around here before." She gave his head a little scratch, careful to avoid the wound. "Where do you live?"

His gold eyes blinked twice at her and he let out another meow.

"You're probably hungry." She stood up and stuck her key in the back door. As she stepped inside he sat down on the top step and waited patiently. "I'll see what I can find."

She flipped on the light switches and the faint smell of baked goods lingered in the air. She walked over to one of the refrigerators and pulled out a carton of heavy cream. Locating a chipped saucer she had dropped while setting up the kitchen, she poured some heavy cream onto it and took it outside to Tom cat.

He rubbed back and forth against her legs as she set the saucer down.

"Drink up my little friend." She smiled as he lapped at the cream with vigor. "It's the least I could do for taking my mind off what happened here."

He ignored her words as the heavy cream was more important.

She waved goodbye to him and closed the door, taking care to lock it. It felt odd to have to do that now. Growing up in Cayuga Cove, she could remember how when she was a child, people wouldn't bother to lock their doors at night. Neighbors trusted each other with spare keys to each other's homes. Children played games of hide and go seek outdoors in the dark, rode their bikes along the desolate hiking trails around the lake, and even camped out in flimsy pup tents in backyards with nothing but flashlights and stacks of comic books. Serious crime was something that stayed downstate. But Mona Clarke's death changed everything. The sense of trust, so crucial to small town life, was being eroded by suspicion and fear. Sadly, Vivienne thought to herself, it might never be the same.

The destroyed product list hadn't turned out as long as she thought it was going to be. She stuffed the items into a clear trash bag and set it alongside the back door to dispose of when she left for the day. She spent some time going through the store front with a feather duster and giving all of the shelves and glass cases a good cleaning. She loved old buildings, but they had less than desirable perk which seemed to be a never-ending supply of dust.

As she changed around the tea display, she thought of Mona. It just wasn't real yet. Perhaps at the funeral service, when she saw her body resting in the casket, it would finally ring true. She no sooner had sat down at the bistro table where she and Mona had had their final conversation when there was a knock at the front door.

She stirred from her thoughts and saw Joshua waving to her. He was dressed in his deputy uniform, looking as dashing as ever. She unlocked the door and smiled. "I'm glad to see you."

"So am I." He smiled back and removed his hat. "May I come in?"

Vivienne paused and put her hand across the door slyly. "Is this business or pleasure related?"

He waggled his eyebrows at her. "Can it be both?"

"Well, in that case." She removed her arm to let him in. "Please make yourself at home."

He ducked inside and gave a little whistle. "Wow. You've really made this store something special."

She shut the door and turned to face him. "Thanks. I tried to make it comfortable and cozy."

He walked around the perimeter, his black boots echoing on the tile floor. "I'm sorry I've been so busy with work. Everyone at the department seems to be on edge lately."

"Given the circumstances, you're forgiven." She walked over to the bistro table and sat down facing him.

He joined her, his knees barely fitting underneath as he set his hat on the tabletop. "I'm awful sorry that your business was caught up in this."

"It wasn't your fault." She sighed. "Just bad luck I guess."

"I wanted to thank you for not breaking your promise that morning about telling everyone." His steel-blue eyes zeroed in on her. "It really means a lot that I can trust you."

She folded her hands together on the table. "I don't like keeping secrets." She loved how neatly he kept his goatee manicured. Probably a regulation for wearing the uniform, she guessed. "But in your case, I made an exception."

"I'm sorry that I couldn't be in the room when Sheriff Rigsbee was asking you questions." He swallowed hard. "If he had found out that I had been talking to you that morning he would have hit the roof and I might have even lost my job."

She nodded in response. "It's okay. It was easier than I thought it was going to be."

His posture relaxed a bit. "It's just a protocol thing."

She remembered how Sheriff Rigsbee has classified them as being in a relationship and she wanted to ask him which of them had said that. But she lost her nerve and just kept nodding at him. "I understand."

He reached over and placed his hands over hers. "How are you holding up?"

She shrugged. "Well, I've delayed the opening until after Mona's funeral out of respect."

"I meant, personally." He added.

"Oh." She thought for a moment about all the business with the grimoire and Nana Mary. "I'm taking things day to day."

"Is that good or bad?"

"Good." She answered. "My life can get surprisingly complicated for a small town girl."

"I could say the same for a small town boy." He replied.

She couldn't believe her ears. He had opened one of his closed doors and she simply had to take action. "You're from a small town too?"

"Sure am." He nodded.

She waited as a moment of awkward silence passed and she could take no more. "So where is that?"

"A little town in the Adirondacks called Indian Lake." He finally revealed. "It's also known as the moose capital of the Northeast."

"I've never heard of it." She admitted.

"I'm not surprised. The population is less than fifteen hundred people."

"So are there really lots of moose around Indian Lake?" She pressed on. "I mean, when you hear something described as the moose capital, you'd expect them to be as common as squirrels."

Joshua grinned. "Well, I've seen plenty of them but probably not as much as squirrels."

She snapped her fingers. "Hey, I almost forgot your gift I made." She stood up from the table. "Stay right there while I get it."

He rubbed his hands together. "I wouldn't dream of leaving."

She hurried into the back room and pulled the apple blossom she had made for him the night before Mona's death from the fridge. With a perfectly browned crust dusted with sanding sugar, it still looked as perfect as the moment she pulled it from the oven to cool. She placed it in one of her logoed cookie boxes along with a plastic fork and a few napkins and carried it out to him. "It's nothing special."

"If you made it, it is special." He corrected as she set it down in front of him.

"You have the honor of getting the first Nana Mary's famous apple blossom." She beamed with pride.

"Hey, that looks spectacular." He wrapped his arm around her waist and pulled her close to him. "I love apple pie."

"It's a very old family recipe." She explained. "I'm sure it will become one of my best sellers."

"Gosh, I wish I could dig in right now and try it." He smiled at her. "But I have to get back to patrolling."

"It travels like a dream." She enjoyed how his arm felt around her. It restored her sense of protection that had been shattered. "I even threw in a plastic fork and some napkins."

He reached into the box with his free hand and speared a piece with the fork. He popped it into his mouth and closed his eyes as a little moan of ecstasy escaped his lips. "Vivienne, this is the best apple blossom I've ever had."

"There is a little trick that'll make it taste even better." She leaned forward and kissed him.

He gave her waist a little squeeze. "Everything tastes better when your lips are warmed up? Yeah, I know that trick."

She giggled and pried herself away before things got too steamy. "I wouldn't want to interfere with an officer of the law on duty."

He winked at her and stood up from the table with the box in his hands. "So, what about that second date I was promised?"

"I'm free tonight."

He scratched his goatee for a moment in pretend thought. "Well, there was this ultimate fighting match I was going to watch…"

"Well don't let me interrupt your time with nearly naked men writhing around inside a cage." She put her hands on her hips in mock protest.

"How about seven thirty at your place?"

She scratched at her chin in response. "Well, I was going to watch these half-naked men fight each other tonight…"

He raised his right hand in the air. "I promise I'll be on time."

"Are we going out for dinner?" She asked.

"Sure, if that's what you'd like?"

She saw another opportunity to get to know him better and decided to jump at it. "How about we have dinner at your place tonight? You provide the table and dishes, I'll provide the dinner."

He was silent for a moment. Then, he looked into her eyes and nodded. "I won't have much time to clean up the bachelor pad for company."

"That's okay." She smiled and raised her right hand. "I promise not to judge."

"604-B Meier Lane. It's a green duplex. My door is on the right."

"See you then, Deputy." She handed him his hat from the table which he dutifully donned.

"I'll be counting the minutes." He grinned and left the shop.

She scooted over to the phone and dialed Kathy's number. "Guess who just got a second date with Deputy Dashing?

"I'm glad you called because I've got the perfect outfit for you to wear." Kathy sounded rushed. "Stop over to the store and pick it up on your way home. I have to go now." She hung up leaving Vivienne to wonder if perhaps her friend was just a little bit jealous about her new relationship. No, she reasoned. If the outfit turned out to be a used potato sack with a piece of hemp rope as a belt, then she'd have to start worrying.

Chapter 13

The *Trade Winds Clothier* was busier than usual with customers. There were several women, all dressed in varying degrees of fashionable attire, clustered near the dressing room area. Each one looked similar to the other. The haircuts were all variations on the same theme with wispy bangs and soft angles. The blond color, shared by the women, again was variations with only subtle highlights and lowlights for any sort of actual difference. Vivienne failed to recognize any of them, but they were keeping Kathy quite busy running piles of clothing over to them, chattering amongst themselves, and simultaneously texting on their smart phones.

Spotting Vivienne standing near the front counter, Kathy gave her a wave and left the armful of new outfits with a strikingly beautiful blond who seemed to be in charge of the others.

"Looks like things are going well here." Vivienne smiled at her friend who returned to her post near the register. "Is there some big sale going on I'm not aware of?"

"You have no idea." Kathy said slightly out of breath from her frantic pace. "They're all here for Mona's memorial service."

"I hadn't heard anything. When is it?" Vivienne hoped it wasn't tonight.

"It's tomorrow afternoon over at *Our Lady of the Lake*." Kathy began to spin one the displays of earrings and bracelets around, pulling a select few pieces of jewelry from the racks. "It's only for close friends and family I'm told."

"Are they close friends or family?" Vivienne pointed discreetly to the group of women who were all giving their opinion to one of their own about the simple black dress she had tried on. The blond leader draped a crimson scarf over the woman's shoulders and nodded her approval.

"Damned if I know." Kathy shrugged. "But they've got money and they're spending it here. I've got no complaints."

The blond leader left the group and joined Kathy and Vivienne at the counter. "Did you find some earrings like I described?"

Vivienne caught a whiff of the same heavy floral perfume that Mona had worn. She stepped aside to allow her easier access to Kathy.

"These have Swarovski crystals." Kathy handed her a pair of silver drop earrings. "They're limited edition too."

Vivienne admired them sparkling in the store's overhead track lighting. "Those are just lovely. Look how they catch the light."

The blond woman turned toward her and smiled. "You get so used to Barney's and Saks." She gave the earrings a little shake. "It's a nice change of pace to shop at little mom and pop places out in the sticks."

Kathy's smile transformed into a frown at the last comment. "We do what we can to keep up. Our social calendar is just crammed with all those fancy barn dances and potluck church dinners."

Vivienne suppressed a chuckle and extended her hand. "I'm Vivienne Finch, by the way. I'm opening the

Sweet Dreams bakery on Main Street in a few days."

The blond woman regarded her coldly, ignoring her handshake offer and instead concentrating on the earrings. "Fiona Meadows."

"Are you family members of Mona Clarke?" She asked.

Fiona set the earrings down on the counter and waved to the group of women. "We're her friends from New York."

Kathy scooped the earrings up and returned them to the display. "I'm afraid I don't have anything fancier in stock. You might want to visit *Meeker Jewelers* down the street."

"I have so many pairs I've never even worn." Fiona yawned. "I'll just dig through some of those."

"I'm so sorry for your loss." Vivienne offered.

"Thank you." Fiona barely raised an eyebrow. She pulled out a platinum charge card and handed it to Kathy. "I'll take the silk ensemble and those two darling scarves."

The group of women approached the counter with their selections of mourning outfits. Most were variations on the little black dress, but a few had chosen burnt reds and warm browns. Fiona smiled at them. "Next stop is the florist, ladies." She glanced at a gold wrist watch on her delicate arm. "We must fill every corner of that drab little church with flowers."

Kathy rang up her purchase to the tune of three hundred and fifty dollars. She swiped the card and then handed it back to Fiona. "Tell Brian I said hello."

"Whom did you say?" Fiona sniffed.

"Brian Amberry, the owner of *Hummingbird Floral*. He's a good friend." Kathy explained as she pulled a plastic garment bag over the silk dress.

"Indeed." Fiona clutched her purchases and stepped aside for the other members to complete their shopping. She turned to face Vivienne. "Are you one of Mona's local friends?"

"Uh, not exactly." Vivienne stumbled with her words. "We knew each other casually."

"I see." Fiona's voice was soft and well-controlled. "Can you recommend someplace charming to have lunch?"

Vivienne doubted Fiona and her fashion clique would find *Clara's Diner* or even *Shanghai Sunset* to be high enough class for their taste. "Have you tried the *Bistro Parisian*?"

"I don't believe so." Fiona arched a finely plucked brow. "Is it very far? These heels aren't made for long walks, especially on those dreadful sidewalks. I think some of those cracks are large enough for a small child to fall in."

Vivienne shook her head. "It's only four stores down from the florist. They have a nice lunch menu." As much as she hated to admit it, Fiona was right. The sidewalks, subjected to the snow and ice of Northeast winters, had not fared well over the years. They were the bane of many a mother pushing her stroller along Main Street.

"I'm dying for a decent salad to nibble on. Seems most of these little towns thrive on the quaint greasy spoons."

"They have wonderful salads there." Vivienne recalled her last visit to the bistro with her mother back in June. The salad was decent sized and quite colorful, but she hardly felt that justified the twelve dollar cost.

Like many of the businesses and boutiques in town, the Bistro relied on the opened designer purses of Fiona and her ilk. The owner rarely left his home in Boston, instead trusting the day to day operation to his executive chef, Valentin Macias.

With their purchases complete, Fiona approached Kathy one last time. "Would you be a lamb and have these sent over to the *Brass Cricket Inn*?"

Kathy, having taken in well over fifteen hundred dollars in sales from the group, put on her best fake smile. "It would be my pleasure to do that."

Fiona handed her back the garment bag and rounded her clique up much like a dog herding sheep. "Thank you most kindly."

They filed out in unison, like soldiers off to war. Fiona bundled her black woolen shawl over her shoulders and stepped out into the cool autumn air. After a quick check of her bearings, she led her troop off to the next destination.

"Thank you most kindly." Kathy mocked and razzed them with her tongue.

Vivienne burst out into a gale of laughter. "I have to admit, you kept your cool surprisingly well."

"These are examples of who Mona wanted to bring here regularly?" Vivienne huffed.

"They might not be the friendliest lot, but you have to admit they dropped a nice chunk of change." Vivienne doubted they would have even set foot in her palace of carbohydrates.

"That's true." Kathy glanced at all the dresses and shopping bags scattered on the counter where the ladies had left them. "They've certainly helped me to reach my monthly sales goal."

"Need some help taking this over to the inn?"

"Sure. But not until after you try on that outfit I told you about." Kathy ducked down behind the counter and pulled out a stunning jade green racer back dress. "What do you think?"

"It's lovely." She ran her hands along the fabric. "But our date is hardly this formal. I'm bringing dinner over to his house tonight."

Kathy's jaw dropped. "Say what?"

"I thought you'd be proud?" Vivienne puzzled. "What better way to find out more about him than seeing where he lives?"

Kathy folded her arms across her chest. "That Fiona woman was right. We are just a bunch of hay seeds here."

Vivienne sighed. "We're just keeping things easy going for now."

"Are you going to seal the deal by crocheting him a gun cozy too?"

"I'll save that for the third date." Vivienne joked. "Better make that the fourth, since I can't crochet worth a damn."

Kathy smiled at her friend and took the dress back. "All I'm saying is that your next date better require the use of this little number."

"It will." Vivienne promised. "Speaking of formal affairs, I wonder why Mona's service is being kept private."

"Probably because they knew no one from town was going to bother to attend."

"I'm serious." Vivienne sighed. "She was always so outgoing and in the spotlight. It just seems strange to have her laid to rest without a fuss."

"I guess that's what Richard wanted." Kathy took a seat on the stool behind her counter. "It hardly seems like something Mona would want, though."

"She was many things, but a shrinking Samantha wasn't one of them." Vivienne agreed.

"You can say that again." Kathy agreed.

The afternoon passed fairly quickly for Vivienne as she helped her friend deliver the fashionable mourners purchases to the Brass Cricket Inn, completed her tasks at the bakery, dropped off some bills to be mailed at the post office, and finally settled into the little oak dinette set in her home kitchen to figure out what to make for dinner.

She had poured over several of the cookbooks and after considering the prep times and the ingredients available in her fridge and pantry, decided upon a simple baked macaroni and cheese. It was comforting and delicious and most importantly it was easy to keep warm in her oven while she prepared for their second date.

Lacking a quality smoked cheddar to elevate her creation, Vivienne resorted to one of the few pieces of cooking advice from her mother. If you can cheat the flavor, go for it. No one but you will be the wiser. She frantically searched her spice rack and came upon the little brown bottle. "I knew you'd come in handy sooner or later." She shook a few drops of liquid smoke into the cheese sauce and stirred it ever-so-carefully into the bubbling orange mixture. She smiled and fanned the steam that rose from her stainless pot toward her nose. Joshua was going to be putty in her hands after eating this.

After combining the pasta with the sauce and

pouring it into one of her vintage harvest gold casserole dishes, she sprinkled the top with bread crumbs and placed it in the oven.

As she about to set the timer, there was a loud scratching sound from outside the kitchen window. In the dim twilight, she saw a pair of yellow eyes watching her. With a frightened gasp, she nearly backed into the gas burners.

"Meow."

She instinctively placed her hands over her heart which had skipped a few beats. "Mister Tom Cat?"

"Meow." He yowled back and scratched at her screen with his front paws.

She crossed over to the window and saw that he had climbed the little white trellis where her morning glories had bloomed all summer. Straddling the wooden diamond pattern planks with his back paws, he blinked a few times. "How on Earth did you find your way here?"

He jumped down to the grass and then darted toward her front lawn.

Intrigued, she followed to the front door and found him sitting on her stoop looking up with those inquisitive golden eyes. "You are nothing if not persistent."

Against her better judgment, she opened the door and he immediately darted up and rubbed back and forth along her legs. He curled his long tail around her calves, purring ever more loudly.

She could feel the nip in the evening air as the temperature dropped. The forecast had called for a heavy frost tonight and she hated to think of him shivering outside without a blanket or a lap to sit upon.

"Why me?" She asked him. "There must be a hundred families in town who have room for a new house cat."

"Meow." He answered back between purrs.

She gestured to her living room. "Come on in."

He placed one paw on the threshold and paused for a moment, as if weighing the consequences of going inside. No doubt he had been on the streets for some time and was not accustomed to being anywhere where there wasn't a quick escape should danger pop up.

As the heat poured out her front door, she put her hands on her hips. "You have to choose in or out, Mister Tom Cat. I don't have time to stand here all night and heat the neighborhood."

He jumped into the living room and immediately began to smell the sofa.

She shut the door and watched as he started to place his paws on the side panel of the fabric. "If you scratch that you'll be spending the night outside."

He regarded the tone of her voice and then stepped away from the sofa. He curled his tail around his body and sat down on the carpet.

"That's more like it." She smiled and petted his head. "But in the morning you're going back outside."

"Meow." He seemed to protest the arrangement.

"Don't try to sweet talk me." She teased and then looked at the wall clock. She had less than an hour to shower, pick an outfit, do up her hair and makeup, and be over at Joshua's. "I'm running late puss. You'll have to fend for yourself for a few hours."

He jumped up onto the sofa and nestled into the small throw pillows creating a little nest. He winked at her and then curled into a comfortable position to enjoy a warm nap.

Not having a litter box or even litter for that matter, she had to improvise as there was no time to go to the store. She rummaged through her cupboards and found a disposable sheet cake tin. Filling it was plain quick cook oats, she hoped it would serve as a proxy bathroom should Tom Cat require one. She also filled a small salad bowl with water and left it nearby in case he required a drink.

As she jumped into the shower and let the warm water dance across her skin, she felt the tension of the day slide away like the shower gel bubbles. She lingered a bit longer than she knew she should, but it was no soak in the garden tub either. That was one of her pure pleasures after a long day, along with a bath pillow and a good paperback book. But she didn't have time for that right now.

Wrapped in fluffy towels, she poked around her bedroom closet for a casual yet flattering outfit and after much debate decided upon a pair of boot-cut denim jeans and a cream colored v-neck sweater. As she admired her image in the mirror, she was pleased that the look turned out exactly like she had hoped.

Guiding the brush carefully through her auburn locks, she shaped it into her usual style and went about putting on her makeup. Although Kathy usually went for more bold looks, Vivienne had always been a fan of the 'less is more' feel. She took care to eliminate shine with matte powder and enhance her cheekbones with a hint of blush. It wasn't exactly a runway model look, but it served her well for many years. She was about to choose a pair of earrings when suddenly the smoke detector went off in the kitchen with a shrill pierce. "I forgot to set the timer." She jumped up from her vanity.

As she ran to the kitchen a thin veil of white smoke poured from the crevices of the oven and she grabbed a dishtowel and waved it frantically at the detector.

Tom Cat growled, his hair standing on end from the kitchen doorway. His tail had puffed out to twice its normal size.

Without thinking, she turned off the oven, turned on the range hood fan, and flicked on the interior light to survey the damage. The macaroni and cheese looked like lumps of coal. "Oh, not tonight." She groaned. "Not this meal." She retrieved the smoldering heap from the oven rack and set it upon the grates above the gas burners.

As the smoke detector ceased its racket, Tom Cat relaxed and jumped up onto the dinette set. He meowed a few times and rubbed his head against the grimoire, which lay open.

"Where did that come from?" Vivienne asked him. "I could have sworn I left it at the bakery." She stared at the pages which she had never seen before. It was the section right after the first journal entry which had looked like a jumble of strange symbols previously. There was a hand-drawn image of a clock face and what looked like corn-husk brooms sweeping counter-clockwise around it. The words 'Tempus Revocare' were scrawled three times below the image.

"Tempus Revocare." She read aloud. It was Latin, but her understanding of the dead language was rusty at best. She had wanted to take it in high school, but mother insisted she take something easier like Spanish instead. They don't even use Latin in the masses during church anymore, Nora rationalized.

"Tempus Revocare." She repeated again. The first word meant time. She knew that because Nana Mary had a grandmother clock that had the words 'Tempus Fugit' inscribed on the brass face. It meant time flies. "Tempus Revocare." She repeated as a rush of cold air swirled into the kitchen.

Expecting to see the window open, she reached to close it only to find it already sealed and locked. The rush of wind pulled the vestiges of smoke from the ceiling and created a miniature funnel cloud that swirled and danced above her head. Vivienne stared in wonder as the tempest danced over to the oven and focused on the burnt macaroni and cheese. As the tendrils of smoke disappeared, so did the burned black color. It faded away to bright orange which then faded to a light brown. The tiny vortex seeped into the pasta and disappeared.

Tom Cat looked at Vivienne and then smacked his lips with his tongue.

She carefully stepped over to the stove and gasped in shock. The macaroni and cheese was perfectly cooked with just a touch of brown on the bread crumb topping. "I don't believe it." She rubbed her eyes in disbelief. "This can't be real."

"Meow." Tom Cat argued and jumped down from the dinette set onto the floor.

She sat down by the grimoire, eyeing the book with new awe. There was no denying what had just happened. Despite all her attempts to explain with logic and science, she was left no choice but to accept what Nana Mary had told her earlier in the day. It was indeed witchcraft and she was most certainly a witch.

Tom Cat rubbed against her legs and then jumped up into her lap.

She reached down and gave his stiff fur a few strokes. "Nana Mary was right all along." She explained to the cat. "This changes everything."

Tom Cat didn't seem to care all that much for the magic display. He looked at her again and licked his lips as if to tell her it was getting past his usual dinner time.

"I've got some cans of tuna in the pantry." She explained. "They'll have to work for tonight."

He meowed back his approval and jumped back down to the floor. He stopped at the water dish and gave the liquid a test with his front paw before lapping some up with his little pink tongue.

Vivienne walked over the pantry and located the can of yellow fin tuna packed in water. "Don't get too used to this, by the way. This is a one-time only special meal." As she opened the can and scraped the flakes onto a saucer, she was glad she didn't read that spell at this particular moment. Having to wrestle a giant tuna in her kitchen would be difficult to explain to the neighbors to say the least.

Chapter 14

Not wanting to set a bad example by being late, Vivienne went just a few miles over the speed limit as she drove across town toward Meier Lane. The setting sun had managed to break through the clouds and illuminate the sky in one of those red/orange colors that no tree could ever hope to match. The nights were arriving earlier and soon it would be dark before most people even sat down for dinner.

She turned onto Main Street and found traffic had slowed to a crawl as she neared the county courthouse and city hall. From her viewpoint behind the wheel, she could make out all sorts of flowers and cards lining the sidewalk to the city facilities. Flocks of onlookers gathered here and there, some holding small candles in memoriam to Mona Clarke. As the funeral services were closed to the public, the public had in turn created its own way to pay respects. The outpouring of sympathy was somewhat surprising, given the controversy she had caused at the historic commission meeting, but in the end Vivienne knew the hearts of most folk in Cayuga Cove were good and they rarely spoke ill of the dead.

As traffic began to clear, she spied Victoria Clemens holding the arm of Mayor Richard Clarke as they walked together and read some of the messages left on condolence cards.

Richard looked tired and much older than usual, Vivienne thought as she drove past. He was clearly overtaken with grief at the sudden loss of his wife and seemed to be relying on Victoria to keep things in as much order as possible during the grieving process.

Her eyes drifted to the grimoire on the front seat. She didn't know why, but she suddenly felt protective of it and didn't dare leave it at home. If it did contain such power, surely it could prove a deadly weapon in the wrong hands.

A squeal of tires snapped her attention back to the road where a silver van pulled out forcing Vivienne to slam on the brakes to avoid a collision. The driver shouted something in an angry voice at the crowd of mourners. Vivienne's headlights reflected off the red lettering along the side of the van. She could clearly make out Suzette Powell's *The Formal Affair* catering logo. The van revved its engine and sped off as Vivienne double checked for any further traffic before continuing on her way.

The smell of the macaroni and cheese filled the air inside the car, and her stomach gave a little growl in response. As she turned onto Meier Lane she had to pay close attention to the house numbers in order to get her bearings. It was one of the streets she wasn't at all familiar with. Unlike the other areas in Cayuga Cove, most of the homes in this area were built in the late sixties and early seventies. There were many ranch and split-level style homes, along with some duplexes that served as rentals due to the lack of any fancy apartment complexes that larger cities had in spades.

Easily enough, she found the green duplex at 604 and pulled her vehicle along the curb to park. She turned off the car and tucked the grimoire into her large purse along with the keys. With the casserole in hand, she walked up to Joshua's door and kept having to fight a persistent breeze to keep the aluminum foil from leaping off the top of the casserole dish.

The front door opened and Joshua welcomed her with a big smile and a warm hug. Dressed in a pair of comfortably worn jeans and a red flannel shirt that allowed wisps of his dark chest hair to peek out from the top two buttons which were left undone, his casual look matched hers perfectly. "Let me help you with that." He took the casserole dish from her grip and guided her into his home.

She stepped into the small foyer and was pleased to smell the faint warm scent of wood smoke. "Thank you."

Setting the dish down on an end table, he slid her jacket down her arms and tucked it into a coat closet where she noticed a few extra deputy uniforms and pairs of polished boots were neatly stored. He retrieved the casserole dish and inhaled deeply. "This smells delicious."

"It's nothing terribly fancy, simple macaroni and cheese." She explained as she followed him into the living room. A robust fire crackled from the fireplace, across from which a simple square table was setup along with place settings, linen napkins, and a bottle of white wine chilling in a bucket of ice.

"I love macaroni and cheese." He licked his lips. "Does it have a crunchy topping?"

"It'd be a sin to have forgotten that." She laughed.

He lifted the foil cover up and smelled it once more. "Is there no end to your talent with food?"

She walked over to a brown leather loveseat and set her purse down on the carpeted floor. "I'm horrible with making fudge." She confessed. "The best I can come up with is more akin to sludge."

"Well that changes things, date's over." He joked as he set the casserole dish on the table.

She shared his laughter and lowered herself down onto the cushions of the loveseat. The leather cushions were soft and supple, cradling her body in a warm embrace. "You have a lovely home here. You're so lucky to have a working fireplace."

"I was surprised it hadn't been replaced with one of those gas units." Joshua stared at the fireplace with pride. "It's just not the same."

"I agree." She watched the flames dance and leap over the split wood. The bottom glowed amber and red, much like the sunset she had witnessed earlier. "It's just not as romantic."

He easily pulled the cork from the bottle and poured some of the wine. "I was thinking the same thing." He took a seat and passed a long-stemmed goblet to her.

"Here's to the lost art of romance." She raised her glass to him.

"I'll drink to that." He shared the toast with her and they both took a sip.

The wine was bright and fruity, with a nice grape flavor. "This is really good. What kind is it?"

"It's from one of the local places around here." He paused for a moment in thought. "Glen Harvest, I think was the name."

"That's the winery that Stephen Clemens owns with his family." Vivienne mused.

"I don't think I know him." Joshua replied and took another sip.

"He's the husband of Victoria Clemens from the historic commission." Although her knowledge of wine was quite limited, she had to admit that this blend was quite tasty.

"Oh." Joshua nodded. "She was the bossy one at the meeting, right?"

"Well, one of the bossy ones I guess." Vivienne shrugged. "There was so much said that night it all seems a blur now after Mona's death."

Joshua swirled the remaining wine in his glass. "I know."

Vivienne scolded herself for bringing up Mona's death again. He probably had dealt with it all day at work and the last thing he wanted to do was spend his off hours talking about it. She took a deep breath and changed the subject. "So, I'm thinking I'm going to aim for a soft opening in four days."

His blue eyes studied her. "No big ceremony?"

"That's not my style, really." She took another sip of wine.

He placed his arm around her shoulders. "You don't care for big crowds either?"

She relaxed and allowed herself to lean against him. "I'm just a laid back country girl at heart." She loved feeling his chest rise and fall with each breath. The faint smell of a spicy cologne drifted from underneath his shirt.

"That's me too." He answered with a chuckle. "Except for the girl part, that is."

He stretched his long legs out and accidently knocked her purse over with the tip of his enormous brown cowboy boots. "I'm sorry about that." He leaned forward to retrieve it. "That's what happens when you have size fifteen feet."

"I can see why." She chuckled in response. "It's okay. Don't tell anyone, but I can be a klutz in the kitchen sometimes too."

"What's this?" He picked the grimoire up from the floor.

"Oh, it's just an old journal from my Nana Mary." She finished off her wine and reached out for it. "I found it tucked in a box with some of her cookbooks."

He flipped it open and glanced at the page. "Whoa. This is from 1692?"

The empty wine goblet fell from her grip and bounced on the carpet as she sat up in alarm. "What did you say?"

He pointed to the first page on the grimoire where the journal entry was posted. "It says March 28th, 1692."

"You can read it?" She blinked in disbelief. "You can actually read it?"

"Yes." He answered slowly. "Is that surprising to you?"

She shook her head. "No. It's amazing me."

"Amazing that I can actually read a book?" He puzzled.

"No," She took the grimoire in her hands. "You are the only person I've shown this too that can see more than just a bunch of blank pages." She flipped ahead to the middle of the book where the pages still looked like gibberish to her. "Can you read this?"

He leaned forward and his brow furrowed. "Not really. It looks like some kind of collection of symbols."

She set the book down on the loveseat and threw her arms around him in response. "I'm not going crazy. Oh, you have no idea how much this means to me."

"Whoa." He pulled away from her. "What's going on?"

"I'm sorry." She fanned her face with her hands. "I know it sounds unbelievable, but this means more to me than you can know."

"Vivienne, I'm not sure I understand what you're trying to say." He gave her a little smile of reassurance. "But I'm happy that you're happy."

"I guess I should start at the beginning."

"Can we talk over dinner?" He asked. "I've been smelling that macaroni and cheese since you came in and it's driving me crazy."

She clapped her hands together. "Oh, yes. I'm so sorry about that."

Joshua stood up from the loveseat and helped her up. "Something tells me you've got a hell of a story to tell."

She looked up at him, the firelight dancing off his finely chiseled features. "You have no idea."

As they enjoyed the main course, and a few more glasses of wine to wash it all down, Vivienne brought him up to speed on her journey of discovery. At first, he seemed to be waiting for her to reveal it was all a prank. After the third glass of wine went down, he lowered his guard and took in every word with absolute undivided attention.

"This is amazing." He marveled. "It might just be the wine talking, but for some reason I completely believe you."

"I can hardly believe it myself." She admitted.

"So you cast a spell on the macaroni and cheese?"

"I guess so." She hadn't found so much as a single charred piece in the entire casserole dish. "But don't ask me how I did it."

"That seems a rather simple spell. Did they even have macaroni and cheese back in Salem?" He chuckled.

"Right now I'd believe anything is possible." She took another sip of wine. "Coming from me, that's really saying something." Her head swirled a bit and she wished she hadn't drunk so much of the wine.

"I'm not a warlock or anything like that." Joshua added as he finished the last of the wine. "Isn't that what a male witch is called?"

"Well that's good to hear." Despite the two of them finishing two entire bottles of wine, she was still quite thirsty. It must have been the heat from the fire, she thought as she held her empty glass out to him. "I don't know about you, but I'm still a little thirshy." She blinked at her mangled pronunciation. "Thirsty. Do you have another bottle?"

"I think there's one more in the fridge, but it's a blush." As he rose from the chair, he held onto the table for support. "That wine really catches up to you after awhile."

Vivienne gave him a goofy smile. "I hardly ever drink, so just a bittle lit and I'm flying."

He laughed at her answer and nearly fell to the floor. "I don't know why that's so funny, but it is."

She stood up from the table and then stumbled over to the loveseat. "Mother would be so embarrassed if she knew I was drinking with a hot man in his own home." She plopped onto the leather cushions. "Oh hell, at this point if I called her she'd probably have us married and having kids by tomorrow. Why don't we just drive down to city hall and get it over with?"

Joshua stumbled over next to her and dropped onto the loveseat. "I can only imagine the news of a shotgun wedding spreading through town. That'd really give the town gossips something to talk about for once, right?"

She crawled over to face him and burrowed her face into his chest. "It sure would. Eunice Kilpatrick would have a field day down at the bank."

He closed his eyes and laid his head back. "I'm too tired to clean up."

"Maybe there's a spell in the book to clean everything up?" She giggled.

"Would you try to make it do my laundry too?" He giggled back. "I could save a small fortune on laundry soap that way."

She waved her hands around in the air. "Oh magic book, do us a favor and clean up this place so we don't embarrass the neighbors."

"You're a poet too?" He asked.

Vivienne responded with a little snore.

He kicked off his boots and closed his eyes as the fire slowly died out. He wrapped his arms around her and surrendered to sleep. Vivienne mumbled something unintelligible and drifted back to sleep along with him.

Chapter 15

She awoke the next morning with a start as the shrill basic ring of the cell phone blared from inside her purse. She stirred from her sleep but was unable to answer it before it went to voicemail.

Joshua blinked his eyes and stretched his arms upwards with a yawn. "What time is it?"

Vivienne rubbed the sleep from her eyes. "I don't know, but the sun is up." She reached into her purse and glanced at the clock on the phone display. "It's half past nine." She couldn't help but notice there were six missed calls, but it was the two empty bottles of wine on the table that stood out the most. Had they really drank that much?

Joshua massaged his temples with his fingers. "I'm glad I don't go in until five tonight. I'm going to need the entire morning to get ready."

Vivienne slipped the phone back into her purse. She rocked her head back and forth, as the loveseat didn't provide the most comfortable sleeping accommodations. "I'm sorry about falling asleep like that. I don't have much of a tolerance for holding my liquor.

"Well, I wasn't exactly sober myself after finishing that second bottle." He agreed.

She wrapped her arms around his shoulders in a warm embrace. "Thank you for being a gentleman."

He nuzzled her left ear. "Thank you for a wonderful second date."

Vivienne was about to respond when a loud knock shook the front door.

"What the hell?" Joshua leapt up from the loveseat. "Sorry about that." He marched over to the door and pulled back the side window curtain to find two police officers waiting on the other side. He opened the door partially. "Greg, Frank. What's going on?"

The taller of the two officers, Greg, was first to speak. "Sorry to bother you Deputy Arkins, but we received a phone call about a possible missing person that you are acquainted with."

Officer Frank interrupted. "Have you seen a Miss Vivienne Finch?"

Upon hearing her name, Vivienne leapt up from the loveseat and ran over behind Joshua. "There's no missing person, officers. I'm Vivienne Finch."

Officer Greg looked at Frank and shook his head. "I told you this wasn't another crime."

"Gentlemen, what is going on? Who called in Vivienne as missing?" Joshua eyed them both with a little bit of resentment.

Officer Frank flipped open his little black book. "The call was placed this morning by Mrs. Nora Finch."

"I should have known." Vivienne fumed and tapped Joshua on the arm. "I'm sorry about this."

Officer Greg tipped his hat. "After what happened to Mona Clarke, we couldn't just ignore the call. With her car parked outside your home, we had to follow up."

"I understand, gentlemen. You were only doing your jobs and I thank you for your vigilance." Joshua looked at Vivienne for support.

Vivienne felt her face flush red. "I truly am sorry for this. As you can see, I'm just fine."

"Sorry to bother you folks." Officer Frank smiled. "You both have a good morning." He turned and walked away as Officer Greg followed.

Joshua shut the door and sighed. "We must be cursed or something."

"I know." Vivienne agreed. "We spoke too soon about having a great second date." She stomped over to her purse and grabbed the phone. "Excuse me a moment, I need to check in with a certain concerned mother."

Joshua nodded and headed for the kitchen. "Would you like some coffee?"

"That would be great." She spoke as she dialed the number and waited for Nora to answer.

Nora answered on the first thing. "Oh, thank God you're alive. I thought they were going to find you dead in the dumpster outside your store."

"Mother, I can't believe you." Vivienne's voice raised a notch. "Sending the police on a search for me? Have you lost your mind?"

"I tried calling you at home and the bakery and then your cell. When I didn't hear back I just started to panic. With a serial killer loose in town, I was more than a little concerned for your safety." Nora frantically explained.

"I was with Joshua." Vivienne snapped. "For the entire night, if you must know."

"Oh." Nora's voice cracked a bit in shock. "I never thought to try calling him. Actually, I don't think I even have his home number."

"Mother, that's not the point." Vivienne took a deep breath and tried to calm herself down. "I do have a social life and you're not always going to be aware of what I'm doing every minute of every day."

"I know that dear." Nora kept her tone neutral. "This murder has just got me all twisted up inside."

"You and the entire town it seems." Vivienne agreed.

"There was a police statement on the local news this morning. The medical examiner ruled Mona's death a homicide." Nora continued. "Can you believe it?"

"My beliefs have been pushed all over the place lately." Vivienne confessed. "Do they have a suspect?"

"I don't know yet." Nora answered. "They're supposed to have another update this afternoon."

"Well, thank you for your concern but in the future please don't send the police out for me whenever I'm out of touch for more than a few hours."

"I'm sorry dear." Nora apologized. "I hope it didn't ruin the date."

"Let's just say it setup a familiar pattern we hope to break in the future." Vivienne smiled at Joshua who returned from the kitchen with two mugs of coffee in his hands. "I love you and I'll call you later today."

"Love you too, dear." Nora replied. "Glad to hear the date went so well last night."

Vivienne shook her head. "Goodbye, Mother." She ended the call and graciously accepted the mug of steaming coffee. "Thank you."

Joshua moved over to the loveseat and sat down. "I put cream and sugar in it."

"That's fine." She took a sip and relished the smell from the steam. There was nothing in the world like the aroma of fresh brewed coffee. No matter how sleepy the senses, it always managed to do the trick.

"So it sounds like things are okay with you and your mother." Joshua smiled. "I'm glad about that. My family was never all that close growing up and it's nice to see that bond still intact."

She joined him on the loveseat. "Yes, she just went overboard because the news reported that Mona Clarke's death has been officially ruled a homicide." Vivienne spoke between sips of coffee.

"I didn't think they were going to announce that yet." Joshua paused in thought. "They must have a suspect in custody."

"Who would that be?" Vivienne asked.

"I don't know. It must have happened after my shift ended yesterday." Joshua shrugged. "There weren't all that many leads."

"I didn't mean to pry." She added. "I just wondered if it was someone local or a random stranger."

"Murder at the hands of a complete stranger is quite rare." Joshua explained. "Unless there is a history of mental instability involved and then it's quite possible."

"There aren't many strangers that come into Cayuga Cove." Vivienne reasoned. "At least, it would be very hard to not get noticed by someone in town."

"I agree." Joshua took another sip of coffee. "I can only imagine what the neighbors are thinking about this morning."

"Well, I don't know anyone who lives on this street." Vivienne said with relief. "So that factor is in our favor." She glanced at the sun streaming through the windows. "But, I really need to get a start on my day."

"I'm working until after midnight tonight, so I guess a third date will have to wait."

Vivienne handed him her coffee mug and stretched her arms up into the air. "Let's hope it's less eventful."

She gathered her purse and the grimoire together. After giving him a kiss goodbye, she crept out the door and let the sunshine warm her face. It was shaping up to be another beautiful fall day. At least, it looked that way until she reached her car and was barked at by Eunice Kilpatrick's mean gray poodle.

"Why, Vivienne Finch." Eunice hushed her little poodle by giving a gentle tug on the pink leash that was embellished with fake gems. "What brings you over to our little neighborhood?" The poodle gave a little growl and bared its tiny teeth.

"Good morning, Eunice. I didn't know you lived on this street." Vivienne's stomach tightened into little knots. Eunice was perhaps the biggest gossip in all of Cayuga Cove, as any of the customers in her line at the Colonial Bank could tell you. In fact, there were really only two things Eunice seemed to delight in for recreational activities: spreading gossip and attending funerals. The latter always struck Vivienne as a bit morbid, but she supposed funerals were filled with a myriad of opportunities to strike conversations in hushed tones without drawing attention.

"Oh, I moved into a home here about a month ago." Eunice's eyes lit up with pride. "One of my customers down at the bank, Audrey Simmons, has a son who works as a realtor. She told me about this little gem and how it was twice the space for the same amount of rent I was paying over on Whiskey Springs

Road."

"Well, that was a blessing." Vivienne reached into her purse and retrieved her keys, hoping it would signal her that it was time to wrap up the conversation.

Eunice ignored her cue. "I couldn't help but notice the police here earlier. Was anything wrong?"

"Oh that?" Vivienne swallowed hard. "No, it was just some routine police business."

"And this little beauty is your car?" Eunice gestured to Vivienne's sedan. "It's so cute."

"Thank you." Vivienne chose that moment to press the unlock button on her key fob. "It never gives me any trouble."

Eunice remained oblivious as her poodle sniffed the rear tire of Vivienne's car and raised his leg to sprinkle it with urine. "I thought maybe the police were trying to enforce that ridiculous odd-even overnight parking."

Vivienne gave her a little smile. "I've already had one parking ticket this month and I certainly don't need another."

"Well, don't let me keep you." Eunice gave the leash a little tug and the gray poodle barked at Vivienne once more. "I feel so much safer knowing a deputy lives here on the street."

"That's great." Vivienne clenched her teeth together and waved goodbye as she slid into her car. As she slammed the door shut she watched Eunice pick up her pace and disappear around the corner. "That's just great." She lowered her head and bumped it a few times on the steering wheel.

Chapter 16

When she had returned home she found Tom Cat curled up on her sofa sound asleep. His golden eyes flickered open to see who was invading his privacy and upon seeing her, stretched his paws out and then curled them over his little head.

"Well, good morning to you too." She shut the door and hung her keys on the entry wall hooks. "At least one of us had a comfortable bed to sleep in."

Tom Cat let out a sigh and returned to sleep.

She went about taking a shower and getting herself ready for another day. With Mona's memorial service taking place, she decided she would go down to the bakery and whip up some sort of dessert for Richard and the many guests that would surely follow back to his home afterwards.

She debated whether or not to let Tom Cat stay inside, but seeing how the temperature had warmed considerably she figured he would benefit from the fresh air and escorted him out as she left her home. Besides, she didn't have a real litter box or any cat food. She made a mental note to stop at the Monarch Grocery and pick up both items on her way to the bakery in case Tom Cat faced another night in the cold. 'Oh, who am I kidding?' She thought to herself. If she was investing in a litter box, she was committing to a long term relationship.

It was half past noon when she arrived at the Sweet Dreams bakery after picking up her cat essentials. After studying several dessert books, she ditched the professional recipes for something more personal from her collection of three by five recipe cards she kept in a candy tin that once held chocolate covered cherries. She went about creating an old family favorite, Treavis cake. The simple Bundt cake, flavored with pistachio and sugared walnut filling, tinted green and finished with a simple sugar glaze, always proved a crowd pleaser. The name was derived from an old family friend, Virginia Treavis, who brought it to many neighborhood potluck dinners over the years. Nana Mary started calling it 'Treavis Cake' and eventually so did everyone else who were fortunate enough to enjoy a slice. After her death a few years back, Virginia's daughter had tucked the recipe into a thank you card for the flower arrangement she had sent to the family. 'Mother insisted you inherit the famous recipe. Nothing would please her more than for you to carry on the legacy.' She had written.

She had no sooner finished drizzling the glaze onto the cooled cake when her bakery phone rang. Seeing Kathy's number on the caller ID display, she answered on the second ring. "What's going on, Kathy?"

"Did you see the news?" Kathy asked.

"That they set the time and date for Mona's memorial service?"

"Who cares about that?" Kathy mused. "You always have your head stuck in a cookbook so you miss the really good stuff."

"Well, I am a baker who works in a bakery." Vivienne set the bowl with the sugar glaze down on the stainless steel workstation. "So what's this sudden news flash?"

"The police arrested Suzette Powell for Mona's

murder." Kathy spit out breathlessly. "What do you think about that?"

"Suzette Powell?" Vivienne couldn't believe it. "Why on Earth would she kill Mona Clarke? The only thing they had in common was that they were both on the historic commission. That's a motive for murder all of a sudden?"

"Who knows with that bunch?" Kathy replied. "I highly doubt it was all sunshine and rainbows between them."

"That's true." Vivienne stared at the Treavis cake on the rotating stand. "I've known Suzette for years. I just can't believe she would resort to cold-blooded murder."

"Do we ever really know our neighbors?" Kathy asked. "Isn't that always what people say when they find out someone who lived among them did something terrible?"

Vivienne thought back to yesterday when she had nearly collided with Suzette's catering van. She seemed to be in an awful hurry and she definitely was having words with someone. "Come to think of it, I saw her van over by city hall where people were gathering and leaving flowers at the makeshift memorial."

"You did?" Kathy's voice brightened. "Did you tell the police about it? Is that why she was arrested?"

"No. It wasn't anything big. I was driving over to Joshua's last night and I almost ran into her van."

"Oh." Kathy's bright tone morphed into disappointment. "I thought maybe you were the key witness to the whole case."

"Oh, please." Vivienne protested. "I did talk to

Sheriff Rigsbee about Mona being in here but frankly he didn't seem to act like my story added anything remotely useful."

"I wonder if you'll be called to the trial as a witness? Wouldn't that be exciting?"

The very thought made Vivienne feel nervous. She had never even served on a jury, but the thought of being grilled by opposing attorneys was just too much. "Perish the thought."

"Well, you never know with these big trials." Kathy added. "Why can't my life be this exciting?"

"You want to trade places with me?" Vivienne asked. "Be my guest."

There was a moment of silence on the line. "Well, not really." Kathy continued. "But I'll take the part of dating a gorgeous sheriff's deputy."

"Thanks." Vivienne glanced at the clock and decided she had better deliver the confection before too much longer. "I'm going to drop off a Treavis cake to Richard's home today. Want to come along?"

"I wish I could but I have a shipment arriving today." Kathy whined. "You really need to start making those for other occasions besides funerals we aren't invited to."

"I will." Vivienne smiled. "Talk to you later."

The home of Richard and Mona Clarke was close enough for Vivienne to walk to from her bakery downtown. In fact, she was glad to get out in the sunshine and take in the majesty of color that the trees were providing to all the residents. With the pink and brown cake box bundled securely with twine, she walked briskly along the businesses on Main Street and turned off onto Presidential Circle where most of the grand homes were located.

The stately Victorian that they had chosen to call home was a three-storied structure with a large porch wrapped around the front. Painted in a pale yellow shade with white trim, it gave no sign of the sadness within its walls. The sidewalk leading up to the front door was lined with a dozen hardy fall mums in alternating colors of burgundy and orange.

As she walked toward the front steps, Vivienne wondered why two people required a home that probably had no less than fifteen rooms inside. Richard and Mona had never had children or any pets. It just seemed like an awful big waste of space, but then again she tried not to judge. They both may have liked the style of architecture and the extra space probably came in handy whenever they threw a fundraiser for some political cause.

She pressed the doorbell and waited with the box in her hands. Her mind wandered back in time to when the home was first built. She imagined maids in pressed uniforms and butlers in tails scurrying about to keep the home neat and tidy for the residents. As the door opened, she recognized one of the blond ladies from the *Trade Winds Clothier* that had buzzed around Fiona. "Hello, I'm Vivienne Finch."

The woman, the one from the group with the darkest blond hair and dressed in a simple black dress, regarded her coldly. "You're late."

"I beg your pardon?" Vivienne blinked in response.

"Where's the rest of your catering staff?" The woman asked. "If it's just you, I don't see how you can possibly have the buffet setup in time before the mourners arrive."

"I think you're mistaken." Vivienne smiled. "I'm not the caterer."

"Oh." The blond woman frowned. "Fiona is going to be furious."

Vivienne handed her the box. "I baked a Treavis cake for Richard. I thought he could use it for when the guests return from the service."

"That was very thoughtful." The woman took the cake and set it down on a dark walnut table with clawed feet beside the front door. "How many does it serve?"

"Oh, about fifteen to twenty, depending on how thick the slices are." Vivienne answered.

"It's a start." The woman sighed. "Thanks again."

"Is there something wrong?" Vivienne asked. "Why aren't you at the memorial service?"

"Someone had to stay back and let the caterers in and since I had hired them it was the logical choice." She glanced down at her gold wrist watch and shook her head. "I can't believe the catering people never showed up."

"Who did you hire?" Vivienne asked.

"*The Formal Affair.*" The woman answered.

"Oh, no." Vivienne truly felt sorry for this woman who had no idea what had transpired. "I think I know why they couldn't keep the commitment."

"Did they go out of business overnight?"

"Well, not exactly." Vivienne couldn't think of a nice way to spin it. "The head of the company was arrested today."

"Arrested? For what?"

Vivienne swallowed hard. "There's no easy way to put this." She fidgeted with her hands as she spilled the awful truth. "She was arrested for the murder of Mona Clarke."

The woman swooned and nearly dropped to the floor.

Vivienne grabbed hold of her and gently eased her into a thrown-like chair inside the grand foyer. "Easy now, have a seat."

The woman shook her head back and forth. "Oh God, Victoria is going to be livid. I hired the caterer who killed Mona?"

Vivienne bit down on her lip. "Did you tell everyone who was catering?"

"No." The woman sniffled. "But they're going to find out in less than an hour. Victoria and Fiona just told me to take care of it and I did." Tears of frustration rolled down her cheeks.

Vivienne reached into her purse and rummaged around for a tissue. Finding one, she handed it to the woman. "Then we still have time to fix this."

The woman snatched the tissue and blew her little nose, which was quite red against her fair complexion. "How are we going to fix this?"

Vivienne knelt down on the floor and took hold of her hands. "I know a place that has fabulous comfort food and can probably make the deadline, but they don't deliver. Do you have a car?"

The woman nodded. "Yes."

* * *

As they pulled into the parking lot of *Clara's*

Diner, the woman whom Vivienne had learned on the ride over was named Samantha Charles, stared up in disbelief at the tacky coffee mug sign. "This is the where we're getting the food?"

"It's our only hope." Vivienne jumped out of the passenger seat. "If we ask nicely, they just might help out."

Samantha seemed hesitant to leave the comfort of her sleek Mercedes. "I've never been in one of these places."

"Then you're really missing out on some good old American comfort food." Vivienne led the way into the diner. "Follow me."

As they stepped inside, Clara was at her usual post by the register keeping order amongst the familiar lunch crowd. "Vivienne, what brings you here?"

"Well, we've got a bit of a problem that I'm hoping you can help us out with." Vivienne spoke in a sugary sweet voice.

"Oh no, I know that tone." Clara shook her head. "What do you need?"

"We need some good food for about..." She looked at Samantha for confirmation. "How many do you think?"

Samantha stared at the locals as if they were wild animals in a zoo. She kept close to Vivienne. "Between thirty and forty people I'd guess."

"Forty people?" Clara raised her voice in surprise which caused the patrons inside the diner to stop gabbing about the weather and sport scores and prick their ears up to catch a bit of juicy gossip to spread.

"We also need to have it ready in less than an hour." Vivienne pleaded. "Do you have any ideas?"

"Vivienne, I don't know that I can help you with this." Clara smoothed the lines of her pink uniform with her hands. "What exactly did you have in mind?"

Samantha decided to help. "The catering company was going to do lobster thermidor, some vegetarian canapés, and crème brulee for dessert."

"Oh, is that all?" Clara rolled her eyes.

"So you can do it?" Samantha replied eagerly.

"Why sure." Clara smiled brightly. "We do that all the time for lunch specials here."

Samantha looked at Vivienne with renewed hope. "You really are a miracle worker."

Vivienne grimaced in response. "Not exactly, Samantha."

Clara put her hands on her hips. "She must be one of Mona's friends?"

"Yes." Samantha answered. "From New York."

"Clara, maybe we can do something like a casserole?" Vivienne offered.

Clara tapped her index finger on her chin in thought for a moment. "I have two trays of scalloped potatoes and ham. That would feed about forty people if they don't take too much."

"They're from New York City. I'm sure they're used to tiny portions." Vivienne smiled at Samantha and decided to class it up for her. "Miss Clara is offering a fabulous and comforting potato gratin."

Samantha nodded. "Oh, that sounds lovely."

"I could have Harold and Stephanie put together some deli spirals. They're quick, easy, and best of all no cooking." Clara continued.

Vivienne nodded in agreement. "A classic no frills canapé just like the catering company was going to do."

"Yes, that would be perfect." Samantha agreed.

"What do you think about four of my famous pecan pies for dessert?" Clara finished.

"They've taken the blue ribbon at the state fair for five years in a row." Vivienne added. "You won't find a better one in all of the state."

"Will five hundred dollars cover it all?" Samantha asked.

Clara's eyes widened. "I'll say it will."

Vivienne nodded. "Given the super rush, I think that's more than fair."

Samantha reached into her purse and pulled out a designer wallet that looked like it was worth more than the diner. She peeled off five crisp hundred dollar bills and handed them to Clara. "Thank you so much."

Clara gladly accepted the money and then dashed into the kitchen. "Harold, drop everything we've got a rush order." She shouted above the sound of clinking plates and metal flatware. "Stephanie, I'm taking over your tables. I need you to start making deli spirals."

Stephanie's eyes twinkled and she quickly removed her server's apron. "I'd love to." She hurried off into the kitchen.

Samantha then peeled another crisp hundred dollar bill and handed it to Vivienne. "This is for helping me."

"Oh, I couldn't take your money." Vivienne protested. "I'm just trying to honor Mona's life."

Samantha blinked back a few tears. "I'm not used to people being so nice to me and not wanting something in return."

"Well, I'm sorry to hear that." Vivienne put her arm around Samantha's shoulder. "But we'll have everything in place and no one will be the wiser. That's how we do things in a small town like Cayuga Cove."

"I hope so." Samantha's mood seemed to brighten and she looked around at the diner's décor in wonder. "So this is what a greasy spoon looks like. I always wondered."

About thirty minutes later, Stephanie brought over a tray of deli spirals and placed them on the counter. "I tried to make these look real special to honor Mrs. Clarke." Stephanie gestured to the food. "I even made some veggie ones in case anyone doesn't eat meat."

Vivienne and Samantha looked down at the delicate spirals that Stephanie had handcrafted with impressive skill. They were elegant and full of colorful fillings of meats, cheeses, and vegetables rolled into kaleidoscope patterns. "They look amazing, Stephanie. I didn't know you liked to work with food design."

"I enjoy it." She beamed with pride. "Waiting tables here, I don't get a chance to do creative things often. But what can you do?"

Vivienne leaned forward and whispered something to Samantha outside of Stephanie's earshot.

Samantha took the hundred dollar bill she had tried to give Vivienne and tucked it into the billfold Stephanie had left for the cups of coffee they enjoyed while they waited.

Ten minutes later, they had all the food carefully packed into cardboard boxes Harold had found in the stockroom of the diner. Cramming them into the trunk space of Samantha's Mercedes, they flew back to the Clarke residence with only mere minutes to spare.

Vivienne helped Samantha set everything up buffet style in the formal dining room and then made a quiet exit as the first cars began to pull in to the driveway from the memorial service.

As she walked along the sidewalk back toward Main Street, the black limousine chauffeuring Richard Clarke drove past. The little purple flags that said 'Funeral' fluttered in the breeze as a line of luxury cars followed slowly behind with their headlights illuminated.

She lowered her head for a moment and took in the tragedy of it all. It was so senseless. But then again, most murders were. When it came down to the fine details, people killed other people over the most trivial of things. Those who tried to find a purpose or logic walked away in frustration. Logic, Vivienne thought sadly, failed miserably in the heat of anger.

Chapter 17

That evening, as she settled into her living room for some quality time with her television, she flipped the channels over and over in frustration. There wasn't anything all that interesting on and she rarely followed any dramatic shows anymore. All too often they were cancelled just as she was getting hooked on the story. Instead, she purchased them when they were released on DVD and only after the show made it past the third season. That way, she was less disappointed when it all came to a sudden end.

Somehow, Suzette Powell's arrest for the murder of Mona Clarke hardly seemed like an appropriate ending to the story of just what had transpired behind her store that awful morning. She wanted to call Joshua and press him for details, but that was simply not a viable option. She knew him well enough that he would never compromise the investigation by spilling details to a civilian. He was too honest for that and she quickly realized it was that very quality that drew her to him.

Then there was the business with the grimoire and her being a witch. Just like Mona's murder, it defied logic and she found herself frustrated with the lack of information surrounding her involvement. If she was indeed a hereditary witch as Nana Mary claimed, why did she still feel so powerless with everything going on?

Her business still hadn't launched. Her last date with Joshua had ended with the police searching for her as a missing person. The magic Nana Mary spoke so fondly of seemed more like a curse than anything beneficial.

From his perch on the sofa arm, Tom Cat stared at her. He had returned at sunset to her front door and pawed it as if he were offended she dared to close it. With his tail held high, he had marched his gray and white body into the kitchen and gave the dry food a test nibble. He pawed at the sparkling new litter box in the corner that was filled with special odor control crystals and decided to demonstrate how pleased he was by tossing some out onto the floor as he dug a little hole and peed.

There was no denying that he was at home and she was powerless to say no to his demands. She would have to make an appointment at the veterinary office to have his vaccinations given and a general checkup to clear him of any unknown diseases. He purred loudly as she ran her hand along his head and scratched behind his ears.

She turned the television off and wandered over to the computer. It had been some time since she had logged onto Social Butterfly. As she clicked on the internet icon and entered her password she found several more people from town wanting to join her friend garden. Some she knew from town, some from childhood, and a few that she thought were complete strangers. She approved those she knew and proceeded to scroll down the status page.

As she expected, there were all sorts of postings about Mona Clarke's service and the arrest of Suzette Powell. Nora was particularly vocal with her thoughts about the situation and she seemed obsessed with forwarding little pictures of candles, rainbows, and weeping angels with messages of condolences on loss.

She grew tired of reading most people's guesses about what had happened and was about to log off when she recognized the face behind one of the friend requests she had earlier dismissed. It was Samantha Charles. She looked more glamorous in her profile photo which was lit softly and posed quite expertly. Intrigued, she approved the request and went back to look for anything she had posted.

Sadly, there wasn't a thing on her personal page except messages of condolences from friends and colleagues. Once more she moved the mouse pointer over to close the program when a little ding erupted from the computer's speakers. Another window opened on the screen and notified her that Samantha wished to chat with her and asked if she was available. Vivienne clicked 'yes' and the window doubled in size.

`Thanks for helping me out today.` Samantha's message appeared on the screen.

"You're welcome." Vivienne spoke back and then chuckled. She proceeded to type the same response in the chat box and click send.

`You were right. No one was the wiser about the food issue.` Samantha replied.

`I told you it would work out.` Vivienne typed back, her fingers unused to working the keyboard.

`I don't know why, but Victoria seemed a little upset with me.` Samantha's response came fast and furious.

`Was the food not up to her standards?` Vivienne typed back.

I don't know. Samantha replied. She didn't say a cross word or throw a nasty look. It was just a feeling.

Vivienne didn't know how on earth she typed so fast. It was all she could do to keep up with the conversation. It was probably the stress of saying goodbye to Mona. She typed.

You think so? Samantha's reply appeared quickly. I hope you're right.

Vivienne found herself warming to Samantha. True, they came from completely different worlds but she felt a kinship to this woman and her worries. She meant well, despite her lack of knowledge of how normal people lived without multi-million dollar apartments and personal assistants. Much like Vivienne, she seemed frustrated at the whole situation. Her fingers hen pecked across the keyboard. Were you and Mona close friends?

For the first time in the chat, there was nearly a minute pause before the answer appeared. Not really.

Oh, I see. Vivienne typed back. Did you come along for moral support?

How about we meet for coffee at that diner and talk in person? Samantha asked.

Vivienne was stunned. She would have thought the Bistro Parisian would be more her style. A quick glance at the clock told her it was twenty past eight. She would have rather stayed in her cozy home with Tom Cat, changed into one of her flannel nightgowns, and had a bowl of microwave popcorn, but there was a chance to find out more about the world of Mona Clark and Victoria Clemens and she couldn't resist the offer.

Meet you there at nine?

It's a date. Samantha answered back and the chat window disappeared off the screen.

Vivienne closed out Social Butterfly and put the computer on standby mode. "Well, Mister Tom Cat, looks like you've got the place to yourself again."

He opened one eye from his nap and meowed in response.

"But tonight I'll be back. I promise." She went into the bathroom to fix up her hair and put on a little makeup.

When she arrived at Clara's Diner, Samantha was seated in one of the booths near the rotating dessert case. She waved to Vivienne.

"Good evening Viv." Harold smiled as he swept a broom along the floor near the back.

"Hello Harold." She replied and sat down with Samantha. Harold was one of the few people that shortened her name and got away with it. She figured that anyone who worked with Clara Bunton, and her finicky standards for twenty-five years, deserved a little slack now and then. As usual, Clara had counted down the daily take and went home leaving Harold in charge for the last hour of business.

"I'm starting to like this place." Samantha looked around the empty diner.

"It has its charm." Vivienne agreed.

Stephanie stopped her work filling the salt and pepper shakers and brought a fresh carafe of coffee over to the two women. "Here you go."

"Where do you keep the coffee mugs?" Samantha asked.

Stephanie slapped her head. "Oh, I'm so sorry.

I'll go get some."

Vivienne laughed. "As I said, it's the charm of living in a small town."

Samantha nodded in agreement. "When we first checked in at the Brass Cricket, I have to tell you that I couldn't wait to head back to Manhattan."

"Why is that?" Vivienne wondered aloud.

"Well, that's just home to me," Samantha confided, "Skyscrapers, four star restaurants, and a social calendar filled with fundraisers and special events."

"I've never been." Vivienne confessed. "But I think it'd be fun day trip. Window shop on Fifth Avenue, maybe take in a show on Broadway?"

Stephanie returned with two mugs and placed them on the table. "Can I get you ladies something to eat?"

"No, thank you." Samantha shook her head.

"Coffee is just fine with me." Vivienne answered.

"What time do you close?" Samantha asked.

"Ten." Stephanie smiled. "But don't rush on account of that. We have lots of cleaning up to do."

"Thank you." Samantha answered back.

Stephanie turned to leave and then spun around on her white sneakers with a squeak. "I just wanted to say thank you for the tip today. It really meant a lot."

Samantha nodded. "You're very welcome."

"I'm putting it in my savings account for school. It's a long way off, but I'm making progress at paying the tuition." Stephanie explained.

"What school do you want to go to?" Samantha asked with interest. "Wellesley? Vassar?"

Stephanie let out a little laugh. "I was thinking more along the lines of Lakeshore Community College."

"I'm sure they have some very nice programs." Samantha did her best to answer.

"It's right here in town and I just might be able to go next fall." Stephanie's eyes lit up with anticipation. "Well, I better get back to work or we'll be here until midnight."

"So, you said on the computer that you and Mona weren't particularly close friends." Vivienne poured a cup of coffee and filled Samantha's mug as well.

"I knew her." Samantha answered. "But Victoria and Fiona were really close with her."

"So you came for moral support for Fiona and Victoria?"

Samantha let out a little laugh. "You think that Victoria Clemens needed moral support? That woman could make Queen Elizabeth feel inadequate."

"Well, I'm afraid I don't know any of them particularly well." Vivienne took a sip of coffee. "Except for Suzette Powell, that is."

"Were you two friends?"

"No." Vivienne clarified. "It's a small town and when you go to social events here they are usually catered by Suzette. I would talk to her from time to time."

"That's good." Samantha nodded. "I was worried I'd say the wrong thing about your good friend and then you'd be mad at me."

Vivienne waved her hand. "It takes more than that to raise my hackles." She chuckled. "Just ask my mother."

Samantha smiled. "Does your mother live in town?"

"Yes, along with my grandmother." Vivienne leaned back against the vinyl booth. "The seeds don't scatter too far here in Cayuga Cove." She studied Samantha's expression for a moment. "So why do you think Victoria is mad at you?"

"Well, it was just one of those feelings you get." Samantha thought back to earlier in the day. "Right after you left, the guests started to arrive and they were hungry. I guided them to the buffet we set up and everyone seemed to enjoy the selections. More than a few people raved about your cake.

"That's good to hear." Vivienne added.

"So a short time later, Richard comes in with Victoria and Fiona at his side. He takes a plate and says how wonderful everything smells and how thoughtful we all were to provide a meal for this occasion."

"So far, so good I'd say."

Samantha nodded and cupped her hands around the mug. "Well, afterwards I see Victoria and Fiona whispering to each other and then point at me." Samantha took a sip of coffee. "I make eye contact with Victoria and she gives me one of those social smiles."

"What's a social smile?" Vivienne asked.

"I'm sure you've seen it before. It's the smile you find on the face of every politician running for office. The one so big it nearly reaches the corners of their eyes."

"Ouch." Vivienne shook her head. "I know that one well."

"If I hadn't known better, I'd have thought she knew what we did with the food."

"I think that secret is safe." Vivienne took another sip of coffee. "They don't seem like the crowd to recognize Clara's cooking."

"It's almost like she wanted me to screw up with the catering and have it blow up in my face." Samantha confessed. "That sounds stupid, doesn't it?"

"I can't think of a good reason why she'd want something like that to happen." Vivienne agreed. "But it doesn't sound stupid. We all get those feelings from time to time."

Samantha put her hands up to her mouth. "Oh God, I wonder if they found out what happened with their purses in the guest room?"

"What about the purses?" Vivienne asked with interest.

"Okay, I'll admit I'm a bit of a klutz when I'm rushed. I was trying to help out by taking coats and purses into a spare bedroom. I put one too many purses on one of those skinny leg end tables and the darn thing flops over." Samantha blushed.

"Those things happen." Vivienne reassured her. "I doubt anything was broken."

"No. Some lipsticks and compacts had spilled out of a few, but I was able to put everything back and no one was the wiser." Samantha paused. "But maybe one of them saw what I did?"

"It could happen to anyone. Besides, if they did see that happen, wouldn't a real friend offer to help?"

"I guess so." Samantha reasoned. "Or maybe they just found another reason to keep me at arm's length?"

"It's their loss if you ask me." Vivienne smiled. "I'd have helped you."

Samantha took a deep breath and sighed. "Well, whatever it is I can't point to anything tangible."

"That's how I feel about Suzette Powell's arrest." Vivienne spoke softly. "I can't point to anything tangible, but it doesn't feel right to me."

"So here we are." Samantha added.

As the evening went on, Vivienne shared stories of her little battles with Nora to lighten the mood. Much to her surprise, Samantha had similar experiences with her mother and the two of them shared quite a few laughs as the coffee carafe was emptied and Harold informed them he was ready to turn off the lights and go home.

"It's been so nice getting to know you, Samantha." Vivienne spoke as she stood by her car.

"I was going to say the same thing." Samantha opened the door to her sleek Mercedes and slid into the leather seat.

A cold wind blew some leaves across the parking lot as the lighted sign above their heads blinked off. Harold and Stephanie emerged from the darkened diner and scurried to their cars with a wave.

"I better get back to the inn before Fiona and the others send out a search party. Heaven knows I don't need to get on their radar any more than I already am."

"When are you leaving for home?"

"Tomorrow morning." Samantha looked a little sad as she started her car up. "I'd stop by your bakery if you were open for business."

"I'll be there baking up new treats all day." Vivienne replied as she unlocked her car. "You should stop by on your way out and I'll give you a little tour."

"I'd like that. If it isn't too much trouble, that is."

"It's no trouble at all. It can get rather boring baking alone all day long." Vivienne confided.

"Then I'll swing by." Samantha waved goodbye. "I'll be checking out around ten."

"I'll be up to my elbows in flour." Vivienne grinned. "Goodnight."

"Goodnight." Samantha shut her door and pulled away onto Spruce Street.

Chapter 18

Vivienne plopped into her car and slammed the door. As she turned the key, the ignition failed to turn over. She pulled it out and tried again. The engine gave a weak little warble sound and then fell silent. "Oh, don't do this to me tonight." Vivienne shook her fist at the sky outside her window. "Is this some kind of test or something?"

Fixing cars was not something she had ever given much thought to. She had always suspected that husbands and boyfriends made repairs sound more complicated than they really were just to have an excuse to stay out in the garage and drink beers in peace. Still, it reasoned that popping the hood and taking a look couldn't hurt matters. Maybe a wire had come loose or a spark plug had popped out? She reached down under the steering column and pulled the hood release.

As she stepped out of the car, a strong gust of wind threatened to push the door closed on her. She forced her way out and was about to grab her purse when another very strong gust caught the door and slammed it shut with a tremendous thud. She yanked her hand back in shock, inspecting that all her fingers were still intact. Thankfully, they were.

She tried to open the door, but it had locked. "Oh, come on." She protested. "This really isn't fair."

She pulled at the handle a few more times, hoping it would just open. But it remained stubbornly closed. She cupped her hands to the window and saw her purse sitting on the passenger seat, the grimoire sticking out slightly. "Tempus Openus?" She spoke futilely. "Lockus Unlockus?" She tried again. "How about just plain old help me out here?" She asked with a sigh.

She would have to call Nora and have her bring the spare set of keys over. She tapped the pockets of the light sweatshirt she was wearing and came up empty-handed. The cell phone, she realized with growing frustration, was still in her purse.

As she looked up at the sky, the moon was full but it threatened to be consumed by angry dark clouds. A storm was brewing and if she didn't hurry along she was going to get drenched. It was only a few blocks to Main Street and thankfully there were several businesses still open late where she could duck in and make a quick call. Wishing she had worn something warmer than the thin sweatshirt, she folded her arms together and trudged along fighting the cold wind with each step.

Spruce Street, she realized, had very few homes on it. At least, it seemed that way to her in the dark of night. The area around the diner was a cluster of light manufacturing type businesses that employed about half the population of the town. Unfortunately for Vivienne, none of them had a night shift.

The wind whipped her auburn hair around back and forth, and rattled the leaves still on the trees above her head. The sound of her footfalls echoed against the brick buildings that had only minimal lighting in their parking lots. She had hoped someone she knew would drive by and offer her a lift, but tonight the road was quite dead. Bad word choice, she thought with a grimace.

As she walked along the first block toward her destination, her eyes caught something darting across the road up ahead. It looked like a large dog. It stopped and stared at her for a moment and then dashed off into some bushes. She stopped in her tracks and considered the fact it might be a coyote that sometimes strolled into town from the fields and woods surrounding the lake. What if it tried to attack her? Did she have anything to fend it off with? She scanned the road around her and found only a small branch that the wind had knocked down from an old oak. She picked it up and decided it was better than nothing.

With the crude weapon firmly in her grip, she resumed her stride toward Main Street. The sound of her footfalls once more echoed off the buildings and she tried to think of something that made her feel safe and secure. Joshua popped into her head. She imagined him walking beside her, his strapping figure imposing fear in those who would wish to do her harm. She could almost hear his footfalls beside her own. Actually, she thought with a start, the sound wasn't in her head. Someone or something was trailing behind her and getting closer.

She craned her head back and caught a glimpse of a shadowy figure walking along the road behind her. She couldn't tell if it was male or female, as it appeared to be wearing a heavy coat or cloak of some kind.

She picked up her pace and so did whoever it was that was trailing her. Her mind raced with questions of what to do next. She considered veering off into one of the parking lots and waiting to see if her stalker followed or continued by. She tried to recall the night class she and Nora had taken to learn self defense against attackers using car keys and elbows as weapons. But in the end, all she could think to do was pick up the pace to a near jog and hope to keep a safe distance between them.

She glanced behind once more to see how close her pursuer was, only to find the street empty once again. She stopped in her tracks and frantically scanned the darkness for any movement. "Hello?" She called out. "Is someone there?"

She didn't really expect an answer, but it couldn't hurt either. With no response, she tightened her grip on the branch and turned toward Main Street. The shadow figure was now ahead of her, standing in the middle of the street. It watched her silently, without moving.

Without hesitation, she turned around and ran full speed back toward *Clara's Diner*. Fueled with fear, her legs moved at a speed she was certain qualified her for Olympic trials in track and field.

The sound of her stalker's footfalls grew nearer and her heart pounded furiously in her chest. Her mind raced with images from horror movies of women screaming bloody murder while a deranged killer chased them with a rusty chainsaw or sharp ax.

Her ankle gave out with a start as she tripped on a sewer grate along the side of the road. With a thud, she tumbled to the pavement and rolled along the cold ground. She scrambled to get up when a gloved hand wrapped around her mouth and stifled her cry for help. "You need to mind your own business, witch." A raspy voice whispered in her ear.

She bit down on the glove as hard as she could and the hand released with a grunt. A rancid smell filled her nostrils and she gagged in response. She swept her legs around and frantically kicked back at her attacker. Her hands frantically searched the ground until she found the branch she had been carrying for protection. She swung and connected a solid thud against the head of the shadow figure.

The figure grunted once more and then lunged at her with both hands extended. The cold gloved hands wrapped around her neck and pounded her head against the pavement. "You'll burn for that," the figure hissed.

The branch fell from her grip and she clawed at the face with her hands. Her fingers snagged onto fabric, a ski mask or some such thing which obscured the features of her attacker. Once more, the rancid smell returned. It was unmistakably the odor of death.

Without warning, a loud howl pierced the air and the shadowy figure was knocked away from her. Free from the iron grip, she rolled onto her side and gasped for air. Tears obscured her vision as she watched a fight break out between her attacker and what appeared to be a large coyote or dog.

The figure swooped and dodged the attacks from the beast, as it lunged and swiped with huge paws. Vivienne went into a coughing fit and tried to stand up but she was too weak. She could only lie on her side and hope that the furry creature drove away the attacker and left her alone.

As she wiped her watery eyes, she could see that what she had assumed was a dog or coyote was actually appeared to be a rather large wolf. It had gray fur, large pointed ears, and eyes that were blue like an Alaskan Husky.

The fight was interrupted when a pair of headlights illuminated them both in the road. Suddenly, a siren blast pierced the air and the familiar blue and red flashing lights flashed bright in the gloom.

The shadowy attacker fled from the scene and the large wolf gave chase after it into the darkness. Alone, on the cold pavement, Vivienne sat up as the police vehicle came to a stop and an officer jumped out.

"Are you injured?" The officer asked.

Vivienne could taste the coppery flavor of blood inside her mouth. She had taken quite a tumble and her body ached in too many places to name. "I could use some help." Her voice was hoarse and dry sounding.

As he came closer, she recognized her rescuer from the morning encounter outside Joshua's home. It was Officer Greg. "I'm going to call for an ambulance, Miss."

"Vivienne." She croaked. "Vivienne Finch."

Officer Greg knelt down in surprise. "Deputy's Arkin's girlfriend?"

She nodded. "I don't need an ambulance. I just need to talk to Joshua."

"Deputy Arkins is off duty tonight, Miss Finch." Officer Greg informed her. "I still better call an ambulance just to be safe."

"He said he was working the night shift." She explained as she coughed again.

"Not that I'm aware of, Miss Finch."

"I don't need an ambulance. I just need a ride home." She was banged up, but she didn't think needed medical care. What she really needed was a good night's sleep in her own bed and some bandages for the scrapes.

"Did someone attack you?" He asked.

She wanted to tell him about the figure but that would involve another trip to the Sheriff's office and more questions and she just wasn't up for it. Besides, she thought to herself, whoever attacked her had called her a witch and she couldn't think of any way to explain the true meaning behind that rationally. Not without getting a free trip to *Cayuga Medical's* behavioral science department for a few days. "No, I've locked myself out of my car at *Clara's* and was walking to Main Street to call my mother to bring the spare keys."

She pointed to the now empty street. "I came upon someone being attacked by an animal like a coyote or a wolf."

Officer Greg nodded as he listened to her. "So that's what it was. It's so hard to tell in the dark."

"I wasn't looking where I was stepping and I tripped on one of those sewer grates and fell." Vivienne explained.

He appeared to by buying her story. "Did you happen to recognize the person who the wild animal was attacking?"

"No." Vivienne felt a chill move through her body at recalling the shadow figure. "It was too dark to make anything out. Whoever it was ended up running off when you pulled up. Why do you ask?"

"Before I found you on the street, I was searching for a missing resident that was called in about an hour ago." Officer Greg added. "I thought maybe it might be them. We get the strangest calls during a full moon."

Vivienne, having had a moment to calm down

and catch her breath, felt well enough to stand. With a little help from Officer Greg, she managed the feat and groaned. "Sorry I didn't get a better look. Would you be able to unlock my car for me?"

"We don't really do that much anymore, but given the night you've had I can give it a try." Officer Greg led her to his cruiser and opened the front passenger door.

She sat down inside the warm vehicle and was thankful to feel the little blast of heat from the vents.

Officer Greg drove them over to *Clara's Diner* where her car was parked in the empty lot. He pulled up next to her driver's side and smiled at her. "Hoods popped? Did you have engine trouble too?"

"Yes." She answered. "It wouldn't start up."

"You can stay in here and get warm while I try to jimmy the lock open for you."

"I won't say no to that offer." She smiled back.

He left the patrol car and walked toward her vehicle with a flashlight in hand.

The heat felt wonderful on her hands as she cupped them over the vents and looked out the window at her car. Officer Greg walked in front of her and suddenly stopped in his tracks. He directed the flashlight into the car and then walked slowly over to the passenger side. She felt for the window button and lowered it. "What's wrong?"

He shook his head at her. "Looks like someone broke into the other side."

She fumbled for the door handle and with some effort extracted herself from the vehicle. "What?"

Officer Greg walked toward her. "Like I said earlier, it's a full moon." He shined his flashlight into the car and examined the damage.

She looked into the driver's side window and saw the shattered bits of broken glass all over the passenger seat. Her purse was tipped over, the contents spilled all over the seats and floor mats. She saw her wallet, her cell phone, but not a trace of the grimoire. "I don't believe this."

Greg walked up next to her. "I'll call it in."

"Can I check my purse to see if anything's been taken?" She asked.

"I'd leave it as is until we write it up."

She took a deep breath and nodded. "I used to think full moons were romantic. Now, I think I've had enough of them."

"Tell me about it." Officer Greg picked up his hand radio and called the incident into headquarters.

Vivienne looked up at the moon that was playing peek-a-boo with the clouds. Had her attacker stolen the grimoire from her car? To most people it just appeared to be a blank journal of no value. But, whoever had attacked her had called her a witch and she suddenly felt more vulnerable than ever. If they could read the spells inside it, what would they do with the power? She didn't want to know the answer. She just wanted to go home, soak in a hot bath, and put on her flannel nightgown. It was what she should have done in the first place.

Chapter 19

Without explanation, the car started up just fine for Officer Greg. She gave up trying to find an explanation for that and just chalked it up to one of life's little flukes. The incident report had taken less time and hassle than she imagined it would, which was a good thing as her energy was fading fast as the night wore on. She would have to drop by *Harrison Insurance* in the morning to put in her damage claim, but at least she was able to drive away and return to the safety of her little Cape Cod home on Sunset Terrace.

The heater in her car didn't keep the chill off from the loss of the window, now covered up with thick plastic wrap she had left in the backseat for wrapping up baked goods. Officer Greg had done his best to rig a temporary fix to keep any moisture out should it rain overnight.

Upon returning home, she greeted Tom Cat and filled his dish with dry cat food. He sniffed it and turned away, rubbing against her legs with a loud purr.

"Not right now." She gave his head a scratch and went to fill the tub with warm water and soak for a good while. Buried deep in lavender-scented bubbles, she rolled a towel up and created a pillow to lay her head against and let the warmth sooth her aches and pains.

She closed her eyes but the image of the shadow attacker kept leaping into her mind. No napping in the tub this time. Given her luck lately, she'd be one of those unfortunate souls who slid under and drowned. Instead, she reached for her soft pink bath mitt and slowly massaged her arms and legs. She groaned now and then when a sharp pain erupted from her movements, but this would help her tomorrow when she had to tackle another day of dealing with the bakery and the loss of her grimoire.

Feeling a bit like a prune, she exited the bath which had gradually grown cool. She wrapped herself up in the fluffiest bath towel she could find in the linen closet and used the vanity mirror to see how bad her scrapes and bruises were. She was happy to discover that other than a scraped right knee, a small cut on her left elbow, and some redness around her neck, she didn't look all that bad. It could have been so much worse, she thought as she slipped into a white flannel nightgown with little blue flowers that Nora gave her for Christmas. After all, she could be wearing a toe tag in the morgue.

She crawled between the soft cotton sheets on her queen sized bed and was soon joined by Tom Cat who jumped onto the bottom corner and made a nest with the rumpled comforter. As he groomed himself and scratched his ears with his back paw, she hoped that a flea circus wasn't laying down tent stakes for an extended run.

That night, she dreamt of being lost in a long corridor filled with red doors that seemed impossibly tall. They were narrow and instead of numbers had strange symbols much like those in the grimoire. She twisted at the knobs to peek inside, but they all proved to be locked.

Frustrated, she walked further down the hall and suddenly one solitary door opened by itself with a creaking groan. She felt a blast of cold air against her nightgown.

With a pause, she contemplated going in. As so often happened in dreams, she was suddenly transported inside the room against her will. The room was black and void of any furniture. A single light bulb, dim and suspended on a long chain, swung back and forth in the cold breeze. A humanoid figure shivered under a gray blanket. It looked like a woman, sitting with her legs folded. Loud sobs could be heard from under the cover and Vivienne was compelled to pull the blanket away.

She found Mona Clarke staring back at her. She was pale and dressed in a simple black dress. In her hands, she held tight to a bouquet of calla lilies. "Don't let them do it." She whispered.

Vivienne knelt down to Mona. "Let who do what?"

Mona looked at the calla lilies in her hand as they burst into flame. She released the flowers, which caught the blanket on fire and forced Vivienne to back away. "Don't let them do it." She repeated.

Vivienne watched in terror as the flaming blanket swirled around and morphed into a large stake. Mona was now tied to it, the flames surrounding her as strange voices shouted from the darkness.

Vivienne awoke from the dream with a start, nearly tossing the pillows around her to the floor in terror. She was covered in sweat, her legs knotted up in the sheets. Releasing herself from the tangled sheets, she was happy to see the morning light glowing softly through the bedroom windows.

After a quick shower, she hopped into a pair of casual sweats that she used for those times when she'd be baking up a storm and covered with spilled ingredients. Tom Cat eagerly ate his breakfast of dry food as she swallowed her daily vitamins and tossed in an aspirin for good measure.

She was out the door and on the road in her newly vandalized car before eight. Her first stop, at *Harrison Insurance,* would prove brief as Matt Harrison was always open well before his posted business hours. She found a prime parking space on Main Street and stepped into the nicely furnished office where his receptionist was busy watering the dish gardens lining the front windows.

After a brief description of her troubles last night, Matt put in her claim and informed her to get two estimates of repair. She was back in the *Sweet Dreams* kitchen by quarter to nine, armed with a slew of recipe cards and dry ingredients. She went about organizing the baked goods according to baking times and started the mixers.

The morning sunlight streamed into the front windows, which had fogged up from the ovens going at full blast. She found that the work definitely helped to take her mind off the events of last night. She lost herself in busy work such as measuring flour and whisking egg whites. There were so many steps to each process and one little screw up could easily spell disaster.

The events of last night had drained much of her energy and she began to question the sanity of trying to run a business solo.

As she popped the first of six dozen peanut butter cookies into the oven, she suddenly had a burst of insight. Stephanie Bridgeman. The sweet girl did her best as a waitress, but it was only a matter of time before all her mistakes caught up and Clara's patience wore thin. Despite her performance waiting tables, she proved with the deli spirals that she had a knack for detail and that was just what Vivienne needed.

She was certain that offered the chance to do something creative, Stephanie would accept the position without hesitation. The only problem would be approaching Clara. Much like her mother Nora, she usually wasn't all that attached to something until someone else expressed an interest.

Vivienne recalled so many spring cleaning adventures of the past as she helped to clear out the spare bedroom in her old home, only to have her hands tied up when she tried to throw anything away. Who did latch hook anymore? Nora decided she would get around to opening that package with the sad clown picture from the late seventies eventually. Sequined blouses with shoulder pads? Nora insisted that they'd be gracing the cover of Vogue magazine any month now. Oddball kitchen gadgets from late night infomercials? They worked nicely for forgotten birthday gifts.

She would have to approach Clara with the same psychology she used with Nora. Convince her that the entire thing was her brilliant idea and offer to help put their plan into action. It wasn't going to be easy. Given the amount of work needed to run her business, Vivienne would have to act fast.

The cell phone in her purse blasted its annoying basic ring and she saw Nora's number appear on the screen. "Mother, I was just thinking about you."

Nora's voice was shaky. "I'm afraid I have some

bad news dear. It's about Nana Mary."

Vivienne went numb inside. "What's happened?"

"She's missing." Nora replied, her voice nearly cutting off as she choked back tears.

"Missing? I don't understand."

There was a pause as Nora blew her nose. "I received a phone call from Whispering Oaks this morning. They've had the police out all night searching for her."

Vivienne's mind whirled around with possible scenarios. "Maybe she went to visit a friend and forgot to tell them?"

"The housekeeping staff found her apartment in disarray." Nora explained. "Her bed wasn't slept in, her microwave dinner was still sitting on the counter, pills all over the kitchen, and there were books scattered everywhere. They think she may have had a 'sundowner' incident."

Vivienne had heard of that terrible affliction. It was usually related to patients who were suffering with Alzheimer's disease. She had read an article that explained a theory that all of the sensory stimulation during the day overwhelmed and caused confusion and stress in the evening. Those afflicted could become angry, depressed, even hallucinate all through the night until morning when the symptoms mysteriously disappeared. "But Nana Mary doesn't have dementia."

"She is declining." Nora replied. "As much as it pains me to admit it, she's been having more and more moments of confusion."

"So where is she? Where have they checked so far?" Vivienne felt the need to jump into her car and start looking.

Nora blew her nose again. "I don't know. I'm just a wreck sitting here not knowing what's going on."

"I'm going to call Joshua and find out." Vivienne went over to the ovens and turned them off. "You stay home and call me if you hear anything."

"I will." Nora ended the call.

Vivienne reached behind her waist and untied the apron that was stained with peanut butter and flour. She dialed Joshua's cell number but only got his voicemail. "Nana Mary is missing from her apartment and I'm going to look for her. Call me as soon as you get this." She was about to end the call when she stopped herself. "I love you." She added.

As she drove along the streets of Cayuga Cove, she was haunted by the memory of her attack, the dream of Mona, and now the disappearance of Nana Mary. It was all just too much to deal with. She held tight to the wheel as she drove a little too fast with no particular destination in mind.

She had always thought of her hometown as a particularly dull place where change came gradually if at all. No one was ever in a hurry to jump onto the latest fad. Chain restaurants and super retail stores didn't bother to expand into the sleepy hamlet. It had been an ideal place to live and work, where you could still sit on your front porch swing and watch the world go by. Now, she felt as if she had taken it all for granted. There was a darker side to Cayuga Cove and lately it seemed to be getting bolder in showing itself.

Without thinking, she came to a dead end at the park located at the end of Lakeshore Drive. She pulled into the deserted parking lot and stepped out from the car into the morning sunshine.

The lake sparkled as gentle waves lapped at the shoreline. It was the deep blue color she had always known, but now it seemed colder and darker than her memory recalled. What secrets lay at the bottom? Rotting wrecks of sunken ferries that used to transport salt mined from under the lake? Jewelry and coins dropped from speedboat passengers out on a joyride? Perhaps, even a few skeletons from murdered souls who were still listed as missing.

She walked over to one of the small pavilions in the picnic area and sat down at a table. There were initials and hearts carved into the wood. Some were from this year, others from years past. There were anniversary dates, summer flings, and even some phones numbers begging to be called for a good time. Without warning, tears began to cloud her vision and she took a moment to have a good cry.

As the tears streamed down her cheeks, she thought of her last visit with Nana Mary. Why didn't she take the time to visit more often? Why didn't she ask more questions about her life, her loves, and even her magic? She regretted not being able to ever have these answered. They would forever remain a mystery.

"What are you crying about honey?" A feminine voice asked from behind her.

She jumped up in surprise to see a young blond woman wearing a blue scarf over her head and a pair of over-sized sunglasses. Dressed in a pair of faded denim jeans and a simple white shirt, she seemed oddly familiar. "I'm sorry. I thought I was the only one here."

The woman tipped her sunglasses down the bridge of her nose and smiled. "It's too nice of a day to be crying on the lakeshore by yourself."

Vivienne wiped the tears from her damp face and nodded. "It is a nice day."

"So what has you so rattled?" The woman sat down across the table from her and removed her eyewear.

"Someone I love is missing and I don't think it's going to end well." She choked up a bit but managed to keep the tears from flowing again. "Everything in my life just seems to be falling apart lately."

"I'm so sorry. Have you checked with Joshua?" The woman asked.

"My call went to his voicemail and I haven't..." Vivienne paused. "What did you say?"

"Your boyfriend is named Joshua and your name is Vivienne Finch. Am I right?" The woman interrupted.

"Yes." Vivienne sniffled. "Have we met before?"

"Yes, too many times to count. You could even call it magical." The stranger replied.

Vivienne squinted as the visage of the woman began to blur and changed into that of Nana Mary. "It can't be."

"It's me, darling granddaughter." Nana Mary smiled back. "I'm sorry to scare you like that but I didn't have a choice."

"How did you?" Vivienne was at a loss for words. Instead, she jumped up from the table and hugged her. "I thought you were dead."

"It's called a glamour spell." Nana Mary waved her hands around like a model showing off a prize on a game show.

"How is it I can see you as you really are?"

Vivienne asked.

"Mortal senses are all easy to fool if you know how to. But a witch's senses are more highly tuned. Your eyes and ears are fooled for a short time, but then your second sight takes over and you can see through the magic. It's all in the grimoire."

"It's gone." Vivienne confessed. "It was stolen from my car last night."

"Before you were attacked?"

"Yes." Vivienne nodded. "You know about that too?"

"These are dark times indeed. We have to be extra careful or we'll both end up dead."

Vivienne sat down next to Nana Mary and took hold of her hands. "I'm so confused with what's going on. None of it makes sense."

"You weren't the only one attacked last night, my dear." Nana Mary continued. "Last night, as I was getting ready to have my dinner, I was interrupted by one of the care staff who looked like Sandy Cumberland from the front reception desk. Only, it wasn't her. She had gone home at five like she always does."

"What happened?"

"Well, this stranger told me that Doctor Mayfield had left some new medication with her and that I was supposed to take two pills with dinner each night." Nana Mary shook her head. "As if I were some stupid child who would never question that."

"Were they poison?" Vivienne wondered aloud.

"I have no idea. I no sooner had grabbed the bottle when I saw through the glamour spell. I couldn't make out their face because they were using another glamour spell underneath the first that obscured their real features. Whoever it was, was working some powerful magic."

Vivienne's eyes widened. "So it was another witch?"

"There's no doubt about that. This is the work of dark magic, my dear. It's evil and it's powerful." Nana Mary did her best to boil down the details. "Whoever it was must have sensed my alarm because they tried to grab me and force the pills down my throat. We struggled and I managed to knock the bottle to the floor and they flew everywhere."

"That explains the pills on the floor." Vivienne nodded.

"So I grabbed one of my heavy hard-bound cookbooks off the counter and I smacked them with it as hard as I could. They fell back against the cabinets and I beat feet it out of there as fast as I could."

"Why didn't you tell security?" Vivienne asked.

Nana Mary grimaced. "What could they do against a dark witch? No, my only option was to get out and disappear."

"Mother mentioned that your apartment was trashed. Were they looking for something?"

"I'm sure it was the grimoire." Nana Mary sighed. "Which probably explains why they came looking for you last night."

"They figured out you had transferred the power to me." Vivienne pondered. "Why not mother?"

"Because whoever it is knows how the power works and can wield magic. They are crafty and dangerous and now it sounds like they have the grimoire in their possession too."

"I'm so sorry about all of this." Vivienne shook her head. "I've really screwed things up."

"No, my darling granddaughter, you haven't." Nana Mary reached out and pulled her into a hug. "It's not supposed to be like this. Besides, that grimoire is rightfully yours. Eventually, it will come back to you. You're both bound by blood."

"I'm just so glad that you're alive. Where are you going to go?"

"I've got a few powerful friends to visit." Nana Mary patted Vivienne on the back. "This is going to require a conclave to fix."

"What's a conclave?"

"It's a gathering of the elder witches in the regional covens. It usually only meets during blue moons, but when a crisis occurs, it can be convened as required. We address problems and dispense justice to those who break the natural laws of magic or practice the dark craft."

Vivienne gave Nana Mary a smile. "You're going to ask for magical help with this?"

"You bet your grimoire I am." Nana Mary smiled back. "It may take some time, so you're going to have to be extra careful. I wish you could come with me, but you aren't practiced enough in the craft to safely travel to the meeting place and the two of us travelling together would draw too much attention."

"I'll watch my back." Vivienne added. "And I've got Joshua to help out too." She snapped her fingers. "Speaking of which, I need to tell you something about him."

"What is it?"

Vivienne looked around the deserted park to

make sure they were alone. "He was able to read the grimoire." She whispered. "Does that mean he's a witch?"

"He can?" Nana Mary expression was one of genuine surprise. "He's not part of the local coven here in town."

Vivienne was disappointed. Joshua continued to remain an enigma and it was really starting to tick her off. "So should I tell him what's going on?"

"Does your heart tell you he can be trusted?" Nana Mary asked.

She paused for a moment. "I want to, but he lied about working the other night. It's starting to bother me a little."

Nana Mary clucked her tongue. "Men are fickle. He probably wanted a night out with the guys to drink beer and watch football. They're all terrible liars."

"I guess so." Vivienne nodded. "He's not like any other man I've ever met."

"So what's the problem?"

Vivienne thought for a moment and felt foolish. "Here I am ticked off about him lying about work, and I'm withholding the truth about who I really am. I guess that makes me just as bad." She sighed. "I don't know what to do."

"Go with your instinct. Look into his eyes and then you'll know if you should tell him." Nana Mary stood up from the picnic table. "Now, I really should be going before I'm discovered."

"What about the police and everyone looking for you? What about Mother?" Vivienne asked.

"There's no time for me to wrap up everything in a nice package. I'll leave that to you." Nana Mary smiled and reached into a pocket in her jeans. She pulled out a tiny purple bag. "This powder will keep Nora calm and she'll believe whatever you tell her. Slip a pinch of it in her coffee or tea when you get a chance."

"What is it?"

"It's a special blend of herbs and magic that I picked up at last Halloween's conclave meeting. She'll believe every word that leaves your lips. Oh, what the politicians would do to get their hands on this stuff."

"What about the police?" Vivienne pressed on.

"Tell them I went to Arizona for a family crisis." Nana Mary took one last look at the lake and all the foliage from the surrounding hillside. "You're a smart cookie, Vivienne. I'm counting on that to keep you alive."

She stood up from the picnic table and kissed Nana Mary goodbye. "I'll do my best."

Nana Mary reached around her neck and pulled off her necklace with the pentagram charm. She handed it to Vivienne. "Put this on and don't ever take it off. It will give you some extra protection."

Vivienne placed it around her neck and smiled. "Is it magically charmed?"

"It is indeed." Nana Mary replied cryptically. "Now I really must be going." She turned and walked away toward the lower playground and woods. She waved one final time before disappearing onto one of the many hiking trails that snaked along the park.

"Good luck Nana Mary." She whispered and stared at the little bag of powder in her hand. How many times had she slipped that into Nora's drinks over the years? That's one recipe she'd have to ask for the next time they met.

Chapter 20

"She's gone to Arizona to visit Cousin Howard and his family." Vivienne lied to her mother after mixing the powder into a mug of orange pekoe tea which she had slurped down alarmingly fast. "She'll be out of touch for awhile but you won't worry about it because she's fine."

Nora nodded accordingly. "Yes, that makes sense now. I feel so foolish for worrying."

"She'll be back before we know it."

"That's right." Nora smiled. "She's very independent for a woman her age."

The powder was amazing stuff. Vivienne thought to herself. Her mother had taken every word as the gospel truth, no questions asked. "You better call Sheriff Rigsbee and let him know what happened."

Nora got up from the table and went to the telephone. "Yes, he'll be glad to know she's not missing anymore." She dialed the number and smiled at Vivienne. "Hello, this is Nora Finch calling for Sherriff Rigsbee. May I speak to him please?"

Vivienne washed up the mugs of tea while Nora explained how she had just spoken to Nana Mary and Cousin Howard in Arizona. Something about a family crisis and Nana Mary had left in a hurry to catch a red eye flight to be at the family's side.

She handed the phone to Vivienne who apologized on behalf of their family for causing a stir. It had taken quite a bit of talking, but at last Sheriff Rigsbee seemed convinced that the facts added up and he called off the search. He asked that given the number of missing person reports called in for their family lately, they try to keep better tabs on each other. Vivienne couldn't agree more.

Afterwards, she called *Whispering Oaks* to explain the situation and apologized for causing any problems. The director of the facility was nice enough, but she could tell from the tone in his voice that he was just a little peeved at the whole mess.

With her cover story in place, Vivienne left Nora's and returned to the *Sweet Dreams Bakery*. It was nearly eleven in the morning and she had to throw away the half-baked cookies in the oven and start the process all over.

As she dumped the cookie dough into the garbage bin, there was a knock at the front door. Samantha Charles waved from outside, her Mercedes parked behind her. Vivienne set the cookie trays on the prep station and went to greet her. "Samantha, I thought I'd missed you."

Samantha grinned. "Did I forget to mention how I always run late for everything?"

"Come in." Vivienne stepped back into the store. "I'm so glad you stopped by."

"This is so cute." Samantha looked around the bakery with wonder. "You've really created a charming little place."

"Thank you." Vivienne beamed with pride. "I don't know if it'll ever open."

"Oh, it will." Samantha gushed. "I'm sure it'll be a smashing success too."

"You're too kind." Vivienne gestured to a bistro table. "Would you like to have some tea?"

"No, I've really got to be on the road in a few minutes if I want to be home before dark."

"Have the others left too?" Vivienne asked.

"Fiona is staying here a few more days to help Victoria with some historic commission thing." Samantha added. "The rest of us are going back though."

"I do hope you'll come back and visit soon." Vivienne pulled out one of her new business cards that sat in a little holder on the table. "I'll ship anywhere too."

Samantha admired the card and opened her purse to place it inside. "Can I have a few more? I'll let everyone know back in the city."

"Sure." Vivienne beamed and handed her a small handful. "I don't have online ordering yet, but I hope to soon."

Samantha placed the cards in her purse and smiled. "Thanks again for being so nice. I don't know what I would have done without your help."

"That's what friends do." Vivienne added.

"We are friends now, aren't we?" Samantha asked.

"I'd like to think so."

Samantha leaned forward and gave Vivienne a hug. "I better get going now. I'll be seeing you on Social Butterfly, right?"

"Sure, from time to time." Vivienne agreed. "If I ever get a chance to visit New York, I'll let you know."

"Don't get a hotel." Samantha insisted. "You'll stay at my apartment. I've got tons of room."

"I'm game for that."

Samantha left the bakery and climbed into her sleek car. She gave a little wave as she pulled away with a friendly honk of the horn.

Vivienne watched her leave and then considered how behind she was on getting product made. There wasn't time to waste anymore. She walked over the phone and called Clara.

As far as convincing people to see things her way, Vivienne was on fire. By three in the afternoon, she had managed to convince Clara to release Stephanie from her employment and hired her on as her new baker's assistant. For the first time in days, things finally seemed to be getting back on track.

"I'm so excited to be working here." Stephanie gushed as she whipped up several batches of chocolate chip cookie dough in the huge electric mixers.

"Are you kidding? I'm the one who should be excited to have such a creative person working for me." Vivienne added as she began to slice the refrigerated checkerboard cookie dough with a knife.

"I feel so creative here." Stephanie stopped the mixers and scraped the dough out of the metal bowls with a large spatula. "Miss Clara was nice and all, but I always felt like she was mad at me."

"That's just how she treats everyone." Vivienne spoke as she slid the checkerboard cookies onto baking sheets lined with parchment paper. "She likes to keep people on their toes."

"Well, it worked like a charm." Stephanie agreed.

Vivienne slid the baking sheets into the oven and set the timer. She looked up at the wall clock. "How about working until six today and then you can come in tomorrow morning at eight?"

"Sure." Stephanie replied. "Are we still going to open in two days?"

"Good grief, I sincerely hope so." Vivienne reached down to the wooden legs on one of the work tables and gave it a little knock.

As she had hoped, their teamwork resulted in one entire bakery case filled to capacity with all sorts of delicious cookies and other sugary confections. Stephanie was quite the helper and her artistic flair was evident on the delicate little designs she had created on some of the iced sugar cookies. She had no sooner said goodnight to Stephanie when Joshua pulled up front in his patrol car and parked. Vivienne stood with the door open, her arms folded across her chest.

"I just got your voicemail a short time ago. I called it in to the department but they told me you found Nana Mary safe and sound."

"Yes." Vivienne nodded. "Where were you?"

"I was asleep all day." He walked up to her dressed in his regulation uniform and hat. "I worked the overnight. It really screws up my internal clock." He moved closer to kiss her but she side stepped into the store.

She had hoped, given the opportunity to confess, that he would jump at the chance. But he didn't and she felt betrayed once again. "That's not what Officer Greg told me last night."

He followed her into the store, allowing the door to close. "You talked to Officer Greg?"

She moved to the tea display and began to arrange the boxes in a new order. "Yes, that would be after I was attacked by some creep last night. I'd have thought you'd have heard about it?"

"Whoa." Joshua crossed over to her with concern. "You were attacked?"

She turned to face him. "That was after I locked myself out of my car at Clara's and was walking to Main Street to make a phone call."

"Vivienne, I'm sorry. I had no idea." He reached out to hold her but she scooted over to the bakery case.

"Look, I get it. You want some time apart and maybe I was moving too fast." She examined the cookies under the soft lights in the case. "You don't have to lie about working to avoid seeing me. If I'm being too forward just say so."

"That's not what I did." Joshua removed his hat and set it on the nearby bistro table. "It's really complicated."

She spun around to face him, her face burning with anger. "You're damn right it is. You were supposed to be working the night shift but you weren't there. I was attacked on the street by some maniac and you weren't there. I thought my Nana Mary was missing this morning and you weren't there. Are you seeing a pattern here?"

"Vivienne, please try to understand. I would never abandon you when you need me." He pleaded.

"If it wasn't for that wild animal, I don't know what would have happened." Her voice cracked a bit.

"A wild animal saved you?" He sat down in the bistro chair.

"I'd really like to be alone right now Joshua." She felt the tears building up and fought to hold them back. "I have so much to do."

He looked up at her with his steel-blue eyes. "I

was there, Vivienne. At least, I think I was."

A single tear dribbled down her right cheek and she brushed it away. "What are you talking about?"

He bit down on his lower lip in frustration. "It wasn't a coyote. It was a wolf."

"How would you know that?" She asked.

"Because I'm pretty sure I was that wolf." His voice was barely above a whisper.

"What?" She blinked in response. "Is this some kind of joke to lighten the mood?"

"It was me." His face was solemn. "I can't believe I'm telling you this, but at this point I've got nothing to lose. I'm a werewolf."

She was about to laugh when she looked into his eyes and noticed they were the very the very same steel-blue eyes that her furry four-legged savior had. She grabbed the other bistro chair and sat down to face him. "I don't know which is crazier. The fact that you say you're a werewolf or the fact that I actually believe you."

He reached across the table and took her hands in his. "It's not something I've ever told anyone. They'd lock me up if I did."

"I thought werewolves walked upright like people? The kind you see in the movies and on television. You know, big burly beasts with sharp claws and teeth that terrorize the town?"

Joshua stared at her for a moment in silence. "They've got it all wrong. When we transform, we literally turn into an actual wolf identical to the regular animal. The only thing different is that our eyes retain our human coloring."

"Do you attack people?" Vivienne asked.

"We keep to ourselves out in the woods mostly."

"Since we're doing the complete honesty thing, I may as well tell you something too, so brace yourself." She took a deep breath. "I'm descended from a long line of magical women which technically makes me a hereditary witch."

The news didn't seem to faze him one bit. He looked into her eyes and smiled. "Not exactly a fairy tale romance that we have here, is it?"

She let out a little laugh and shook her head. "It depends on the author, I suppose."

"I had a feeling there was something different about you when I saw that book of yours the other night." Joshua admitted.

"You could read it." She added. "No one else except Nana Mary could do that."

"Is she really okay?" Joshua asked with concern in his voice.

"Yes. She's gone to summon help from the elder witches." She replied. "We were both attacked by someone who can use magic, and to make matters worse, they stole my grimoire in the process."

"Did she fly on a broom?" He asked with a little grin.

"I doubt it." Vivienne cracked a smile. "I don't think balancing on a wooden pole would be very comfortable. Give me a big first class seat with champagne and warm nuts any day."

"Well, I have no memory of what happens when I assume wolf form." Joshua confided to her. "I'm sorry I can't tell who attacked you last night. But, I'm glad I could at least help a little bit."

"So is your entire family made up of werewolves?" Vivienne asked. "Is that why you're so secretive about your past?"

"We don't form the same sort of family bonds like humans do. After we mature, we leave home and rarely ever go back. It's like that with most were-creatures, I guess."

"You mean there are more than werewolves?"

"More than you could possibly imagine. For every animal, there is most likely a were-creature existing out in the world."

Vivienne became fascinated with the man before her. He was something other than human, just like her, and it felt insanely good to talk so openly about events that defied reality. "I have so many more questions to ask."

He looked at his watch. "I really do have to work tonight. Can I answer them tomorrow?"

She nodded. "I'm sorry I was cross with you earlier. It's just been such a terrible past few days."

He stood up from the table. "I can't blame you for being suspicious. It happens to me frequently." As he grabbed his hat and put it on, he looked around the store. "Do me a favor and don't stay late tonight."

"I was getting ready to go home right before you showed up." She stood up and walked over to him. "I can't take any foolish chances right now."

"Good." He wrapped his arms around her waist and pulled her close. "I'm going to have the guys keep a close watch on your house tonight, in case your attacker decides to come back."

She kissed him on the lips. "I appreciate that."

"Do you want a patrol to check on your mother's home too?" He asked.

She thought for a moment. "My mother isn't a witch."

"Now I'm confused."

She smiled at him. "Despite what you may have heard from the gossip mill around town, she's just a regular mortal. I'll explain more about it later."

"If anything suspicious happens tonight, I want you to call. I don't care how trivial it seems."

"Don't worry about that." She fiddled his badge with her fingers. "I promise."

He gave her another kiss and then walked to the door. "Are you ready to lock up?"

She nodded. "I just need to get my purse and we can call it a night."

He followed her out to the back alley where she locked up the bakery for the night. It was the first time she didn't feel weird about being near the dumpster. She pointed to the broken passenger window of her car. "They didn't use magic to steal the grimoire."

"I see that." He scratched his chin. "Maybe it was just some dumb kids from town?"

"My insurance will cover the repair." She replied as she climbed into the car. "I just have to get two estimates." She turned the key and the engine revved.

"Just one more thing before you leave." He knelt down to face her. "I love you too."

"I'm never the one to say that first." She admitted. "So you just think about what that means when you're on patrol tonight."

He laughed. "I'm honored."

She pulled away and sped off for home before the darkness arrived.

Chapter 21

Vivienne was filled with new hope after she returned home for the night. The bakery was filling up with product thanks to hiring Stephanie as an assistant. She and Joshua had finally opened up with the truth about each other and they now shared something few people ever could understand. Nana Mary was off to a secret location seeking magical assistance from the elders at the conclave. Mother, having drunk the magic powder, had believed the cover story and went back to worrying about when she could expect grandchildren from her successful matchmaking venture. Her life seemed to be getting back on the right track.

As she sat down with the chicken breast she had baked for dinner, she cut up a few pieces for Tom Cat, who pawed at her legs, and turned on the television to look for something interesting to watch while she ate.

Tom Cat batted the pieces around on the floor like toys, while she flipped through the channels and stopped when she saw Mayor Richard Clarke addressing a crowd on the local news report. She turned up the volume and listened with interest.

"It is with great sadness that I address you tonight. Having spent a great deal of time with family and friends over these last painful days, I must confess that I have failed the good people of Cayuga Cove." Richard looked terrible.

His dark hair was limp and blew awkwardly around his head as he faced the microphones from the local news crews. There were dark circles around his eyes from a lack of sleep, and his cheeks looked sunken in as if he hadn't been eating. "After the arrest of Suzette Powell, I knew I could no longer keep this secret shame inside. I stand here before you tonight to admit that I have been involved in an ongoing affair with Ms. Powell for several months now."

This was followed by a storm of camera flashes and a chorus of questions hurled from the gathered reporters that surrounded the Mayor. He put up his hands to shield his eyes from the flurry of light. As it died down, he straightened his tie around his neck and gripped the edges of the small podium from where he was speaking. "I have failed as your Mayor to lead this office with the dignity and grace it deserves. More importantly, I have failed as a husband to keep my vows of marriage. So I am prepared to face the consequences of my actions."

He looked blankly into the cameras. "I am stepping down, effective immediately. The city council has appointed Victoria Clemens as acting Mayor, and I can tell you she is more than dedicated to serving the citizens of our fair town. She will assume this role for the next thirty days, after which a special election will be held if someone chooses to run against her. If not, she will serve the remainder of my term and I'm sure she will lead with the honor and integrity that my late wife so often remarked about her dear friend. Thank you all and God bless our little town."

He gave a little wave from the podium. "And now, Madame Mayor, will you please do us the honor of addressing the people?"

Victoria Clemens stepped up to the podium looking radiant in a tan business suit with her hair pulled back into a simple bun. "The honor is mine, to serve the citizens of this wonderful town. I accept the challenge to make Cayuga Cove the destination that Mona Clarke dreamed of. It is with deep sadness that I mourn the loss of my dear friend, but I feel so blessed to honor her memory by picking up the torch she lit and carrying it to the finish line."

There was a little cheer from the assembled crowd. Victoria put up her hands to stifle it. "My friends, I only ask that we come together as a city to make it a home we all can be proud of." To heal the wounds of the past," she gestured to Richard by her side, "To blaze a trail of innovation for the future." She gestured to the city council members who were watching off to the side. "I thank each and every one of you for your faith in me to lead you there. Good night."

Vivienne stared at the television in disbelief. She was wrong about Suzette Powell after all. Maybe it was a fatal attraction type of murder? With Richard's confession, the case against her was definitely taking a more certain turn. She speared a piece of chicken with her fork and chewed it thoughtfully.

After washing and drying the dishes from dinner, she answered the phone when Kathy called.

"Did you watch the news tonight?"

Vivienne opened the cabinet where her dishware was stored and slid some plates on the top of the pile. "I sure did. Can you believe it?"

"I was working late at the store, so I didn't know about it until Eunice Kilpatrick stopped in." Kathy explained. "She knows everything."

"Oh?" Vivienne closed the cabinet and turned the florescent light over her sink off. "I'm not surprised."

"She told me that you were seen over on Meier Lane the other morning leaving Joshua's duplex." Kathy snickered. "You got caught, you naughty girl."

"We didn't do anything." Vivienne clarified. "I had too much wine and feel asleep on the loveseat."

"God, if I had a nickel for every time I used that excuse." Kathy continued. "So things are going well?"

"We've certainly moved forward in our relationship, I guess you could say."

There was a pause as Kathy tried to phrase her curiosity. "In what way would that be?"

"Well," Vivienne paused, "we've both said the 'L' word to each other."

"Who said it first?"

"Does it really matter?" Vivienne sauntered into the living room and plopped down on the sofa.

"As I live and breathe, Vivienne Finch let down her walls." Kathy's voice rose slightly with excitement. "I guess that means this is getting serious."

"It means we're both very happy with how things are going." Vivienne countered. "And yes, it's getting serious."

"I'm so happy for you two." Kathy replied. "The next time Nora gets a notion to play matchmaker, will you send her my way?"

"Are you sure you really want me to do that?" Vivienne laughed. "I've had my fair share of duds to weed out."

"True." Kathy mused. "But she may be on a hot streak. Does Joshua have any handsome single brothers?"

"Let's not start raiding the family members just yet." Vivienne chided.

"I know." Kathy sighed. "I'm starting to think all the eligible men in Cayuga Cove are either gay or married or both."

"Both?" Vivienne pondered.

"Well, Eunice told me that that Suzette's husband, Brad, swings both ways." Kathy was all too eager to gossip. "She had heard that he went to New York with Tristan from the antique store behind Nathaniel's back."

"I wouldn't put much stock in everything that Eunice says." Vivienne added. "We're talking about a woman who has a nativity scene at Christmas that includes three wise men and two lawn jockeys. She's not exactly an open book on diversity."

"Well, I wouldn't be surprised if he has moved on to the men. After all, there are only so many women in this town."

"He never dated me." Vivienne was quick to reply.

"Me either." Kathy added.

"Just don't call me and say you're dating Richard Clarke anytime soon." Vivienne warned.

"Please, like I'd even consider dating that sleaze."

"Well, they say women are attracted to men with power and money." Vivienne reasoned. "Can you really blame Suzette for having an affair after how her husband has blatantly carried on like a drunken frat boy over the years?"

"No." Kathy agreed. "Brad has cheated on her with so many other women I'm actually kind of glad she gave him a taste of his own medicine."

"Well, she certainly chose a high profile man to

do it with." Vivienne swatted at Tom Cat who tried to claw the sofa arm with his paws. He dashed off with a defiant meow. "But why kill Mona?"

"Mona could have found out and told her to back off." Kathy guessed. "Or maybe she threatened to kick her off the historic commission and the Women of Small Business Association?"

"So you go out and murder someone? That just seems like a crazy step to take."

"Isn't that always the case with those things?" Kathy asked. "What do they call them? Crimes of passion, right?"

"Sounds like one of those tawdry movies on television." Vivienne put her feet up on the coffee table and leaned back.

"I'm sure the trial will be the main event to see when it starts."

"I'll bet Eunice Kilpatrick takes time off from the bank just to have a front seat in the courtroom." Vivienne said with a laugh.

"Hell, I bet she'll try to get on the jury." Kathy laughed back. "So now we have Victoria Clemens as Mayor. Could this week possibly get any worse?"

"She's been by Richard's side ever since this terrible thing happened." Vivienne replied. "She certainly seemed confident and capable addressing the crowd tonight. Maybe we misjudged her?"

"I wish I could move up the rungs of the ladder as fast as she did." Kathy mused. "Lowly commission member one day, Mayor the next."

"Some people are just lucky like that." Vivienne let out a yawn. "Did I tell you I hired Stephanie Bridgeman to help me out at the bakery? She's been such a blessing."

"Did Clara fire her?"

"No." Vivienne smiled as she recalled her little foray into reverse psychology. "I convinced her it was the best idea."

Kathy laughed. "Well, she certainly wasn't a good waitress but her heart is in the right place."

"She's very talented." Vivienne yawned again. "We're shooting for opening in two days."

"It sounds like you're pooped." Kathy finished up the conversation. "You better get to bed soon."

"Good idea." Vivienne agreed. "Keep me posted if you hear anything else from Eunice."

"You know I will. Goodnight." Kathy hung up.

Vivienne clapped her hands as Tom Cat appeared from the kitchen. "Are you ready for bed now?"

He cocked his head to the side and meowed.

"Let's go." She turned off the table lamp and headed for her bedroom.

Chapter 22

"Stephanie, can you hand me the orange frosting?" Vivienne asked as she decorated an individual cake shaped like a pumpkin.

Stephanie handed her the heavy metal bowl laden with homemade vanilla frosting. "That's looking great."

"Thanks." Vivienne smoothed some more orange onto the cake and sculpted it along the ridges, adding some bumps for a little more realism.

Stephanie busied herself with creating little green fondant leaves and vines to adorn the cake with. It was going to be on the center pedestal in the front window for the grand opening. "I think it's so clever making the raspberry-lemon cake look like a pumpkin."

"Let's hope the customers think so too." Vivienne rotated the stand to examine her work. "I'm ready for some of those vines and leaves now."

Their morning routine was working like a well-oiled machine. As the morning hours disappeared into lunchtime, they had almost filled the second display case with cupcakes and whoopie pies. All that was left for the afternoon was to bake some apple blossoms, some fruit tarts, and a few pies.

Vivienne sent Stephanie off for her lunch hour and asked her to swing by the *Monarch Grocery* on her way back to pick up some more apples. She brewed herself a cup of tea and settled into one of the bistro chairs as the first of her pumpkin pies baked in the ovens. She sorted through the mail that had arrived earlier, thumbing through the usual assortment of flyers from vendors and suppliers asking her to choose them for her business needs. A complimentary issue of a new fashion magazine that promised to help her find that 'fall runway look for less' briefly caught her interest before she put it down.

She pushed it all aside and admired her store. It was finally coming together and she felt confident enough to open for business nice and quiet tomorrow morning. No big crowds, no ribbon cutting, no fuss.

The front door opened and the bell overhead jingled. Joshua knocked on the wooden frame. "It smells amazing from out here." He beamed. "Are you busy?"

She stood up from the table and straightened her apron. "I'm on a lunch break." She admired the way the sunlight seemed to frame him like an aura. Dressed in a pair of khaki pants, a blue polo shirt that matched his eyes, and a pair of boat shoes worn sockless, his classic good looks never failed to dazzle her.

He held up a takeout bag from Shanghai Sunset. "So I'm just in time to bring the vegetable mei fun?"

Her eyes brightened. "You brought lunch? That's so sweet."

He walked it over to the table and gave her a kiss. "I figured this was a good choice."

She opened the bag and pulled out the little white containers, some plastic forks, napkins, and some packets of soy sauce. "It's perfect. I was in the mood for Chinese again."

"You ever had cellophane noodles before?" He asked as he sat down to join her.

She nodded. "There's this great little buffet out

near the outlets."

Joshua opened his box of noodles. "Never been there, but I'd like to check it out sometime."

"You have to be careful at the outlets. Most of the time, you're paying close to retail anyway. But sometimes, you get lucky and find a good deal." Vivienne opened a packet of soy sauce and drizzled it over her food.

"So I figured this might be a good time for you to ask some questions." He wrapped some noodles around his fork and slurped them into his mouth.

"I'm glad you said that." She twirled her fork and took a small bite.

"I'm off today, so I've got lots of time." He smiled.

"What led the sheriff to arrest Suzette Powell?"

"Oh? I thought you were going to ask questions about my condition."

"It's probably not the best idea here in the bakery where just anyone could walk in." Vivienne patted her lips with her napkin.

"I'm not really at liberty to talk about the investigation." He reminded her.

"You know I won't tell anyone." She pressed. "After all I've been through, you can at least give me one or two answers."

He set the fork down and folded his arms across his chest. "I suppose I do owe you that much. Fire away."

She thought for a moment. "What evidence did you have to arrest her? Richard Clarke didn't confess about his affair until last night."

"There was a fingernail fragment imbedded near

Mona's wrist." Joshua kept his voice low. "When all of the commission members were brought in for questioning, Suzette Powell had a broken fingernail on one of her fingers."

Vivienne leaned forward in her chair. "What about fingerprints?"

"None were found on the weapon or anywhere else." Joshua shook his head. "It's the damndest thing."

"So how did you link the fingernail to Suzette?" Vivienne continued.

"She agreed to DNA testing and the results came back positive as a match." Joshua shook his head. "I really didn't expect that because she was so cooperative during the questioning."

"I suppose the affair with Richard only made the connection more powerful." Vivienne thought aloud. "You're going to think I'm nuts, but I still have a hard time believing she'd resort to murder."

Joshua took another bite of his lunch and nodded in agreement. "There's not much we can do about it now. It's in the hands of the lawyers from this point."

"I suppose so." Vivienne sounded defeated. "Maybe I'm just paranoid because of everything that's happened to me over the past week."

"You're not paranoid." Joshua reached over and took her hand in his. "You're nothing short of amazing."

She felt her cheeks blush. "Oh, stop."

He brought her hand up this his lips and kissed it. "You're probably going to be busy well into the night."

She nodded back. "I'm taking the plunge and

opening tomorrow morning. Unless, God help me, someone else ends up dead in my dumpster tomorrow morning."

"That's not going to happen." He reassured her.

"I'm going to hold you that promise."

He released her hand. "I'd like to be your first customer."

"I don't think there will be a line at the door. If you're here at eight you've got an excellent chance."

The bell jingled as Stephanie returned with a paper bag from the *Monarch Grocery* in her arms. "Oh, you have company."

"Stephanie, you remember Deputy Arkins." Vivienne spoke up.

Stephanie set the bag down on the counter. "I almost didn't recognize you out of uniform. Nice to see you again."

"And you as well." Joshua replied.

"We were just having lunch and catching up." Vivienne batted her eyes at Joshua.

"I was telling Vivienne how great this place smells from the outside."

Stephanie unloaded the apples from the bag and grabbed a peeler from the utility drawer. "She's going to have the whole town beating down the door to buy things every day."

"You both are too much." Vivienne protested as she closed up her Chinese container. "I'll save this for dinner later."

Joshua handed her a fortune cookie. "Don't forget this."

She accepted the treat and cracked it open. "Fortune favors the bold." She read aloud.

Joshua mouthed the words 'in bed' to her with a grin.

She laughed. "Now it's your turn."

He cracked the fragile yellow shell open with his hands and pulled the slip of paper out. "A penny saved is a penny earned."

Vivienne mouthed the words 'in bed' at him and winked. "Good advice."

He winked back and started to gather up the contents into the bag. "The cookies never lie."

"I better finish those whoopie pies." Stephanie went to work giving them some privacy.

Vivienne kissed him and took a moment to tuck in a small tuft of his chest hair that poked out of his neckline. "You almost make me want to play hooky with my own store."

"I understand." He gestured to the space around them. "You have this to keep you occupied today. I'll try to think of something nice to do on the weekend."

"It's a date."

After Joshua left, Vivienne returned to the work area behind the counter where Stephanie was busily piping cream cheese filling onto pumpkin flavored whoopie pies. "How are things going over here?"

"I just had the most unpleasant encounter with Mary Ellen Bryce." Stephanie said as she took the tops of the whoopie pies and sandwiched them to the lower frosted halves.

"I didn't know you two were friends." Vivienne grabbed the orange frosting to start another pumpkin cake.

"We aren't." Stephanie continued. "But she used to come into Clara's all the time and sit in my section.

After a while, I didn't even have to ask what she was going to order. Every time it was the same old thing. A bacon, lettuce and tomato sandwich on toasted wheat with no mayonnaise cut into quarters and she wanted it served with the bread and butter chips instead of the dill spear."

Working in the schools, Mary Ellen was all about routines, Vivienne thought to herself. It was no surprise she ordered her own life much the same. "So you obviously saw a great deal of each other at the diner." Vivienne dipped a small spatula into the icing and smoothed it over the rounded cake.

"Yes, and she was friendly enough. She even tipped me a little more than usual whenever she'd ask about when I was going to start college. She always told me how important it was to get a good education."

"Mary Ellen does take pride in her school and her former students." Vivienne agreed. "So what happened?"

Stephanie slid the tray of whoopie pies onto a slotted holding cart and pulled out another dozen ready for filling. "She was ahead of me in line, so I decide to say hello and let her know that I'm working for you now."

Vivienne slowly rotated the cake pedestal and began to sculpt ridges for the pumpkin décor. "She was probably on her lunch hour from the school."

"She kind of just nodded back. So then I tell her how sorry I was to hear of Mrs. Clarke's passing."

"There's nothing wrong with expressing condolences. They did serve together on the historic commission." Vivienne replied as she evened out a patch of frosting on the cake.

"Well, she turns around and she looks really mad. Like, her face was kind of red and it looked like she might start crying at any moment." Stephanie recalled. "She then gets this funny look on her face and says that I change jobs more often than some people do underwear."

Vivienne stopped decorating the cake. "She did?"

"Oh, it gets better." Stephanie nodded. "She then told me that Mona Clarke and Victoria Clemens were both a bunch of hypocrites who only served their own interests."

"That's odd." Vivienne wondered. "They didn't seem mad at each other during the historic commission meeting."

"Well, she certainly had a gripe about them today." Stephanie finished. "I thought she was going to bite my head off before she paid for her groceries and stormed off."

"The more I hear about this historic commission, the less I find I know about how it really worked." Vivienne confessed. "Perhaps it's better to not know these things?"

"Just don't bring up the subject around Mary Ellen anytime soon." Stephanie sighed. "I know I sure won't."

By six in the evening, Vivienne and Stephanie had done the impossible. Every bakery case, every pedestal, every tray and shelf was lined with a selection of delectable baked goods to tempt the most finicky of customers.

"It looks stunning." Stephanie remarked as she and Vivienne stood at the front door looking in.

"It wouldn't have happened without you." Vivienne gave her helper a hug and wiped her brow. "We're all set."

"Do you want me to come in early?" Stephanie asked.

"Would you mind coming in at seven?"

"I'll be here." Stephanie untied the strings from her apron. "Finally, we have something good for the news to report."

"No media or big hoopla tomorrow morning here. We're keeping things nice and simple and quiet for the first day." Vivienne agreed. "We're overdue for that." She untied her apron. "Let's clean up the kitchen and go home."

Having the evening free, Vivienne stopped on her way home at the *Monarch Grocery* to pick up some wet cat food for Tom Cat. She had heard that the moisture helped to keep the animals hydrated and their kidneys healthy. Having lacked a proper diet for some time, she wanted to make sure her new companion would be with her for many years.

Pushing her cart along the pet aisle, she admired a little display of cat toys. There were plastic busy balls, catnip filled mice, and even strips of cardboard that were supposed to attract cats for sharpening their claws. She decided on the cardboard, hoping Tom hadn't made a mess of her sofa arms during her absence.

Moving down the aisle toward the canned food, she was surprised to find Cassandra Pembroke adding several cans of cat food to her cart. She had never had much contact with her in town, but the chance to speak to another Historic Commission member was something she wasn't about to throw away. She pretended to reach for a can of food and accidently bump her. "Oh, I'm sorry…"

Cassandra turned around. "It's all right."

"Cassandra, how are you?" Vivienne feigned surprise.

Cassandra took a moment to respond. Her eyes widened as recognition occurred. "Vivienne, it's nice to see you too. I'm fine."

"Much the same on my end." Vivienne smiled. "I'm just picking up some food for my new cat." She reached for some cans, not caring what brand they were.

Cassandra took notice of what she was grabbing and put her hands out. "Oh, no. You don't want that brand."

Vivienne retracted her arm. "Why not?"

Cassandra shook her head. "It's crammed with fillers and ash. It's incredibly unhealthy for your animals."

Vivienne was sure that it had to be healthier than eating garbage out of dumpsters like Tom Cat had been doing, but she smiled politely and cocked her head to the side. "I had no idea. What do you recommend?"

Cassandra scanned the shelves and reached for a line of golden colored cans at eye level. "This one is all natural. It's the only kind I ever feed my own babies."

Vivienne eyed the price on the shelf and gulped. Almost two dollars a can, she couldn't believe it. "Well, a mother always wants nothing but the best for her babies."

Cassandra nodded. "I wish my children were as

easy to please."

"How are they?" Vivienne grabbed a few cans of the expensive food, vowing to ditch them in another aisle after the conversation. She knew Cassandra had four children and none lived at home.

She counted each of them off on the fingers of her right hand. "Colton is married and living in the Hamptons. Caroline is a violinist with the New York Philharmonic. Christopher is working at a brokerage firm on Wall Street, and Caleb is in his second year of law school at William and Mary."

"My goodness, they sure are keeping busy." Vivienne, like many in the town, had often seen Cassandra's children frolicking on the lake with speed boats and jet skis during the warm summer months. "But I'd expect nothing less from your children."

"I hardly ever see them anymore." Cassandra spoke softly. "They've come to resent my choice to leave Manhattan behind."

"It's not like you moved across the country." Vivienne reassured her.

"Well, Peter still lives in New York, so they just gravitate to him more." She sighed. "Their father is the one who opened most of the doors, so I can't really blame them for being closer to him."

"Speaking of New York, I had the pleasure of meeting one of Mona's friends from there." Vivienne eased the change of conversation quite expertly. "Do you know Samantha Charles"

"I know of her." Cassandra clarified. "She was in the group that came with Fiona Meadows, wasn't she?"

"Yes. She's such a sweet young woman." Vivienne spoke.

"Hard to believe she's associated with Fiona Meadows." Cassandra sniffed.

"Why do you say that?"

Cassandra leaned closer to Vivienne. "You know that online magazine that was brought up at the historic meeting, *A Byte of the Finger Lakes*?"

"Yes." Vivienne nodded.

"It's run by a publishing house in New York that's headed by none other than Fiona Meadows." Cassandra folded her arms across her chest. "Can you believe the nerve of her to show up for the memorial after running a scathing piece like that?"

"Mona said she was misquoted in the article." Vivienne recalled from the night of the meeting. "Do you think Fiona changed it on purpose?"

"I don't know." Cassandra rolled her eyes. "But I'm telling you something isn't right about this whole murder business. Suzette Powell and Mona had their share of disagreements over the years, but they never came to blows."

Vivienne thought for a moment. "But she was having an affair with Richard under Mona's nose."

Cassandra shook her head. "Peter had a mistress in New York but I never told the children about it. I'll admit some days I did fantasize about pushing that little hussy right off that penthouse balcony, but it never went beyond that."

"I'm sorry." Vivienne put her hand on Cassandra's arm.

"It's ancient history now." Cassandra patted her hand. "What on Earth would push Suzette to the breaking point to lose control like that?"

"We may never know." Vivienne reasoned.

"So you think she did it?"

"I know things look that way, but I can't say that I'm entirely convinced." Vivienne clarified. "Now this business with Fiona Meadows and the magazine has me wondering even more."

"My phone has been ringing off the hook." Cassandra went on to explain. "First it was all about Victoria taking over as Mayor and then Mary Ellen kept me on the phone for over an hour going on and on about her problem."

"Has she been getting angry calls about the cost of the new school uniforms again?" Vivienne opened the door for Cassandra to spill the goods.

Cassandra looked around to make sure no one was within ear shot and she waved her closer. "You didn't hear this from me, but she told me that Richard had earmarked some grant money for new playground equipment that Mary Ellen was going to use as damage control for the uniform fiasco last month. Well, out of the blue, Richard called up Mary Ellen and told her that he's had a change of heart and the money was going be used to fund a small park memorial in honor of Mona."

"No wonder she was mad." Vivienne remarked.

"That's not all." Cassandra continued. "Mary Ellen had gone out of her way to convince her associates on the school board to support Richard's campaign last fall and he won in a landslide thanks to the Educator's Union supporting him. So naturally, she felt stabbed in the back and rightly so if you ask me."

"Whatever happened to our sleepy little town?" Vivienne asked.

"This has been going on for years." Cassandra remarked. "Small towns look peaceful and quiet. The sad truth is we are just better at cloaking deception from outsiders."

Vivienne tapped her foot against her shopping cart. "I'm not at all convinced that Suzette Powell killed Mona. People need to know about all these other things."

"What can we do?" Cassandra asked. "We're not exactly in a position to change anything that's happened."

"I think I'm going to see if I can talk to Suzette." Vivienne replied.

"She's locked up in jail. I doubt they'll let you see her, much less talk to her."

"Well, I have a connection that might be able to make that happen." Vivienne replied. "What can it hurt?"

Chapter 23

"That's insane." Joshua's voice raised a notch. "No. Absolutely not."

"What about Fiona Meadows and this magazine business?" Vivienne pressed on. "Suzette might have some information about that and it could change things."

"Why are you so concerned about Suzette Powell now?" Joshua asked.

"Because the more we find out about this situation, the more things start to fall apart." Vivienne reached out and stroked the back of his neck with her hand. "Mary Ellen Bryce has been stabbed in the back by Richard Clarke, who it turns out was having an affair with Suzette Powell. Victoria Clemens is now Mayor, thanks to his confession on the news. There's so much more to the story."

"Vivienne, this could be dangerous. You've already been attacked once this week."

She leaned back against the loveseat in Joshua's apartment. "That probably had more to do with the grimoire than Mona's murder."

"You don't know that." Joshua reasoned. "I think you should leave the investigation to the professionals."

"But they're on the wrong track." Vivienne pleaded. "They're focusing everything on Suzette and maybe that's exactly what the real killer wants."

Joshua took a sip of the lemon-lime soda that was in his hand. "Even if I could get you in there, Sheriff Rigsbee would rake me over the coals if he found out."

"What if he insists that I go talk to her tonight?" Vivienne battered her eyes.

"How do you propose we make that happen?" He asked.

She reached into her purse and pulled out the little purple bag of powder that she had used on Nora. "With a little help from some good old-fashioned magic."

Joshua's eyes widened. "You're going to drug him?"

"Not drug him." Vivienne explained. "Just use a little magic powder to make him see things our way It's kind of like truth serum, only it makes the other person believe whatever you say."

Joshua shook his head. "Magic powder, magic books, I'm starting to miss the simple life back in Indian Lake. All we had to deal with was rogue werewolf attacks."

"So you'll help me?" She asked hopefully.

"We're even after this?" He asked.

"Absolutely." She kissed him on the cheek. "Now let's get this into his coffee.

* * *

It was nearly dark as Joshua led her into the Sheriff's office. Vivienne had brought one of her apple blossoms from the bakery and a freshly brewed cup of coffee.

Joshua waited in the hall outside the office where Sheriff Rigsbee was tipped back in his chair reading a file with this boots propped up on the desk.

He gestured for Vivienne to go in.

She knocked on the open door and smiled. "Sheriff Rigsbee, I just wanted to apologize to you in person for that whole business about Nana Mary."

Zeke Rigsbee looked up from the paperwork on his desk. He resumed his usual rigid stance, setting the file down. "Apology accepted Miss Finch."

Vivienne set the apple blossom and coffee down on the desk. "I'm having my opening tomorrow for the bakery and I thought you deserved a little treat for being so nice about everything."

"You didn't have to go to any trouble, Miss Finch." He eyed the apple blossom with interest. "But since you came all this way..."

She reached into her jacket pocket and pulled out a plastic fork and a napkin. "Please enjoy the sample and by all means stop by when you get a chance. I've got my famous raspberry-lemon cake too."

He speared a bite of the apple blossom and smiled. "You sure know how to bake." He reached for the coffee and downed some. "Deputy Arkins is a lucky man."

"You're too kind." She took a seat in front of him. "The coffee is a special blend I'll be selling at the shop. There's a hint of vanilla in it."

Zeke picked it up and swallowed another gulp. "It really hits the spot."

She decided to test the effects of the powder. "You know, I was thinking it might be a good idea if you let me go visit Suzette Powell."

He stared at her blankly. "It might be a good idea? Sure, I think that actually might be a good idea."

"I think you should let me visit her and make

sure everything is okay." Vivienne continued. "You should have Deputy Arkins escort me to the holding area."

"Miss Finch." He looked at her with glassy eyes. "I'd like you to go visit with Suzette Powell and check on her. Deputy Arkins will escort you to the holding cells." He reached for the phone and pressed one of the interior line buttons. "Jerry, Deputy Arkins and Miss Vivienne Finch are coming down to see Suzette Powell." He appeared to listen to a question on the other end. "Yes, it's fine with me. I'll send them right down."

Upon hearing the conversation, Joshua stepped into the office. "You wanted to see me Sir?"

Zeke smiled warmly. "Yes, Deputy Arkins. Will you escort Miss Finch down to holding so she can visit Suzette Powell? I think it's a very good idea."

"No problem, sir." Joshua marveled at the effects of the magic powder. He looked at Vivienne. "If you'll follow me, I'll lead the way."

Vivienne rose from her seat and took his arm. "Thank you Sheriff Rigsbee. You relax and enjoy the rest of that apple blossom and the coffee."

"Oh, thank you Miss Finch." He speared another piece of the baked treat and let out a little hum of pleasure as he chewed.

As they walked toward the holding area, Joshua whispered in Vivienne's ear. "You never used that stuff on me, did you?"

"How can you even think that?" She whispered back.

"I'm dating a witch." He answered softly. "I don't think these types of questions are out of line."

She gently poked him in the side of the ribs with her elbow and they walked downstairs to the holding cells. "The effects will wear off in about an hour or so. So we better hurry."

They decided it would be best to have Joshua stay outside with the officer on duty and keep him from hearing what Vivienne was asking Suzette.

As Vivienne stepped into the area where the cells were, she had no trouble locating Suzette as she was the only person in custody.

She was dressed in an orange jumpsuit and her hair was a bit messy and untamed as she nervously chewed on her nails. She sat up from the bunk in surprise. "Vivienne Finch? What are you doing here?"

Vivienne felt sorry for her. The smell wasn't as bad as she imagined it would be. It was a mix of heavy antiseptic cleanser and metal. "Suzette, I came to see how you were holding up and ask you some questions."

"Is my lawyer here?" She looked to the side from behind the bars of her cell.

"This isn't official." Vivienne spoke softly. "I have some questions to ask if you're okay with that. I'm sort of doing my own little investigation."

Suzette shook her head. "I didn't kill Mona Clarke." She gripped the bars on the cell door with her hands. "No one believes me."

"I believe you." Vivienne folded her arms across her chest as the heater didn't seem to doing much of anything except make clanking noises. "Maybe we can put some of the missing pieces together and figure out what really happened?"

"I only wish my lawyer seemed as concerned as

you." Suzette answered. "What did you want to know?"

"Well, first we need to talk about the affair with Richard Clarke."

"I didn't do that either." Suzette gripped the bars so tightly in response that the color from hands blanched. "They said he confessed to it at a press conference? Is that true?"

"He did." Vivienne nodded back. "Why would he lie about that?"

"I don't know." Suzette began to tear up. She pulled her hands back through the bars and wiped her face. "It's like they're all trying to frame me. What did I ever do to deserve this?"

"Are you aware of the physical evidence the police found? Your finger nail was embedded in Mona Clarke's wrist?"

"Yes, my lawyer told me about that." Suzette produced the finger where her nail was indeed broken off although it looked entirely possible it had been nervously bitten. "I don't know how it was broken."

"So how did it end up embedded in Mona's wrist?"

Suzette sobbed and shook her head in frustration. "I can't answer that because I honestly don't know. Before you showed up I started to wonder if maybe I was crazy and had a split personality or something. Maybe my lawyer could get me off the hook on a temporary insanity charge or something?"

Vivienne shared in her frustration. Suzette didn't have as many answers as she had hoped for. "Where were you the morning when Mona was murdered?"

"I was out walking the hiking trails by the lake."

She answered. "I'd put on a few pounds over the summer and I wanted to get in shape before the holidays came around. You know, sort of give myself a little wiggle room for all those sugary treats."

"Did anyone see you?"

"I don't think so." Suzette shook her head. "After the summer tourists leave, the park is pretty deserted. It was just me and the geese."

"It is pretty deserted this time of year." Vivienne agreed. "So you don't have anyone to verify your location that morning."

Suzette looked up at the ceiling of the holding cell where the heating unit continued to make annoying noises. "I wish I did because then I wouldn't be here."

"Did you know about the magazine interview with Mona before the meeting the night of the Historic Commission meeting?"

"Yes." Suzette answered. "I overheard Victoria telling Mary Ellen about it right before we walked into the meeting." Suzette squinted as she thought back. "Mary Ellen said something about how she was glad someone else was going to look like the bad guy on the committee for once."

"So they knew about it?" Vivienne wondered aloud. "Most likely because Fiona and Victoria are so close."

"Who's Fiona?" Suzette asked.

"A friend of Mona's from New York City." Vivienne answered. "She runs the publisher that produces the online magazine."

"Mona said she was having a lawyer look into things." Suzette offered. "Why would she show up at the memorial service if she was getting sued for libel? Doesn't that seem rather tacky?"

"Maybe Fiona was snooping around to find out if Richard was still pursuing legal action?" Vivienne thought aloud.

"Or maybe Richard wasn't involved with the legal process at all?" Suzette offered. "Maybe this was something Mona was pursuing and he didn't even know about it?"

Vivienne snapped her fingers. "I never thought of that."

"Maybe Fiona was the one who murdered Mona?" Suzette pressed on. "Vivienne, you have to find out who did this. Don't let me get sent away to prison for something I didn't do."

"I'm trying to help out the best way I can." Vivienne reassured her. "I wish I had more questions but I can't think of anymore right now."

Suzette reached through the bars and took hold of Vivienne's hands. "You've given me hope that I'm not going to rot in here. That's a start."

Vivienne suddenly felt light-headed and slumped against the bars of the cell. Everything faded to black and then she heard voices. People were arguing. Her vision cleared and she found herself seated in Suzette's position during the Historic Commission meeting. She was compelled to chew on her nails as the audience started to grow restless. The microphone squealed with feedback and she reached out to cover it with her hands. Another pair of hands reached over hers and she felt one of her nails break off.

"Vivienne, can you hear me?" Joshua's voice called out to her from the crowd.

Vivienne awoke on the floor of the holding area. She blinked a few times as she came around to her senses. "What happened?"

"You fainted." Suzette replied from the other side of the bars.

Joshua helped her up from the floor. "Are you okay?"

"I think so." Her head was still foggy from the strange vision that had filled her mind.

Jerry, the officer on duty, scratched his chin with concern. "Should I call an ambulance?"

Joshua put his arm around her shoulders and she leaned against his chest for support. "No, I'll take care of her. I think we've had enough for tonight."

"Don't forget about me in here." Suzette pleaded.

Vivienne gave her a weak nod and walked alongside Joshua and Jerry as they left the holding cells.

Jerry returned to his post at the door. "Hope it's not the flu starting early. I'm saving my sick time up for when Cynthia has the baby."

Joshua helped Vivienne to the elevator. "No, she's just been running on fumes all week."

Vivienne looked up at Jerry as the elevator arrived and the door slid open. "When is the baby due?"

"Probably around Christmas time which will work out great come tax season." Jerry's eyes lit up with excitement. "But Cynthia's hoping it's after New Years."

They stepped into the elevator. "As long as it's healthy, that's all that matters." Joshua pressed the button to return them to the ground floor.

By the time they had reached the main lobby, Vivienne was back to feeling like herself again. "I have to tell you something when we get outside." She whispered in Joshua's ear.

"Okay." He whispered back and said goodnight to the officers on duty.

As they stepped out into the chilly night air outside the Sheriff's office, Vivienne felt more alert. "I had a vision of the historic commission meeting."

"What did you see?"

"It was as if I were Suzette sitting in her chair. I saw the microphone and it started to get that awful feedback."

"I remember that happening." Joshua interrupted. "Werewolf hearing is more sensitive than human."

Vivienne struggled to recall the details. "I put my hands out to cover it up and then someone put their hands over mine and broke one of my nails."

"Who did that?" Joshua asked.

"I couldn't see." Vivienne replied.

"Which side did the hands come from?"

Vivienne thought for a moment. "It was Victoria Clemens. She reached out to pull my hands away.

"Are you positive?"

Vivienne inhaled some of the cold air. "So that's how Suzette's nail must have been broken. It had nothing to do with Mona Clarke at all."

"So how did her nail end up embedded in Mona Clarke's wrist?" Joshua asked.

A strong gust of wind whipped across the steps of the Sheriff's office and Vivienne shivered. "I don't know. The vision ended right after that happened."

"So you think that Victoria Clemens had some part in this?"

Vivienne shrugged. "Visions aren't going to help in a court of law. We're going to need to find some tangible evidence."

As they started down the stairs, Officer Frank Borden knocked on the glass door to get their attention. He opened it partly, fighting the wind. "Deputy Arkins, you never signed off on that incident report from yesterday."

Joshua stopped in his tracks. "I forgot all about it."

"I hate to bother you on your day off." Frank apologized. "But we need to send it to Albany by tomorrow or there's going to be hell to pay."

Joshua reached into his pocket and handed Vivienne the keys to his car. "You'll catch a death of a cold out here. I'll be just a minute or two."

"It'll be all heated up by the time you come back." She smiled. "You don't need any more trouble at work."

He rushed back into the station with Frank on his heels just as her cell phone rang. It was a call that was automatically forwarded from her business line to her personal cell after hours.

"Vivienne, this is Samantha. Thank God I took your business card with me." She said breathlessly over the phone.

"Is everything okay?"

"I found something in my purse when I got home and when I discovered what it was I thought you should know right away." Samantha explained. "Remember when I told you I had knocked the purses over after the memorial service?"

"Yes. I do." Vivienne's interest was sparked. "What did you find?"

"A memory stick with a computer file on it." Samantha continued. "I popped in my laptop to see if I could figure out who it belonged to."

"Who did it belong to?" Vivienne asked.

"Victoria." Samantha's voice cracked a little. "But that's not why I called. It was what I found on the memory stick that you need to know about."

Vivienne, freezing in the cold air, tried to coax the information out of Samantha a bit faster. "I hope it's something that sheds some light on this case. The police here are completely on the wrong track."

Samantha jumped at the bait. "It had the original interview with Mona Clarke from the online magazine on it and another file with some additional quotes to add to the story."

"What additional quotes?"

"There was something about running for mayor herself and how the townsfolk rarely get things right when they vote on issues." Samantha continued. "Not the sort of things you'd say to get elected, that's for sure."

"Yes, my friend Kathy read that article the night of the historic commission meeting." Vivienne recalled. "So, Victoria put new material in the interview to screw Mona Clarke? Why would she do that to her best friend?"

"There was also a note from Victoria to Fiona demanding she make the editor of the magazine add the new answers into the story or she would use her contacts in New York to yank advertisers from all her group publications. It was rather nasty." Samantha finished.

"You're kidding?" Vivienne felt her jaw drop. "How soon can you have this sent to me?"

"I'll have it sent overnight air to you and I'll make a copy here just in case. I hope it can help you with your investigating."

"Oh, believe me this will help." Vivienne turned her back as a gust of wind whipped up. "More than you can know."

"Keep me posted on how things are going." Samantha finished. "Talk to you soon." She ended the call.

Vivienne hurried down the steps, the cold wind whipping her hair against her face. She pressed on the key fob and unlocked the doors to the Jeep.

Fighting against the wind, she forced the passenger door open just enough to get inside. She reached over and stuck the key in the ignition and started the car. Her fingers went to the heat controls and she cranked it up way into the bright red color along the dial. She couldn't wait to tell Joshua about what Samantha had found. While not quite a motive for murder, it certainly would open a new avenue for the police to investigate.

Once again, she admired how neat and clean he kept his vehicle. She wished her own car would stay as pristine and have that new car smell. She sniffed the air to get a whiff. Her nose rewarded her with the smell of something rotten and yet at the same time sweet. It was the most peculiar smell she had ever known. Thinking he had left some kind of takeout in the back seat, she turned around to locate it when a shadowy figure reached out and snatched her from the backseat.

Some sort of rag was pressed against her nose and mouth. A new smell, a mixture of alcohol and nail polish remover, made her feel woozy. She tried to resist, but the touch of her attacker burned with searing cold, making her entire body shake. She only managed a single honk of the horn before her hands slipped off the steering wheel.

Her arms and legs felt suddenly heavy. Despite her efforts, she could do nothing more to resist. Her eyelids grew heavy, fluttered, and then everything went black.

Chapter 24

Vivienne found herself sitting in a field on a warm evening just after sunset. The grass was tall and swayed in a gentle breeze as hundreds of fireflies glittered against the night sky.

Joshua was next to her, sitting Indian style amongst a group of robed people who were formed into a circle as the gentle beat of a solitary drum thumped along with a slow, rhythmic beat.

"Hero and villain, lad and lass, all answer to the hourglass." A feminine voice droned in time with the drum. It was Mona Clarke, dressed in a white robe with a torch in hand. She smiled at Vivienne and then knelt down and touched the flames to the base of the wood pile. It roared to life with a great whooshing sound. "Round the wheel spins, wrong and right. Darkness falls into the light." Mona chanted as she stretched her arms up into the night sky.

The bonfire blazed from the center of their circle, as the drum beat picked up pace. Vivienne watched the sparks from the crackling wood leap into the air. She clutched Joshua's hand tightly and tipped her head back to look at the stars above.

"I love you." He spoke softly.

"I love you too." She leaned forward to kiss him when the flames suddenly disappeared and were quickly replaced with a wave of dark water. It splashed outward and swept her away from the circle with a thunderous crash.

Vivienne awoke with a start, her face wet from lying in a shallow puddle of water on a cement block floor. She tried to move, only to discover that her arms and legs were tightly bound with a thick braided rope. She rolled onto her back and gasped in surprise. A sunken, hollow face watched her from above. Whoever it was looked very old, and in the poor light she was unable to tell if it was male or female. Dressed in a black hooded robe, it seemed happy to remain in the shadows away from scrutiny.

The familiar rotten, yet sweet, smell from Joshua's car returned and she had now found the source. It was her captor. "Why are you doing this?"

The figure cocked its head to the side as if it didn't understand her question.

She inched her way back away from the solemn figure, until her movement came to sudden stop against a large barrel. It smelled of grapes and upon closer inspection she recognized it was one of those huge oak wine casks where the aging process occurred. "Where's Joshua?" She asked again.

The figure remained stoically in place. Through a series of awkward stretches and movements, she was able to at least sit upright on the floor. She tried to loosen the ropes, hoping her movements didn't attract attention. "I'm guessing this is a wine cellar." She looked around for anything that might help to cut the ropes but the room was just a bunch of huge casks and barrels stacked along shelves and a little table loaded with stained towels used to wipe up drips and leaks. "I've never actually been in one before."

The sound of a door opening from the far end of the room caught Vivienne's attention. Footfalls, the clack of high heels, echoed in the large area. "He won't answer your questions." Victoria Clemens stepped out of the shadows, her arms folded across her chest.

"Victoria? What's going on?" Vivienne tried to reason with her.

Victoria ran her hand along one of the many barrels stocked full of fermenting wine. "You are in a wine cellar, but sadly it's going to be your final resting place."

Vivienne wriggled back and forth against the ropes which bound her. "Why are you doing this?"

Victoria walked over to the cloaked figure and ran her hands along the fabric. "You certainly are inquisitive for a baker. I'd almost dare say you're even better than the local police, but that isn't too difficult to do now is it?"

Vivienne could feel the rope loosening a bit around her wrists, but she was far from getting free. "I'm not just a baker."

"That's right." Victoria grinned. "You're also a novice witch who happened to lose her little spell book." She clicked her tongue. "So it looks like magic isn't going to help you out of this one."

"Victoria, why did you do it?" Vivienne asked. "Why did you kill your best friend?"

"You'd like that, wouldn't you? To know all the answers and then wait to be rescued by your deputy boyfriend just in the nick of time." She laughed. "I'm afraid to disappoint you, but that just isn't going to happen." She whispered something to the cloaked figure and it shambled off leaving them alone in the wine cellar.

"Since you seem to know about the spell book, I'm guessing you're a witch too."

Victoria slowly walked over toward Vivienne. "I've been called many things by many people, but that particular adjective just happens to be true this time."

"You won't get away with this." Vivienne reasoned. "You think after Mona's murder, my disappearance isn't going to cause a stir?"

"Oh, I'm counting on that." Victoria cooed. "You see, this town has had so many bad things happen recently you'd almost think it was a cursed."

"I don't believe in curses." Vivienne could almost slip her right wrist out of the rope.

"And that's why you'd never be anything but a baker and a mediocre witch." Victoria stopped just shy of Vivienne's feet. "You don't have the guts or the foresight to become a great witch."

"If becoming a great witch means doing what you did, then no thank you." Vivienne shook her head.

Victoria laughed out loud. "Color me so surprised." She paced back and forth between the wine casks. "I tried to be patient with life but you know what? It just isn't fair and the people that play by the rules get run over and pushed into the ditch."

Vivienne tried to use reason to buy some time for Joshua to find her. It was a long shot, but at the moment it was all she had. "Using dark magic is playing with fire, Victoria. Why would you risk it? If the Elders found out..."

Victoria glanced down at her with a look of pity. "A dead witch tells no tales, so they aren't going to find out." She tapped her hand along one of the larger casks. "It's such a shame to have to stuff you in one of these casks, but think of it this way. You'll be pickled in one of the very best wines in the Finger Lakes." Her lips curled into a smile. "If the wine ages just right," she said smugly, "Perhaps even a gold medal winner for Glen Harvest winery?"

"Was Mona a witch too?" Vivienne asked.

Victoria rolled her dark eyes. "Stop talking about that stupid woman. She wasn't even part of the big picture."

"Well, you killed her. So she must have had something on you."

Victoria shook her head. "She was a puppet. Something I was able to manipulate until she started to get a little too comfortable with the power I was giving to her."

Vivienne freed her one wrist and then slipped the other out with barely a twitch. "I think you killed her because of something to do with the online magazine interview."

"You really are a lousy detective, Vivienne." Victoria sneered. "You just can't put the pieces together and it's killing you." She gave a little laugh. "Well, drowning in a vat of freshly pressed grape juice is what's going to kill you, actually." She laughed again. "It's not as violent as say being stabbed outside your bakery with the scissors that were going to be used to cut the ribbon for your grand opening."

Vivienne sprung herself forward with a cry and slammed against Victoria's legs, knocking her off balance. She fell to the wet floor with a thud.

Victoria whirled around and kicked at Vivienne with her heels. "Help me." She screamed as loud as she could. "She's getting free."

Vivienne ducked and weaved, as Victoria's sharp heels came dangerously close to hitting her face.

She grabbed the rope and tried to lasso it around Victoria's torso.

Victoria grabbed hold of Vivienne's hair and yanked back hard with a grunt. "Stephen." She screamed again. "She's free."

Vivienne's legs were still bound, so she remained at a disadvantage on the floor. She frantically tried to unravel the rope. She yanked and pulled on the braided cord, but it was no use.

Victoria scooted back and got to her feet. She raised her arms in the air and chanted something that sounded like Latin. One of the wine vats over Vivienne groaned and tipped forward threatening to crush her.

With quick thinking, she rolled backward just as the barrel came crashing down onto the floor and split open like a ripe melon. One hundred gallons of red wine splashed out like a crimson wave and swamped the floor with a foamy wet mess.

The cloaked figure shambled into the room and appeared next to Victoria. "Kill her." She screamed in anger.

Vivienne, soaking wet with wine and still bound at the legs, could only watch as the cloaked figure walked over the shattered cask and reached out with claw-like white hands. Without thinking, she threw her hands up and repeated the only spell she had ever used. "Tempus Revocare. Tempus Revocare. Tempus Revocare."

The liquid began to bubble as if it were boiling. The cloaked figure lurched toward her, stepping into the foaming mess. Suddenly, the liquid swirled up into a vortex-like shape and pulled the figure into its center. Wood beams floated off the floor, nails flew this way and that. In a matter of seconds, the wine cask re-assembled back together trapping the liquid and the cloaked figure inside.

"No." Victoria screamed in frustration. She raced toward the now intact cask on the floor and tried to roll it over Vivienne. It proved too heavy, and she only managed to rock it slightly back and forth.

Vivienne, safe from attack for the moment, wasted no time in working on freeing her legs. She frantically began to undo the knot. At last, the rope slipped down past her knees and she was able to free her legs. While the cask barrier had given her the time she needed, it now became yet another obstacle between her and freedom. She tried to push it away, but had no better luck than Victoria had trying to roll it forward. All at once, the lights went out and the door slammed shut with a thud.

It took a few moments, but Vivienne's eyes began to adjust to the sudden darkness. There were several pieces of electronic monitoring equipment that provided a weak, yet useful light from their LED display panels. Working her hands along the casks, she felt spigots on the lower end that could function as a foot peg to stand upon. Perhaps she could climb over and make a quick escape? With no time to waste, she raised her right leg up as high as she could and put her foot on the metal spigot. Using her arms, she pushed against the cask and managed to climb up enough that she could make out the outline of the door thanks to the bright light behind it. It had to be the exit.

As she leaned her weight against uppermost edge of the wine cask, her cell phone dug into her side. She reached down and yanked it out, overjoyed at her sudden luck.

But her joy soon turned to disappointment as the phone was too weak to get a signal down in the cellar. She was, however, able to use the screen as a flashlight. She continued to climb over the cask and stopped when she came upon the pale white hand sticking out from the wooden beams like a spigot. It looked to her as if the wood had grown around the arm creating a water-tight seal. The flesh resembled paraffin wax, flat and plain in the feeble light. Upon closer inspection, she was shocked to see that the fingers and palm were completely smooth and devoid of prints or lines.

She didn't know what exactly the thing inside was, but she was pretty sure it wasn't going to get out. As she moved her other arm to the side of the arm, it lurched forward and grabbed her. She let out a scream of terror but the icy grip was painfully cold and once more she felt dizzy.

The wine cellar faded away and was replaced with the hazy image of a brightly lit bar area that was filled with colorful bottles of wine.

Victoria was standing in front of her, a glass of red wine in her hand. "Stephen, I can't fathom why you are content with just sitting back and running your family's winery. Don't you have any ambition to be something better?"

Vivienne, much like what had happened with Suzette Powell in the holding area, realized she was experiencing another vision of the past through the eyes of another. Only this time, she was seeing it through Victoria's husband, Stephen Clemens.

"What is this lust for power all of a sudden?"

Stephen replied. "I swear, every time you and Mona Clarke spend time together you just come back more miserable."

"I'm not miserable spending time with her." Victoria set her wine glass down on the tasting room bar. "I'm miserable because I'm married to someone who's happy making a life here in the sticks."

"We've got money, Victoria." Stephen argued. "More than most people in this area have. But that's not good enough for you, is it? I'm not good enough."

"You're drunk." Victoria started to walk away when Stephen reached out and grabbed her roughly by the arm.

"I'm drunk because that's the only way I can stand to be around you anymore." Stephen raised his voice.

"Let go of my arm or you're going to regret it." Victoria snapped.

"Mother was right about you." Stephen let go of her arm. "You only married into this family for the money."

Victoria reached for her wine glass and tossed the liquid in his face. "And you're a little man who will never do anything except run a little business that his parents created out in the middle of nowhere."

Stephen reached for the open bottle of wine on the bar but lurched forward. His hands went up to his chest. "Victoria…" He grunted. "Can't breathe…"

"Stephen?" She suddenly flew at him with concern. "What's wrong?"

"Can't breathe…" He dropped to his knees. "Call an ambulance."

Victoria frantically ran over behind the bar and

reached for the phone. "I didn't mean to make you so upset." She turned to face him. "You can't die on me yet. We have so much more to accomplish."

Stephen dropped to the floor with a groan and then went silent. His vision of Victoria blurred.

Victoria raced over to him and knelt down. "I need you still." She whispered and took his hand in hers. "I refuse to let you leave me like this." She yelled. "Stephen, do you hear me. I refuse to allow this to happen."

The vision faded to black and Vivienne found herself back in the wine cellar. Only now it was illuminated with all sorts of black candles and she was lying prone on a table. Victoria was dressed in a black robe and she waved her arms in the air and chanted. She stood before a simple table that had a small cast iron cauldron resting above some lit sterno canisters. "I pull you from the darkness of death to do my bidding." She brandished a small knife and dragged it across her palm, drawing a river of blood which she dripped into the cauldron. "I borrow thee from the realm of shadow and command you to serve me."

Vivienne could only watch in horror, trapped inside the memories of Stephen, as his re-animated body twitched and groaned. It sat up stiffly from the table and swung his pale legs over the edge. "I obey." The voice was raspy and garbled.

Victoria grabbed a small basting brush off the table and dipped it in the cauldron. She swirled it back and forth and then pulled it free, coated with a sticky syrup-like mixture. "You will follow my orders without question or hesitation."

His head bobbed up and down. "I will obey."

The voice, low and sepulchral, had a strange echo to it that sounded anything but human.

"Give me your hands." She commanded.

Stephen extended his arms and she took hold of his hands and turned them palm side up. She took the brush and painted his hands with the concoction. The fine lines and prints sunk deeper and deeper within the pale flesh and then disappeared altogether, appearing very much like the hands of a store mannequin.

Once more, the darkness swirled around the vision and Vivienne was suddenly transported to the dumpster outside her store. The voices of Victoria and Mona Clarke grew louder as they walked down the alley.

"Victoria, I don't know why we have to look at the parking situation this morning. I've got a very busy schedule with the bakery opening." Mona's voice said.

"The sooner we address this problem the sooner we can move forward with the plan." Victoria replied as they both rounded the corner from the alley. "Boy, there's a real nip in the air today. There's no doubt fall is coming." She rubbed her black leather gloves along her arms.

Mona put her hands on her hips, the giant pair of scissors in her grip. "Actually, there is something I wanted to ask you about and it may as well be now. It's something that's been bothering me since last night's meeting."

"What's that dear?" Victoria asked.

"It's about that magazine article that Kathy Hemmings brought up." Mona tapped the scissors against her leg. "My lawyer has been doing some investigating into the situation and he informed me that the publisher is under Fiona Meadows' company."

"I had no idea." Victoria's eyes widened.

"Actually, I think you had plenty of ideas." Mona continued. "You see, there was a file sent to that magazine shortly after I gave the interview. After some legal pressure from my lawyer, the editor sent it as proof he wasn't printing libel."

"What was on the file?"

Mona set the scissors down on the pavement. "It was a follow up with the very quotes that I thought they he had made up to sell copies. Only, these appeared to be written by me."

Victoria eyed the scissors. "That's strange."

"When I checked the date of the file, it just happened to be created the day you and I spent in my home office going over the plans for the Main Street refurbishment." Mona explained. "So I can only assume that for some reason you took it upon yourself to sabotage me. You created those quotes and you sent them from my own email address so not to arouse suspicion from the editor."

"Yes, you've got me there." Victoria nodded. "Frankly, I'm surprised you were able to figure that out given how self-absorbed you've become lately."

"Excuse me?" Mona's voice went up a tone.

"You are so high and mighty you don't even recognize someone you went to high school with." Victoria mocked. "Hello?" She tossed her hair with her hands.

Mona shook her head in bewilderment. "What's going on here?"

Victoria continued. "We were on the cheerleading squad together at Elmira Free Academy."

She tossed her arms into the air with a little cheer. "Go Blue Devils."

Mona eyed her carefully and then the spark of recognition appeared. "Missy Collins?"

Missy nodded. "I was counting on you to be so into yourself that you'd never recognize me. You made it all too easy."

"You look completely different." Mona's jaw dropped. "Why did you change your name?"

"I had to because of you." Missy replied. "You see, I never got my knight in shining armor to save me like you did. After high school, I moved to New York to try and become a fashion model but the competition was just too fierce and I never could land a job. I was a little fish in a big pond. Before long, my accounts ran dry and I was faced with the prospect of moving back to Elmira with mother."

"We all fall down from time to time. The moment we pick ourselves up and continue is what truly defines us." Mona added.

"Spoken like a true politician." Missy shook her head. "I had landed a full time job at a small pharmacy in the city and was making just enough to get by. Making a nice little normal life for myself and almost forgetting how bad things really were."

Missy ran her gloved hands along Mona's expensive jacket. "Then, one night, you blew in like a diva demanding a prescription for your husband after hours. I said hello but you didn't even recognize me. All you saw was a tacky plastic name tag and the stupid blue uniform. You got your way with the manager, thanks to your new social connections, and left without even saying thank you."

"I had no idea." Mona sympathized. "You should have said something that night."

Missy stepped away from her. "I don't want your pity, you stupid cow." She hissed. "I eventually had to move back to a cramped apartment in Elmira with my mother and take a job in the grocery deli." She whirled around in the alley, swept up in sweet nostalgia. "Remember when I was voted most likely to succeed in the year book?" She posed against the brick wall of the bakery. "Prettiest smile, best body, class flirt and where did it all get me?" She frowned. "A menial job at the local grocery deli wearing one of those tacky store uniforms and a stupid name tag, that's what I got. Weighing and slicing ham and turkey for bored housewives who accused me of giving pieces with too much fat or forgetting to charge the sale price."

"Missy, I don't know what you want from me." Mona shrugged. "Life is what we make it out to be, for better or for worse."

"Why did you get the better? How is that fair?" Missy sneered. "Even back in high school, all you wanted was to steal my head cheerleader position", Missy retorted, "Because that's all you can do lacking any sort of real talent. Things never change and you're living proof."

Mona shook her head. "Yes they do. My God, Missy, it's like someone waved a magic wand and changed everything about you."

"Funny you should mention magic, really." Missy smiled. "Did I mention the part about being a witch and being able to use magic?

"What?"

Missy nodded. "Of course, if I played by the

rules of magic I'd still be an ordinary mortal. You see, I was the generation that was supposed to be skipped. Mother had told me the truth and how she couldn't violate the rules of magic to alter my life. I begged her, pleaded with her, but she just wouldn't budge. So one night, her brakes mysteriously failed and she ran head on into a tree. Magic couldn't save her after all."

Mona gasped. "You murdered your own mother?"

Missy grinned. "The magic passed to me, the moment she died. I vowed then and there to get back the life that should have rightfully been mine all along. With some carefully crafted spell work, Missy Collins became the fabulous Victoria Clemens. I gave myself a head of hair with the perfect texture and color, flawlessly toned skin that tanned and never burned, and a body with no unsightly sags or cellulite. When I looked in the mirror I didn't even recognize myself and neither did you."

Mona recoiled in horror. "But you've got a fabulous life here. Look at you, you're Victoria Clemens now." Mona gave her a little smile. "You've created a brand new life that is far from that grocery store."

"You mean having a little winery out in the sticks with a dead husband?" Missy put her hands on her hips. "I don't think so."

"Stephen is dead? When did that happen?" Mona backed up toward the dumpster.

"He had a heart attack a few days ago." Missy revealed. "Before I could finish my plan to get back the life you stole from me."

"I didn't steal your life." Mona fired back. "I made it with a little bit of luck and a lot of hard work."

Missy paced back and forth in short circles. "It was all so simple but you had to start poking around and mess it up." She rubbed her hands together nervously. "The magazine scandal was supposed to create enough chaos that Richard would step down and leave a vacancy for a new mayor, my husband."

"But he's dead." Mona pointed out.

"But still under my control." Missy replied. "I created a spell that made him appear alive and quite healthy to mortal eyes. Then, all I would have to do was work a little magic on the city council, have Stephen drop dead of a heart attack when I chose, and take over as Mayor in his place. It would be my small start to a bigger picture in politics. State Senator, Governor, maybe even President someday?"

"You're insane." Mona turned to leave. "I think you really need some serious psychiatric help."

Missy clapped her hands together. "Stephen, grab her."

Mona whirled around as the reanimated corpse of Stephen leapt out from behind the dumpsters and seized her in his grip. His cold hand wrapped across her mouth and muffled her started scream.

Missy walked up to her with a grin. "That's right, babe. You've tangled with the wrong witch and now you're going to pay for it."

Mona tried to wiggle her way free but it was no use.

Missy picked up the giant scissors and held them to Mona's chest. "Playing by the rules with magic wasn't working fast enough so I found a short cut. A little detour to the darker side of magic gave me the answer I was looking for." Missy pressed the scissors harder against Mona's chest. "In order to get closer to Richard, you had to die and someone else had to take the blame."

Mona shook her head in response. Her eyes watered.

"Suzette Powell always has a way of getting on my nerves. I really can't stand the woman. Always biting her nails and acting so mousy, she reminds me of how I used to be back in New York. She's a dull, average nobody who never gets noticed." Missy grinned. "Pinning it all on her just sort of makes this a two-for-one deal."

Mona cried out once more and kicked Missy in the shin.

Missy started to fall backwards, which caused Stephen to lurch forward to save her in response. Unable to move away, Mona fell onto the scissors which impaled her through the chest. She crumpled in his grip.

"You stupid idiot, I almost got stabbed myself."

Stephen let Mona drop to the ground with a thud. She moaned and then went still.

Missy reached into her charm bag and produced Suzette's fingernail. "Stephen, press this into her wrist and be quick about it."

He did as she asked, jabbing the fingernail into her soft pink flesh. The sound of the sanitation truck roaring down the alley interrupted them. "It's time to leave. Stick her in the dumpster and let's get out of here."

Stephen did as she asked and picked Mona up from the ground. He placed her gently on her back in the dumpster and then disappeared into the alley just as the truck approached and everything went dark.

Vivienne awoke to the smell of natural gas. She was still trapped in the *Glen Harvest* wine cellar, in the dark, only now she had full knowledge of what had happened to Mona Clarke.

As she pulled herself up from the floor, she heard the hissing sound coming from the far end of the room. The pipe that served as the main line had been severed and the space was filling up fast with flammable gas. The wine cask where Stephen's body had been encased was shattered on the floor once more, with no sign of him anywhere. She bolted toward the door leading out of the cellar when the door opened and Stephen stood at the threshold. In his lifeless hand, there was a single book of matches. He pulled one free and prepared to strike it and start the conflagration that would kill them all.

"No." Vivienne screamed in horror just as something gray leapt from behind the door and snagged the matches from his hand. Vivienne watched in shock as Joshua, in wolf form, scampered over to her and dropped the matches at her feet.

She quickly grabbed them and looked at the reanimated form of Stephen with a mixture of pity and disgust. "It wasn't your fault. You need to let us go."

Stephen stared at her with his cold, dead eyes. He started to shamble toward her. "Light the match." He repeated over and over with his new orders.

The werewolf growled at him and leapt into the air in a vicious attack. Vivienne, taking advantage of the distraction, made for the door to escape. When she reached the threshold, she ran right into Victoria, who she now knew to be Missy Collins.

"You're not going anywhere." Missy smacked Vivienne across the head with the grimoire she had stolen.

Vivienne recoiled for a moment. "You're a murderer and you've violated the magical laws."

Missy sneered. "There's only room for one big witch in town and that's me." She slammed the door shut and locked it from the other side.

Vivienne furiously yanked and pulled at the handle but it wouldn't budge.

"Light the match, Stephen." Missy yelled from the other side. "Do as I command."

Stephen picked up the wolf with both arms and hurled him against the wall of casks. The wolf yelped in pain and rolled to the ground, transforming back into the naked form of Joshua.

Vivienne rushed over to him. "We have to get out of here. The gas is going to blow this place sky high any minute." She grabbed some stained towels that were used to clean up drips from the casks and draped it across his lower half to cover his nakedness.

Joshua shook his head and moaned. "Vivienne, I've been tracking your scent for hours. When I came out of the station both you and my car were gone." He wrapped the towel around his waist and knotted it.

Stephen clumsily picked up the book of matches.

"There's no time to explain." Vivienne looked around in desperation and then focused on the taps which allowed the wine to be drawn from the barrels. She rushed over to the one directly across from Stephen and started to yank on the spigot with all her might. "Joshua, help me pull this out."

Joshua jumped up from the floor and limped

over to the spigot. Together, they managed to yank it out. A river of red wine poured out, but the pressure wasn't nearly strong enough to reach Stephen.

"Back up." Joshua ordered.

Vivienne side stepped. "Whatever it is you're planning to do, you better hurry."

Stephen ripped a single match from the book and prepared to strike it across the coarse surface.

With a primal growl, he threw his arms back and then forward at the cask. The wood splintered and shattered as a wave of red wine blew outward, knocking Joshua and Vivienne to the floor.

The wave of red wine crashed over Stephen, drenching him and the matches in one fell swoop.

Joshua quickly got to his feet and pulled Vivienne up from the floor. "Let's get out of here."

"Lead the way." She spit out a mouthful of wine.

Stephen, now soaking wet, tried to strike the matches but they wouldn't light. The soggy cardboard just disintegrated in his featureless hands. He stared at them like a lost child.

Vivienne's attention turned to the locked door. "Can you smash that open too?"

Joshua nodded and with a ferocious growl slammed into the door with all his might. It fell forward into a stairwell. Joshua grabbed the door by the handle and tossed it inside the cellar. "Follow me." He ordered.

As they both raced up the stairs into the tasting room, a flash of lightning and a clap of thunder shook the structure.

Vivienne pointed to the lit exit sign above a set of double doors. "That way." She sprinted out the front door as a vicious thunderstorm swirled overhead.

"What now?" Joshua asked as he followed behind her into the gravel parking lot of the winery.

Vivienne caught a glimpse of Missy standing near the vineyard with her hands in the air. Oblivious to their escape, she had her back to them chanting something that seemed to make the storm grow worse.

"Run like the wind." She said and pulled him with her.

They had only a minute to spare as a large bolt of lightning erupted from the storm and struck the winery tasting room. It exploded in a huge fireball, knocking them both to the ground with the concussive pressure as a clap of thunder stung their ears.

When they looked up a few seconds later, there was only a flaming pile of rubble that burned like a great bonfire. The orange and yellow flames reached up toward the clouds in angry defiance.

"No." Missy screamed furiously having noticed their escape. She picked up the grimoire and began chanting another spell.

The thunderstorm flared with a strange greenish light as Vivienne held tight to Joshua. Whatever spell was about to hit them, she was certain it was going to end with their mutual demise. "I love you." She yelled tearfully at him.

He was about to speak when his eyes widened in surprise. "Vivienne, what is that?"

She turned around to see several spikes of lightning arching to the ground and creating a grid of electrical energy around Missy. "I don't know."

Five cloaked figures slid down the lightning bolts, each taking a place apart from the other. They raised their arms and shaped the electrical energy into the shape of a pentagram.

A shrill scream from Missy pierced the air. The pentagram flashed like a strobe as a whooshing sound, much like the air escaping from a balloon, erupted and flung Missy and the figures up into the swirling storm clouds. There was one final crack of thunder and then the clouds began to dissipate allowing the stars to shine once again.

Joshua sniffed the air. "Where's Victoria? I can't smell her anymore."

Vivienne got up and ran over to the spot where Missy and the figures had been. The field grass was bent, reminding her of the pictures of crop circles from tabloid magazines. There, in the center, was her grimoire. She picked it up and held it to her chest.

Joshua stepped beside her. "What the hell was that?"

Vivienne could feel the slight tingle of magic in the air. It was so subtle; she could easily mistake it for common static electricity if she didn't know any better. But, she did know better. Somehow, she knew this was the magic of the elders. "She's been arrested by a higher power than the police." Vivienne tried to explain.

"I don't want to know." Joshua shook his head. "Do I?"

"You better get out of here." Vivienne looked at Joshua. "You'll never be able to explain what happened and why you're dressed only in a flimsy towel."

Joshua kissed her as the sound of sirens from the volunteer fire department sped toward the ruins of the *Glen Harvest Winery*. "I love you, Vivienne Finch."

"I love you too, you furry beast." She kissed him back as the sirens grew louder. "Now hurry up and get out of here."

"What about you?"

"I'll figure something out." She smiled. "See you back home."

He turned around and ran with unnaturally fast speed. His limbs elongated, fur covered his body, and a few seconds later the towel fluttered to the rain-soaked ground as the werewolf disappeared into the woodlands.

She walked over toward the parking lot where Joshua's Jeep was parked haphazardly taking up several spots. Bits and pieces of the structure had rained down upon the vehicle, but by some minor miracle it appeared mostly unscathed.

The fire truck screamed into the lot and she waved at them. Two burly men in heavy gear jumped out of the cab and approached her. "Are you hurt?"

"No. But I'm sure glad to see you."

One of the firemen draped a thick blanket over her and led her to the truck. "Was anyone else inside?"

"Stephen Clemens, the owner." She shook her head sadly at the flaming remains of the winery. "I don't think he made it out."

"We'll look for him."

Vivienne nodded back solemnly.

Chapter 25

When she returned to Cayuga Cove a few hours later, she couldn't believe her eyes. The local police had blocked off the area around Stephen and Victoria's home with yellow crime tape.

Parking Joshua's car along the curb, she made a beeline for the gathering of police and fire vehicles. Sheriff Rigsbee and several officers were standing off to the side.

Sheriff Rigsbee turned around in surprise. "Vivienne Finch. Why am I not surprised to see you here?"

"Victoria Clemens tried to kill me tonight." She explained. "She trapped me in the *Glen Harvest Winery* and cut the gas line."

"What are you talking about?" Sheriff Rigsbee eyed her cautiously smelling her wine-soaked clothing. "Have you been drinking?"

"I've been doing some investigating about Mona Clarke's death and I found out she isn't who we thought she was. Her real name was Missy Collins and she's had a vendetta against Mona for years. Suzette Powell is innocent."

"We know all about it."

Vivienne shook her head. "How could you know that? I was on my way to explain everything to you."

Sheriff Rigsbee regarded her for a moment and then ducked under the police tape. "Victoria Clemens called me personally and confessed to everything tonight. By the time we got to the house it was too late, she had hung herself."

She followed him to his car. "She committed suicide?"

He nodded. "She left a note explaining everything. Would you come down with me to the station so I can add your incident to the report?"

"Yes." She stepped into his car.

As they drove away, he gave one last look at the scene before them. "It may not have been pretty, but at least justice was served."

"I suppose it was." She still didn't understand just what had happened in her absence.

"Justice was served, darling granddaughter." Sheriff Rigsbee's image blurred and was replaced by that of Nana Mary.

Vivienne's hands flew to her mouth. "Nana Mary?"

She pulled the car over to the side of the road. "Victoria Clemens or Missy Collins, whichever you prefer to call her, has been under investigation by the elder witches for quite some time."

"How did you know her name was Missy Collins?"

Nana Mary reached over and pulled the necklace with the pentagram out from underneath Vivienne's shirt. "We could see it all with this. It's sort of like a hidden camera, broadcasting what you see into the minds of the elders in the conclave."

"Even my thoughts?" Vivienne wondered.

"Even those." Nana Mary smiled.

"I've been having these visions." Vivienne explained. "It's like I'm seeing things through someone else's eyes."

Nana Mary nodded. "Tactile recall. It's one of

the more rare gifts that just so happens to be your special power. That's why I was under orders from the conclave to give you the talisman that would allow them to view everything."

Vivienne took a deep breath. "What is this tactile recall?"

"You'll learn to control it better over time. But basically, if you are in physical contact with someone, you'll be able to sense their thoughts." Nana Mary replied. "It will come in quite handy, especially when someone is lying to you. You see, people often think of what they're trying to cover up when they fib. The police have lie detectors to bring the guilty to justice, witches have special powers and talismans."

"But I keep passing out afterwards. That doesn't seem like a good thing for me in the end."

"Every gift has a safety trigger to avoid it being misused. It's the natural law of magic." Nana Mary explained. "Something that Victoria chose to ignore when she delved into the forbidden arts."

"So the conclave punished her?" Vivienne shuddered.

"It was the only way to stop her. She was becoming far too dangerous. We had always suspected that she killed her mother, but we had no way to prove it."

"Until I came into the picture, that is." Vivienne paused for a moment in thought. "How did you get her to write a confession?"

"The elder witches are experts with spell work. She was easy to charm and once under their control she had no choice but to spill all the gory details on a long detailed note."

"Where is Sheriff Rigsbee?" Vivienne asked.

Nana Mary chuckled. "He's under the control of one of witches gifted with mind control at his office. Right now, he's been fed the information he needs to finish the investigation and free Suzette Powell."

"Isn't that just one piece of the mess to fix?" Vivienne wondered. "How are we going to make this look like a natural event?"

"The conclave is on top of it. When something of this magnitude occurs, they call in a specialist team to clean up the damage. You'd be surprised to know how many world events have actually been staged to cover things like this up."

"So no one will ever know the truth about us?"

"They're not ready for such knowledge, darling granddaughter." Nana Mary winked. "Perhaps one day they will be, but in the mean time we must remain hidden from site."

Vivienne leaned over and gave Nana Mary a hug. "I don't know what to say except 'thank you'."

"You're welcome, my dear. Now, I better drop you off and then head back to my apartment. The specialists should almost be done with the cleanup and we need to be in our places before the time wrinkle spell is cast."

"Do I want to know what a time wrinkle is?"

"Let's just say it stitches events together so it all makes sense to mortal minds." Nana Mary laughed. "But when it occurs, you're going to feel a little bit nauseous."

"Great." Vivienne groaned.

"It only lasts a few seconds. If you head home and go to bed, you might even sleep through it."

"That sounds like a plan." Vivienne yawned. "I still have a business to open tomorrow morning."

"Good girl." Nana Mary smiled and then drove her back home. "Save an apple blossom for me."

★ ★ ★

"Thank you so much. I'll have that cake ready next Thursday." Vivienne waved goodbye to the last customer of the day. She was dead tired, but the raw energy from everything that had happened propelled her through. As she walked over and locked the door, she turned the little sign over to closed.

Stephanie printed out the daily cash receipt and nodded with a smile. "Wow. I think this will make you happy."

"How much did we make?" She walked over to a bistro chair and sat down.

"Seven hundred and forty-three dollars and some change." Stephanie beamed. "What do you think?"

"I think I'd love to sleep in tomorrow morning." Vivienne smiled back. Her adventure the night before had pulled muscles she didn't even know she had.

"You're the owner, you can do that." Stephanie replied as she tore off the receipt and began to count down the cash drawer.

"I can do that, can't I?" Vivienne mused. "Oh, but it wouldn't be fair to you."

"I love this job." Stephanie replied as she counted out a stack of twenties. "If you think I can handle it, that is."

"I know you can handle it, Stephanie." Vivienne

agreed. "So you open and I'll come in around ten."

"I'll be here." Stephanie jotted down a figure on some lined notebook paper and moved on to the pile of tens and fives in the cash drawer.

A knock on the door interrupted their conversation. Vivienne turned around and noticed Suzette Powell waving from the other side of the glass. "Suzette?" She rushed over and unlocked the door. "How are you doing?"

"I don't know how to thank you." Suzette stepped in from the chilly evening air. "I didn't think anyone was going to believe me."

"It wasn't just me. Sheriff Rigsbee was running an investigation the entire time that I wasn't even aware of." Vivienne felt a little guilty with sticking to the conclave's cover story, but she knew it was for the best. "Samantha Charles was the one who found the memory stick in her purse."

"But you were the one to put them on the right track." Suzette gushed. "I would never have thought a nail biting habit could have almost landed me in prison for murder." Without thinking she stopped her right hand from going into her mouth.

"It almost worked." Vivienne replied. "But thankfully, her suicide note was quite detailed."

"It was almost like she couldn't live with the guilt." Suzette pondered. "Well, you look extra busy today. I just wanted to stop by and thank you for all you've done."

Vivienne gave her a warm hug. "Just throw some catering gigs my way now and then and we'll call it even."

"Do you happen to have Samantha's number? I

wanted to call and personally thank her too."

"Sure." Vivienne wrote it down on one of her business cards and handed it to Suzette.

"Thanks." Suzette waved goodbye and then disappeared onto Main Street.

"She's lucky to have friends like you." Stephanie said.

"We're all lucky." Vivienne added and locked the door once more. "Now, let's make a list for tomorrow's baking."

Stephanie finished counting the drawer and handed Vivienne the bank bag. "Here you go. The first official bank deposit."

"May there be many more to follow." Vivienne smiled.

Chapter 26

Five weeks later, on Halloween, Vivienne set her fat pumpkin on the front step next to Joshua's. She had carved a happy face with a gap-toothed grin on the pumpkin to welcome the children arriving for trick-or-treat in contrast to Joshua's fearsome looking pumpkin with sharp teeth and slanted eyes. Dressed in a black cape and wearing a purple witch's hat with little foil spiders dangling from the brim, she lit each of the candles and admired the view. Tom Cat cast a wary eye from his comfy perch she had installed on the living room windowsill. He gave a little meow and then curled up for an early evening nap.

So much had happened since that fateful night that almost was her last. Richard Clarke had come clean about the alleged affair with Suzette Powell. He explained that Victoria had blackmailed him about how he and Mary Ellen Bryce had influenced the educator's union for votes. Upon her death and suicide note confession, he once more apologized and moved down to Florida shortly after to start a new life. The city council decided to hold a special election in six weeks time which just so happened to fall on Election Day. Two candidates decided to run, but only one was met with almost universal praise. Cassandra Pembroke was sure to win thanks to her no nonsense approach to situations.

Mary Ellen Bryce was forced to resign from her position in the school and moved out West as the damage to her reputation was too great to repair. The expensive uniforms were ditched in favor of a dress code which still preserved order without hurting the wallets and purses of the parents. She was replaced by a young man from Ithaca who was much more in step with the students and quickly bonded with the staff and mended bridges that Mary Ellen had so easily burned.

The historic commission was disbanded after a generous private grant funded a complete redesign of Main Street, courtesy of millionaire hotel heiress Samantha Charles. She ended up buying the former Clemens residence shortly afterwards and made plans to start using it as her new summer home. True to her word, she had kept Vivienne busy with special orders to be shipped to New York City for all sorts of special events. The famous Treavis Cake, being the most requested item of all.

Nora had calmed down greatly, now that her daughter was in a healthy and happy relationship. She still stopped in at the bakery nearly every day to check up on how things were running. She limited herself to one query a week as to when a wedding day might be set, which Vivienne thought more than fair. But that still didn't stop her from sending gift subscriptions for bridal magazines every chance she got.

Nana Mary continued to enjoy her life at *Whispering Oaks,* where she continued with her winning streak at the weekly bingo games. She offered guidance to Vivienne, as she began to study the grimoire and its plethora of spells and charms.

Stephanie Bridgeman continued to demonstrate a talent for decorating that surprised even Vivienne. She was eager to learn new techniques and was soon creating her own loyal following with her cute animal cupcakes that kids couldn't resist. Her green frogs with a pink taffy tongue had become the most popular with boys and her dragonfly with a candy stick tail proved irresistible to girls.

As for Joshua, he had received a special commendation from Sheriff Rigsbee for his dedication in bringing Mona Clarke's investigation to a close. He continued to demonstrate an uncanny ability to find missing persons that no one in the office could match. It was all in the nose, he would joke to the others.

A gaggle of laughing children bounded down the road all dressed in their Halloween finery. Vivienne watched them race up the sidewalks with plastic bags flailing in their hands. "Trick or Treat." They shouted at the pink home across the street.

Joshua stepped outside and joined her on the front steps with a big bowl of candy. He had decided upon a classic Hollywood Wolfman costume and gave her a little nibble on the ear. "Aren't we flirting with danger here?"

"What do you mean?" Vivienne asked as she snagged a piece of strawberry licorice from the bowl.

"Showing our true colors so boldly to the world?" He winked.

"It's Halloween." She smiled at him. "The one night of the year we can be ourselves and no one will look twice."

Joshua set the bowl on a little plastic table next to the steps and sat down. "What time is the coven meeting?"

"It starts at five minutes to midnight." Vivienne sat down next to him. "But Nana Mary wants to leave by eleven so we get a good seat for the festivities."

"I don't suppose you can tell me what goes on during these meetings."

Vivienne bit off a piece of the licorice and shook her head. "I've been sworn to secrecy."

"That's a shame." Joshua dug through the candy bowl and pulled out a peanut butter cup. "Because I was going to tell you about what we werewolves do when we meet on full moons."

"You know, there are some secrets I think I can live with." She laughed.

Joshua chewed the chocolate confection thoughtfully. "Probably for the better, I'm sure."

"My darling, it's just a little witchcraft." Vivienne put her hand under his chin. "I'm a good one, remember?"

"No." He smiled back at her. "You're the best." He kissed her fully on the lips as another group of children ran up the sidewalk to them.

"Oh, gross." One of the boys dressed as a pirate stuck out his tongue. "If that's your trick, can we have our treat now?"

Vivienne and Josh laughed and filled their bags with goodies. "Happy Halloween." They spoke in unison as another wave of children descended upon them.

Coming Soon!

Yule be the Death of Me: Book Two of the Vivienne Finch Magical Mysteries.

It's the height of the Christmas season in Cayuga Cove and the residents are preparing for the annual holiday gingerbread house competition. With the Sweet Dreams Bakery a smashing success, Vivienne and her assistant Stephanie create a charming reproduction of a Victorian home landmark they are sure will snag the top prize. However, when an anonymous 'Santa's Naughty List' starts appearing on utility poles and community event bulletin boards all over town, exposing the less-than-savory deeds of many local residents, the holiday spirit quickly turns sour. When the first name mentioned on the list is found murdered a few days later, the gift of suspicion leads to holiday panic. Vivienne must catch a cunning killer before her own goose is cooked!

About the Author

J.D. Shaw is a 2008 graduate of the prestigious Odyssey Writing Workshop run by Jeanne Cavelos, former senior editor at Bantam Doubleday Dell. During his six weeks in the program, he worked alongside such award winning authors as Barry B. Longyear and Nancy Kress.

He lives in Elmira, NY with Sam, an indoor tiger cat, who seems to think that sleep is just wasted time between feedings and spending quality outdoor time with his pal, the neighborhood stray, Mister Tommy Cat.

This is his first novel in the Vivienne Finch Magical Mysteries. He is currently hard at work on the next book in the series.

'Like' *The Vivienne Finch Magical Mysteries* book page on Facebook and stay informed on all the latest news, contests, and events.

Made in the USA
Lexington, KY
12 September 2014